A Heart Restrained

by
Jennifer Wilck

Scarred Hearts Series

A Heart Restrained

Cover Art by *Jennifer Greeff*

The Wild Rose Press, Inc.
PO Box 708
Adams Basin, NY 14410-0708
Visit us at www.thewildrosepress.com

Publishing History
First Edition, 2023
Trade Paperback ISBN 978-1-5092-4818-6
Digital ISBN 978-1-5092-4819-3

Scarred Hearts Series
Published in the United States of America

"Wouldn't you enjoy this more if it were in English?"

She paused and shifted so she faced him, one leg bent under her, the other dangling off the edge. "Absolutely not! Telenovelas are so much more emotional than American TV."

"Why don't you at least research online to find a plot summary?"

"I'm happy with the way things are," she said. "I don't need to hear the words to feel the story."

"But…you're crying."

She smiled through her tears and wiped her cheeks. "I know."

Staring at her, his heart rate increased, and he tamped the panic her tears caused. At first, he thought pain caused her tears, but her rapt attention to the screen made him realize otherwise.

Why would she want to do this to herself? And how could she enjoy a show she couldn't understand?

He should leave, before she recognized his complete lack of comprehension. But her rapt attention to the screen fascinated him. She was smart—his business dealings with her had proven it. Yet she focused as if she understood her show.

She stared at the TV screen, but he couldn't take his gaze off her. Her skin, despite its bruising, was luminous. Her lips were parted, and she gripped the edges of the sofa cushions until her knuckles turned white. This close to her, heat radiated from her body. He could hear a faint sigh.

If she were this passionate about a television show, how passionate would she be if he kissed her?

Dedication

To all the women I know--friends and family--whose strength I admire and strive to emulate. Thanks for being my village.

Chapter One

Caleb Zeno raised the volume on one of his four seventy-inch flat-screen TV monitors mounted on his office wall to better hear an interview on his competitor's station. The interviewee was the one bright spot in the show's otherwise dismal ratings. The subject's brown hair was pulled into a high ponytail, and her blue eyes sparkled.

"—Fiona Hamilton's online lifestyle brand has become the 'go-to' stop for…well…everyone!" The interviewer laughed. "Tell us, Fiona, how do you do it?"

Fiona smiled. She had even, white teeth and a dimple in one cheek. "Thanks, Tara. I try to make Love, Laugh, Live a virtual best friend you'd turn to for advice."

"And how do you do that?"

"Well, I was always the person my friends came to when they needed help—finding the best bargains, figuring how to correct wording, or making healthy and delicious recipes. In addition to offering private consulting services for select clients, I turned my advice into a website."

"Which now has over one million subscribers."

"One million, one hundred twenty thousand."

"Impressive."

Caleb muted the rest of the interview and turned to

his computer. Examining the latest stats from his company's lifestyle website, he frowned. His had only half the number of subscribers as Love, Laugh, Live. Drilling down, he reviewed the analytics. Most were women in their fifties. Some in their sixties. He was satisfied they met the needs of that age group, but unfortunately, their numbers were dismal in the key demographic he coveted, the eighteen- to thirty-four-year-olds. Only ten percent of his company's subscribers fell in that range.

He drummed his fingers on the glass and stared out the floor-to-ceiling windows overlooking Los Angeles and its entertainment mecca below. As the CEO of WW Media, the number one media conglomerate in the country, he expected his various holdings to be successful. All of them. His lifestyle website wasn't.

A knock on his door interrupted his musings. He motioned in Amanda Sherwood, his head of marketing.

"Hey, Caleb. I'm on my way to a meeting across town, but we just ran the projections for first quarter next year, and I wanted to give them to you."

Caleb reached for the folder. "We need to talk about Totally Tempting."

The woman frowned. "Sure." She eased into the seat across from Caleb's desk. "What's up?"

"We've got the fifty-plus age bracket covered—good job—but we need to improve our standings with the eighteen to thirty-four demos. What are we featuring to appeal to them?"

Amanda tapped her phone's screen a few times. "Well, this month we're featuring golf resorts. Next month we're highlighting investment strategies for retirement. And the following month we're focusing on jazz clubs."

All perfect for most of their audience, the older demo, but nothing was *tempting* to their target. "We need new features. Love, Laugh, Live is killing us. We're missing the mark with key younger demographic."

"Okay, I'll conduct market research studies."

Leaning in his chair, Caleb wished for something more creative. They'd never overtake Love, Laugh, Live with a run-of-the-mill solution. "I think we need a different approach. Maybe even start over."

Her eyelids widened. "It's a small part of our overall market share. I'm not sure starting over is the best use of our resources."

She had a point. Instead of talking to Amanda, maybe he should be talking to his investor relations department. It might be time to consider acquiring a more successful lifestyle website.

When Amanda left, Caleb pressed a button on his desk, and his assistant's voice interrupted the quiet.

"Becca, I need to you schedule an appointment for me."

****

Fiona removed the mic and handed it to the production assistant. Smoothing her black pencil skirt, she turned to Tara with a wide smile. "Thanks for the interview, Tara. It was a pleasure talking to you."

Tara nodded. "The pleasure was mine. It's not often I get to interview someone whose products or brand I use. I check your website daily."

Fiona's pulse increased. Nothing made her happier than hearing how much people loved her website. "I'm so glad. What do you like best about it?"

"Your site draws me in. There's never a time when I log on to look for one thing without exploring at least three other things I didn't know I needed but somehow can't live without."

"Ha! It's not the first time I've heard that." She grabbed her purse and extracted a business card. She recognized a potential client when presented with one. "I also provide high-level personal shopping and consulting to select private clients. Call me if I can ever be of assistance to you."

Outside the station office, she climbed into her silver BMW and leaned her head against the seat. The company she'd built herself had been her sole focus for the past five years, and she'd done a damn fine job with it. Tara's comment filled her with pride. She hummed and checked her phone before leaving the parking garage. Her assistant had left her a message.

"Hey, Fiona, the interview was great. You got a phone call from a Caleb Zeno of WW Media. He wants to schedule a meeting with you to discuss the website and your consulting services. I scheduled it for Monday lunchtime. He's going to get back to me with the details."

She checked her calendar. Patricia had indeed scheduled the lunch meeting with the CEO of WW Media, her website competitor. A bead of excitement kicked in. If her parents could see her now. One interview on a morning show, and the number one media conglomerate CEO wanted to schedule a meeting. From his lifestyle website, he catered to an older demographic than she did. So why did he call? Maybe he wanted to hire her personal consulting services. Although most of her clients were female, she helped the occasional man polish his look or incorporate a healthy diet into his lifestyle. A sharp stab of pride sliced through her. A few more appointments like this, and maybe she'd finally be able to convince her parents she'd made the right decision by not working for someone else.

She stowed her cell phone in her large, black leather purse and pulled out onto the road, turning on some music. As usual, LA traffic was heavy, and it took her forty-five minutes to drive the six miles to her office. She never should have taken her car. By the time she pulled into her parking space, the excitement and sense of accomplishment from the interview had waned. Her building was in a refurbished warehouse that also housed a tech company and an import/export business on a quiet side street. As expected, Patricia sat at her desk.

"You nailed the interview, and you conveyed our messaging perfectly."

Fiona smiled. An easy task when her brand was her personal style. "Thanks. And Caleb Zeno? Did he say what he wanted? He's our competition."

Patricia winked. She grabbed her coffee cup and headed toward the kitchen. "He was eager to meet with you ASAP. His assistant was vague—she just mentioned discussing a business opportunity."

Fiona laughed. Most of her male clients were uncomfortable with the idea of asking a woman for help. She flopped onto the turquoise sofa next to her antique cherry desk. "Then I'm just the woman for him," she called.

"That's for sure," Patricia said, returning with two steaming cups and offering one to Fiona. "He didn't sound pleased about waiting until Monday, but I didn't want to make it any sooner and make you sound too available."

"You're impossible." Fiona laughed.

"True, but you love my coffee."

"I do." In addition to Patricia's to-die-for coffee, the petite redhead was a marketing genius and gushed about how Fiona's brand distinguished itself from others. She could break everything into site hits and numbers and body language and word choice. Fiona had hired her because of her expertise and was thankful for it every day. She was glad Patricia had given her five days before her meeting with Caleb Zeno. It gave her plenty of time to research his company and specific areas where she could offer her assistance. High-powered men were usually easy to research.

Three hours later, she wasn't so sure. His extensive bio gave no personal information, but plenty of company information. He owned numerous companies and his wealth was obvious. Deciding to look one last time, she searched his name and "philanthropy."

Bingo.

A few articles mentioned his name, linked to CAST Ltd. CAST had backed a few charities— including a botanical garden offering therapy through horticulture. Did he like plants? There weren't any photos of him at the garden, and the article only briefly mentioned his name, unlike one of his other partners, Simon McAlter.

She continued scrolling. Another charity established a coding school for underprivileged kids. Computers weren't much of a stretch for a media mogul, were they? Except again, his name wasn't the one most associated with it. She shook her head and powered off her computer for the day.

Worst case, she'd attend the meeting and learn about his interests there and follow up with suggestions a day or two later. It wasn't ideal. Still, it had been one day. She wasn't ready to admit defeat.

****

The 1920s décor of The Fonda Theater didn't jibe with the electronic cacophony of the heavy metal punk band performing on the stage, and Caleb shifted in his seat to get comfortable.

"Aren't they absolutely amazing?" His sister Lexie leaned over, gyrating to the music.

They were something, all right, but amazing wasn't the word he would use to describe them. More like eardrum-shattering loud. However, the joy on his younger sister's face overrode his true feelings, and he nodded, feigning enjoyment for her sake. Several years younger than him, he'd protected her from the day she was born. Although no longer a vulnerable, helpless child, he still protected her, and he would do anything to make her happy.

"Thank you so much for coming with me," she said, when the lights came on after the third encore.

They rose, pressed into the crush of people trying to leave.

"I didn't like the idea of you going alone." His sister was a grown woman and capable of taking care of herself, but anything could happen at a concert. He would have spent the entire night worrying about her otherwise.

Lexie shook her head. "Steve planned to come with me, but work called at the last minute. A client crisis or something. I'm glad you came. It's more fun with someone." She shrugged, taking a step forward.

"Safer, too."

Lexie turned, and her nostrils flared. "I'm not five, brother dear."

It didn't matter how old she was, he'd never stop protecting her. Just because they were no longer threatened by their father, didn't mean there weren't other ways she could get hurt—like being trampled in a crowd. He reached forward and tapped the guy in front of his sister who jostled people around them and looked about to crush her. "Watch out."

The guy opened his mouth to speak, looked at Caleb's stony glare, and mumbled an apology. He smelled of weed. Curving his arm around his sister's shoulders, Caleb held onto her, then used his other shoulder to wedge his way through the crowd.

"Wait, Caleb, I want to use the bathroom."

He sighed but maneuvered through the crowd to the restrooms and leaned against the wall for what seemed like a long time. Finally, Lexie returned. Once outside on the sidewalk, free of the stifling fumes that passed for air, he looked at his sister with concern.

"Are you okay?"

She laughed. "Of course I am."

Knowing he'd kept her from being trampled, he let himself relax and walked with her to his electric blue Ferrari F60.

"I had so much fun," she exclaimed, practically bouncing with excitement. "I know you're not a huge fan of the group but—"

"Lexie, I'll take you to any concert you want, anytime." He much preferred accompanying her to a concert for a group he disliked than have her go alone.

Safely ensconced in the car, she spoke in a low voice. "You don't have to protect me anymore, you know." She placed a hand on his arm. "It's time you started focusing on yourself. Find someone to make you happy…"

He patted her arm and focused on steering his car out of the garage into concert traffic. "I'll always look out for you. My company is doing well—" *Except for the lifestyle brand.* "—and I have you and Steve and my friends. I'm happy."

"Are you? I can't ever tell with you."

He'd learned long ago not to show his emotions. "I am."

Of course, he was.

Chapter Two

It took every ounce of restraint Fiona possessed not to let her jaw drop when Patricia led Caleb into her office. The huge man somehow dwarfed the office she'd thought until now was open and spacious. More than six feet tall, his muscular shoulders were so broad his suits must be custom tailored. His shaved head somehow managed to draw attention to his molten chocolate eyes. She blinked, taking in his firm jawline, high cheekbones, and slightly crooked nose. All the oxygen in the room disappeared.

He reached across her desk and grasped her hand.

"Ms. Hamilton? I'm Caleb Zeno."

His large, tanned hand with trimmed nails squeezed hers, breaking the spell. Realizing her window of opportunity to make a good first impression waned, she stretched her mouth into what she hoped was a smile. "Call me Fiona."

Her voice wavered, heat raced up her arm from contact with his firm handshake, and her heart beat a tango in her chest.

Good lord, no one had prepared her for meeting with…with…him.

He nodded, and she pointed to one of the shabby-chic painted chairs on the other side of her grandmother's antique desk. Never in her life was she relieved to have a physical buffer between her and a potential client. He waited for her to sit before doing so himself.

Fiona wondered if such a large man would shatter the fragile looking chair and breathed a sigh of relief when he didn't.

"Would you like something to drink?" she asked.

"No, thank you." His deep voice resonated low in her belly. She pressed her palm against her middle.

She'd never seen a man so still. He sat and stared at her, as if he were assessing her. His scrutiny made everything and everyone else fade away. Her skin heated.

His face was a mask—a gorgeous one, but a mask, nonetheless. Not a muscle moved. The silence thickened. He was uncomfortable. Shouldn't be surprising—many high-powered, successful men had trouble asking for help. Her first step was to help him relax.

"I appreciate your coming to my office."

He looked around, as if memorizing every detail of her eclectic space. Did the vibrant colors and textures of the mismatched furniture give off the homey atmosphere she'd striven for?

"You're welcome." His gravel-like voice gave her the feeling he didn't know what to make of her or her services. Before she could start in on her spiel, he shifted positions and leaned in his chair. "I saw your interview with Tara Kincaid."

She smiled. "What interested you about it?" Since her research ahead of time didn't net results, maybe he'd offer a clue now she could use.

His gaze moved from her eyes to her mouth and to her eyes again, making him once again, shift in his chair.

Did her smile make him uncomfortable? Or her direct questions? If he wanted her help with improving his image in some fashion, then he must answer a few questions at least.

"Your subscriber numbers are impressive. How many private clients do you have?"

He looked forbidding, and she shifted in her chair. This man needed her to soften his image. If she could get him to talk about himself a little and establish a rapport—anything to make him more comfortable and to appear more human. But first, she'd answer his question.

"About ten, right now. I like to keep the number of private clients small, so I can give them a personal touch. But I'm able to take on a few more." She leaned forward. "Your company is quite impressive, but there's not a lot of information online about you. Are you originally from Los Angeles?"

He stiffened. "No." Then, as if he were making a concerted effort, his body loosened a fraction, and his gaze swept the room. "How large is your outfit? Are you the only one who handles your clients? What about your lifestyle brand?"

She frowned. Eliciting information from him was impossible. Helping him was going to be a challenge. "For Love, Laugh, Live, I do most of the research, along with my assistant, Patricia. Occasionally, I'll hire guests to feature their expertise. For my private clients, however, it's just me." She studied the man across from her. Her mind went in a million different directions. His one-word answers were driving her crazy as were his questions about her business. Did he expect less than exceptional service from her?

"I'm well aware of your business successes," she said. "What about your outside interests? What do you enjoy in your free time?" She smiled. Again, he didn't return it.

Icebreakers weren't going to work with this man.

He leaned forward in his chair. "Are those click numbers you quoted Kincaid accurate?"

She bristled. Did he think she'd lie on national television? "Of course, they are." He'd know if he'd done any research into her company. Maybe he wanted her to sweat.

"Mr. Zeno, as I'm sure you're aware, I work with a variety of select clients as a high-level personal shopper and consultant, in addition to managing my website. I'd love to help you, but I'm going to need you to tell me what you're looking for."

He shifted, his mask in place once again. "Help me? I don't need your help. I want to buy your company."

****

She laughed.

Out of all the possible responses, he hadn't expected laughter. He hated people laughing at him. Too often, it reminded him of his father laughing at him while Caleb protected his mother and sister. Because the man's laughter never expressed joy. It always preceded verbal abuse. He blinked. However, Fiona's velvety laugh was kind, and her sapphire irises sparkled with humor, not malice.

He pushed away from the desk. Velvet and sapphires? The only velvet he should think about lined the box of the expensive single malt scotch he'd bought on his most recent trip to Scotland. The only sapphire he should think about was the necklace he'd helped Steve choose for Lexie's upcoming birthday. He shouldn't associate those things with the woman sitting across the table from him.

"Are you kidding?" she asked, leaning forward when she'd calmed. Her perfume wafted around him, a delicate, flowery scent, which should have annoyed him. Instead, it enticed him, making it almost impossible to concentrate.

What the hell?

"I don't kid about business," he said.

The rosy flush began at the V of her cream blouse, moved its way along her graceful neck, and wrapped itself around her delicate jaw and cheekbones. Fascinated, he dug his fingers into his thigh to stop from touching her skin, to see if it felt as warm as it looked.

This was a business deal. Attraction to her played no part.

"Why?" she asked.

Her sapphire—*dammit, blue*—eyes bore into him, and he got the distinct impression she could see into his soul. He didn't let anyone see into his soul. Ever. He barely acknowledged having one. Gritting his teeth, he focused on making his expression blank, on ignoring everything about her.

"Why what?" He put extra effort into making his tone business-like.

"Why do you want to buy my company?"

"Because it's successful and will fill a void in mine." He slid a folder across the table toward her. "This is my offer."

She didn't even bother to open it. "My company is not for sale."

He raised an eyebrow. "All companies are for sale, for the right price."

Her nostrils flared. "Mine isn't."

"Open the folder. You'll be pleased at what I'm offering you."

She pushed away from her desk, and his breath caught.

"You know nothing about me. You don't know my professional goals." She stood. "I will not sell my company to you." She took two steps toward him.

An unaccountable urge to rise consumed him.

"Don't look so distraught," she said. "I'm sure there are plenty of companies dying to take your money. But if you decide you want to revamp your image, call me."

The smile she gave him made his heart thud in his chest. His mind whirled at her suggestion. He was distraught. No one read his emotions, ever. This meeting was unexpected. He and his investor relations team had put together a generous offer with an even more generous buy-out package, including shares in his company. And she hadn't even looked at it.

****

"Oh my God, Patricia!" Fiona called, closing the office door behind Caleb, and tossing her heels across the room. "Patricia!" She'd never been so glad to end a meeting in her life.

"What, what, what?" Patricia peeked around the doorframe of the kitchen.

"He wanted to buy the company! And his arrogance, like I'd jump at whatever number he offered." She couldn't decide whether to be annoyed or flattered.

Patricia walked into the room. "What did he offer?"

"I have no idea. I didn't look at it," she said. "Here I'm thinking he wants to hire me, and he just wants to take over." His overbearing personality knocked her off kilter.

Patricia sat at her desk. "Well, we're more successful than his lifestyle brand. You should be flattered."

Flattered? Maybe.

"He sure was sexy, though." Patricia returned to her desk.

Sexy as sin. Her body heated.

Patricia stuck her head around the wall separating her from the rest of the office. "By the way, you're blushing."

"I am not." *Dammit, I am.* She stalked to the bathroom, ignoring Patricia's laughter, and splashed water on her face.

He *was* sexy as sin. Her body tingled from being near him. But to want to buy her company? He was crazy.

Men like him used their power and wealth as a right, as a means of trampling over everyone in their way. Well, she might not be as wealthy or as powerful as Caleb Zeno, but she would not be trampled. She would be prepared the next time. Because with men like him, there was always a next time.

She dried her face, grabbed a cup of coffee, and returned to her desk. Next time, she'd have the upper hand, because despite Caleb's attempts to hide his feelings, she could read them. Discomfort, confusion, and surprise played across his face. He'd replace his mask, square his shoulders, and feign indifference. But he hadn't been as successful as he thought. She was observant. Next time, she'd use the ability to her advantage.

Chapter Three

What the hell had just happened? Caleb shut his office door and sank into his chair, relieved to be in his monochromatic office instead of Fiona's chaotic profusion of colors, textures, and laughter. How she got any work done, he'd never know. He rose and paced to the windows and back again. That woman, that infuriating, beautiful, infuriating woman! She'd thrown him off course, almost made him forget his name, much less his purpose for meeting with her.

He'd met tons of stunning women before, and they'd never affected him like this. He'd never allowed it. But one whiff of her perfume, one touch of her hand, one note in her voice, and he lost it. He hadn't explained his business strategy, hadn't lulled her with justified compliments about the strength of her business, hadn't offered his compelling reasons why she should let him buy her company.

He'd sat there. Dumbstruck. Asked questions any moron could have found the answers to in three minutes flat. Until she'd laughed at him.

He had a sense of humor, just like everyone else. He laughed too—when someone said something funny or did something humorous. Although, for the life of him, he couldn't remember the last time it had happened. He shook his head. It didn't matter.

The sound of her laughter played in his head, and

he shook it, trying to rid himself of it. The only other person whose laughter stuck in his head was his father's. The man would laugh while belittling his mother or while making his sister cry just because he could. It didn't matter he, his sister, and his mother had left his father and built a new life, he couldn't forget the man's laugh.

Fiona's laugh brought joy, and he was no longer that scared little boy. Even still, the sound of it provoked a response in him, one that made him forget his identity and purpose.

And as a result, his offer of a sale had gone nowhere.

Pushing away from his desk, he grabbed his gym bag from the closet and headed to the top floor to his executive gym. He needed to clear his head.

Caleb spent a half hour lifting weights, and another half hour running the track on the roof of the building. Dripping with sweat, he changed into swim trunks, dove into the pool, and began swimming laps. Twenty minutes later he hoisted himself out of the pool, dried off, and changed into his work clothes.

"Becca!" he called to his assistant, returning to his office.

She met him at the door.

"I need to schedule another meeting with Fiona Hamilton. This time, have her come to me."

"Your schedule is pretty tight..." she said.

"I don't care what you move. Just make it happen."

At the end of the day, Caleb stopped at Becca's desk. "Did you reach Ms. Hamilton?"

Becca nodded.

"And?"

She sighed. "She said no."

****

"I'm not meeting with him again, Patricia. Don't even bother asking me or checking my schedule."

Fiona shut her laptop and grabbed her purse. "I'm going home and forgetting all about him. See you tomorrow."

On her way home, she stopped at the store for chocolate ice cream. After the day she had, she wanted to curl up with a gallon and a spoon and watch TV. Entering the lobby of her building, she grabbed her mail and walked the flight of stairs instead of taking the elevator—she needed to offset her impending calorie dump. As she stuck her key in the lock, her new neighbor's door opened.

"Oh, hey!" Lexie said. "I thought you were my brother." She eyed Fiona's bag. "You stopped at The Creamery. I love that place!"

"After the crappy day I had, I'm having an ice-cream fest." She raised the container. "Want to join me?" She hadn't known the woman long, but Fiona couldn't help but like her.

Lexie laughed. "Oh, it looks so yummy! I'd love to, but Steve and I are waiting for my brother to come over for dinner. He hasn't seen the place yet. I'm hoping to get him to unpack a few boxes for me, too."

Fiona grinned. "Have fun!"

Letting herself into her apartment, she plopped the grocery bag on the biscuit, onyx and gold metallic granite counter and turned on the light. On the wood floor, two ants scurried along the grain.

"Ew, gross." She stepped on them, put the ice cream in her Subzero freezer, and went into her bedroom to change. Kicking off her pumps, she threw her cream silk blouse and chocolate brown pencil skirt into the dry-cleaning bin and dressed in pewter athletic shorts and a magenta tank top. Cobalt fuzzy flip-flop slippers soothed her feet. She surveyed herself in the mirror and laughed. While she strove for a peaceful and professional look at work, at home, she adored color.

In the living room, she turned on her computer and checked her personal emails and social media. When she finished, her stomach rumbled, and she went to the kitchen to find the ice cream. She turned on the light and screamed.

Trails of ants were everywhere—crawling from the overlooked ice cream ring on the counter, to the floor, and along the walls.

And crawling across her slippers.

"No! Go away! Get off me!" She hopped around, her shrieks bouncing off the kitchen's sunflower yellow walls, walls which before now had been cheery, but right now showed off the creepy trail of ants.

Pounding on her door silenced her screeches. Brushing her hands across her arms and running in place to keep them off her feet, she opened her door and gasped.

In front of her, looking like a Roman warrior with proud bearing, fisted hands, and muscles tensed, stood Caleb Zeno. A flash of surprise flickered before he banked it. If he was arrogant before, he was forbidding looking now. A long-sleeved T-shirt stretched across his broad chest, accentuating his sculpted muscles underneath. He stood with legs apart, leaning forward, as if he were ready to pounce.

"What are you doing here?" She fidgeted, her skin

itchy. The last thing she needed after today's disastrous lunch and this evening's attack of the ants, was a visit from him.

"Are you all right? Is someone hurting you?" He made no effort to hide his perusal of her body before his stare pinned her. Her skin tingled, but from the ants or him, she didn't know. She rubbed her arms.

"No one is hurting me. I'm fine."

"Don't deny it," he growled. "You screamed." After another quick glance at her, he angled his head to peer into her apartment.

"I wasn't…oh." Heat flooded her face. She bent her arm behind her and scratched her back and neck, before looking at her toes. Three ants crawled across her slipper, and she screeched, jumping, and shaking her foot.

Looking at her like she was crazy, he moved her out of the way, and stormed into her apartment.

"Hey, I didn't say you could come in!"

"What's going on? Is someone here?" He gave a cursory glance into the living room before turning around, hands on his hips, glaring. "Are you on something?"

Her head whipped around, and she fell back as if he'd smacked her. "Who the hell do you think you are? Of course, I'm not *on* something! And what gives you the right to force your way into my apartment when I didn't give you permission to enter?"

Hands on her hips, she glared at him, until a tickle on her neck made her shriek.

"Why are you screaming?"

She brushed her hand across her neck and held it out to him, the offending dead insect in her palm.

"Ants." She tried to keep the wail from her voice. She didn't want anyone to know about her reaction to the infestation, least of all, him.

"Ants?" He stilled, his mask in place once again, except for one raised eyebrow.

"All over my kitchen. And me."

He stepped close, so close she could smell his scent—a mixture of mint and spice—and feel the heat radiating from his skin. His gaze raked her once again, before he flicked an ant off her shoulder. She jumped, unsure if his touch, or fear of the ants, caused her skittishness.

"Show me." His controlled voice remained forceful, but no longer commanding.

At least if she brought him to the kitchen, he'd be closer to the door. Turning in silence, she led him to the source of her problem.

He looked around. "Vinegar and a spray bottle."

"Excuse me?"

"Do you have vinegar and a spray bottle?"

She shook her head.

He strode from her apartment, and her stomach dropped. As uncomfortable as his presence in her apartment made her, he'd offered a distraction from the vile insects. But a minute later he returned with a large bottle and started spraying.

Reaching with tentative movements around the ants for paper towels, she followed him, cleaning after he sprayed. His movements were spare and sure, and she tried not to compare him to an avenging angel.

When he finished, he turned and leaned forward, shrinking her kitchen to little more than a closet. "Why are you crying? What's wrong? Did you get bitten? Are you allergic?"

She blinked, embarrassed he had caught her tears. Her adrenaline rush disappeared. "No, it's nothing. You don't need to worry. I just *hate* ants." Most guys were uncomfortable around weepy women, but she wasn't weepy. He needed to relax.

"They're gone now. Clean your kitchen with bleach and use traps. If they return, call the landlord."

She followed him to the door. "Why were you here?"

He crossed the hallway to Lexie's apartment. At the threshold, hand clasping the doorknob, he turned. "Lexie's my sister."

****

Closing the door inside his sister's apartment, Caleb exhaled in a whoosh. The tightness in his chest eased. The screams made him run to Fiona's apartment instead of Lexie's. Only he hadn't known it was Fiona's.

He acted on instinct, believing someone was in danger. The sight of Fiona trembling—her tears—had been like taking a baseball in the chest. He went straight into his Mr. Fixit mode. But now his brain accelerated into overdrive.

Why the hell had he had such a strong reaction? It was ants, not a murder. He passed her door in the hallway, scanning the numbers for Lexie's. Once he realized who it was, he couldn't turn around and abandon her.

She'd laughed at him without even considering his business proposal. Of course, he didn't like her. Just because his body fixated on her scent, and he had an urge to touch her soft skin didn't mean anything.

"There you are!" Lexie exclaimed and raced over to give him a hug.

Caleb swept her into his arms, kissed her cheek, and planted her on the ground. Her husband, Steve, had followed her into the foyer, and Caleb shook his hand.

"Sorry."

"What happened to Fiona? Is she okay? Do I need to go over to her?" As usual, his sister spoke a mile a minute and worried about everything.

"She's fine. She had an ant problem."

Lexie shuddered. "Ugh. I hope they don't come over here!"

Steve rubbed her back. "Don't worry, sweetheart."

"Dinner is ready, so come sit, please."

Caleb forced himself to focus on the conversation and the food. But his mind kept traveling to the annoying woman across the hall. He'd never seen anyone wear so many bright colors.

"Earth to Caleb!" his sister teased. "This is the second time you've drifted off. Should I put your food in a bag for you to eat on your way to wherever you wish you were?"

He shook his head. "Sorry. Bad day."

Lexie frowned. "Oh no, what happened?"

He did not want to get into this with his sister. "I'm trying to work a difficult business deal."

"Oh, well, I'm sure you'll prevail. You're brilliant." She tore off a piece of bread. "Speaking of brilliant, what did you think of my neighbor?"

He didn't want to discuss her neighbor. "No one who's afraid of ants is brilliant."

"Hey! You're not fair. Have you seen her website? It's amazing. I love it!"

"You know it? I thought you liked Totally Tempting."

Lexie blushed. "I tried your site, Caleb, and it's great, of course. But there's something about Love, Laugh, Live that is just…I don't know…I just love it."

He growled under his breath, and Steve laughed.

"Lex, I don't think your brother likes you helping the competition."

She rolled her eyes. "Well, if you tried it, you'd see how great it was. You should get to know Fiona. I think you'd like her."

"No thanks, I'm good."

Lexie opened her mouth to respond but paused. As much as he wanted to fidget under her scrutiny, he remained impassive.

"What do you want, Lexie?"

She arched an eyebrow. "Nothing."

He stopped chewing. Her tone didn't say "nothing."

"It was nice of you to help her get rid of bugs. Maybe I'll invite her over here one day, with you, so you can get to know each other better."

"Not necessary, Lex." The steak, which had been savory a moment ago, dried to shoe leather.

She smirked. "She's beautiful, smart, and has the damsel in distress thing you always like."

He swallowed with difficulty. He didn't want a damsel in distress. Never had. It had always been foisted on him. The responsibility drained him and was the exact reason why he didn't want to get into a relationship with anyone.

"You don't know me as well as you think you do, Lexie. Let me be."

"You seem sure of yourself, Caleb. But not everything is as black and white as you think it is."

Caleb rose and took his plate to the kitchen. "Seems to me you shouldn't be arguing with me *before* you ask me to move furniture and boxes."

Lexie gasped. "How did you know?"

Steve laughed. "You're transparent, sweetheart. Besides, I might have given him a little warning."

She frowned at her husband. "What did you do that for?"

"Well, we men have to stick together."

Caleb looked at him. "Nice to know you have my back."

Steve nodded.

As Caleb rolled his sleeves to help his sister unpack, he banished all thoughts of Fiona and his sister's conversation. The only relationship he and Fiona had was one where he bought her company. He didn't mix business with pleasure. Never had and wouldn't start now.

Chapter Four

She reached for his head and ran her hands over the smooth skin, tracing the lines of his skull and the back of his neck. His growl acknowledged her touch. His hands caressed her body, leaving a trail of goose bumps in their wake. He licked his way across her collarbone and between her breasts. Soft sighs escaped her lips as he took first one breast, and then the other, in his mouth. Flipping her over, he ran his fingers along her spine. She shivered. He blew soft hot breath across her shoulders. The tiny hairs on her arms rose and glancing down, a trail of ants made their way toward her fingers. She screamed.

The scream woke Fiona from her dream—or nightmare—and she sat up, her body shaking and achy. She gasped—the bald man in her dream was Caleb.

She frowned. Just because he'd helped her with her ant problem didn't absolve Caleb from his arrogance. He wasn't someone she should be fantasizing about—fantasy would be reserved for someone who would sweep her off her feet, shower her with love and affection, speak kind words, and smile often.

Twitchy from the imagined ants, she jumped out of bed. When she arrived at work an hour earlier than usual, she was exhausted and cranky.

"Morning, Ms. Hamilton." The mailman greeted her at the door.

"Morning, Earl." She took the stack of mail, waved goodbye, and entered her dark office. Flipping the lights, she sifted through the stack of envelopes. For a web-based company, she sure got a lot of snail mail. A large manila envelope caught her attention. She unsealed it and grabbed the stack of papers clipped together inside. The top page was a letter. She looked at the stationery header and frowned. She read the first paragraph and fumed. She stared at the bold signature and huffed.

No. Freakin'. Way.

Fiona grabbed her phone and dialed. A female voice answered, and she inhaled, remembering it wasn't the secretary she had a problem with right now.

"May I speak with Caleb Zeno?"

"He's out of the office right now. May I take a message?"

Hoo boy. "Yes, this is Fiona Hamilton, and I—"

"Please hold on, Ms. Hamilton. I'll put you right through."

Out of the office my—

"Caleb Zeno."

No hello? Fine. "You have a lot of nerve sending me those papers."

"You didn't let me explain my proposal at our meeting. I thought you should see it before you make your decision."

"I'm not interested in your proposal. As I already told you, my company isn't for sale."

"Fiona, you should consider the benefits you'd receive from my ownership before you dismiss my terms. I'd like to meet with you to discuss it further."

Was this guy for real? "I don't know how to make

it any clearer to you, Mr. Zeno. I am not interested in your terms. I'm not selling my company."

"Don't you owe it to your customers to at least think about it?"

"Owe my customers? The fact you'd call them customers shows how little you understand my business." She heard his intake of breath, but she was on a roll and wasn't about to stop. "I give my heart and soul to my clients. I speak to them as I would a trusted friend. It's in everything I recommend, everything I advise, everything I put together. It's as much about how I make them feel as in what I advise. I don't recommend anything I wouldn't suggest to my closest family member. My clients are my virtual family. And I would never, ever turn them over to an uncaring, inconsiderate millionaire who wants to add my company as a notch on his spreadsheet!"

She ended her tirade and swallowed. Had she said all of that?

"Read my proposal." His voice was calm, distant, final. "Goodbye." He ended the phone call before she had a chance to say anything.

Which was a good thing, since her heart thumped, and she gasped for air, preventing a response.

The phone thunked as it landed on her desk, and she sank into her seat. She wasn't a confrontational person, but Caleb brought out the worst in her. Another reason not to sell her company to him—if she couldn't handle being around him, how could she recommend her clients to him?

As luck would have it, this wasn't a situation she had to ponder. She wasn't going to read the unwanted proposal, and all the money in the world wouldn't make her reconsider going into business with a man who'd seen her reaction to ants. Centering herself, she spent the rest of the morning weeding through phone calls and emails from people who had seen her interview. Her click rate and site visits were through the roof. Several of the calls and emails were for her personal consultation services, and she handed those over to Patricia for scheduling.

By lunchtime, her stomach growled, and she needed a break. She took the sandwich she had packed and a bottle of water from the fridge and walked outside to the park across the street. In the distance, the Pacific Ocean glinted in the sun. It reminded her of the occasional summer trips to the beach with her parents. She'd been happy, carefree, even if her parents had had to scrimp and save to afford it. But she remembered the laughter, how much love they showered on each other and her. All around her, couples enjoyed the warm day—holding hands, sitting together on the benches, kissing under a tree. A wave of melancholy swept over her. The car accident that took her parents seven years ago had taken away a good chunk of her sense of belonging.

Her phone rang. "Hi, Lexie." Her chest warmed at the sound of her new friend. It was nice to have someone in such a big city.

"Steve and I are celebrating my birthday with a barbeque on the beach tonight. It's not a gift thing at all, and I'm sorry for the late notice, but do you want to join us?"

"I'd love to!"

If Caleb wasn't there.

****

By the time six o'clock rolled around, Caleb wanted to relax on the beach. He hoped Lexie hadn't invited Fiona. He rolled his shoulders, still tense from their confrontational phone call this morning. Not many people dared to yell at him. Fewer were able to make valid points while doing it. But he still believed buying her company was the best thing for both of them.

He changed into black and gray board shorts and a white T-shirt and plucked a navy towel from the linen closet. In the kitchen, he grabbed a six-pack of beer and a tray of his marinated ribs from the fridge before driving toward the beach.

As expected, Lexie and Steve were in their usual spot—halfway between the road and the water. He'd recognize her bright red and orange beach umbrella anywhere. Lexie threw herself at Caleb.

"I'm so glad to see you," she said, hugging him tight. His insides warmed. Leave it to his emotional sister to greet him as if they hadn't just seen each other this past weekend.

He patted her back, met Steve's gaze, and nodded. "Happy birthday. Great night for the beach."

"Even if you had to pry yourself away from work," she teased.

"I'd never miss your birthday." He handed the beer and the ribs to Steve and sat in the beach chair she'd brought him. Stretching his legs, he soaked in the early evening sun, dug his heels into the sand and let the lapping waves lull him. As friends of Lexie or Steve arrived, he waved or nodded. He knew them all, but as his sister had said, he didn't do small talk, and he saw no reason to change.

Closing his eyes, he willed away the tension of the

day.

"Hey, Lexie, sorry I'm late."

His muscles tensed. He recognized her voice. It was modulated, smoky. He opened one eye at Fiona's approach. A floppy red hat sat on her head. Large sunglasses hid her eyes. A white, gauzy cover-up covered her body, but hinted at curves he craved. She reminded him of a starlet from the 1950s. His nerves hummed.

"Oh I'm so happy you came!" His sister grabbed Fiona in a hug.

He forced his muscles to loosen, focusing on each one in turn. By the time he'd finished, the two women were seated a few feet away under the umbrella.

"Fiona, you know everyone, right?"

As Fiona looked around, a few people introduced themselves.

"And of course, you know Caleb."

Fiona's face stilled. A flush started in her cheeks and moved to her hairline and down her chest to the edge of her just revealed bathing suit.

Interesting.

She removed her sunglasses, exposing stormy blue irises.

They reminded him of the ocean as the fog rolled in.

"I do," she said.

He nodded. He didn't know what to say. How *did* one carry on a non-professional conversation with a professional adversary? Especially one from whom he'd just received a tongue lashing. She hadn't said anything to Lexie about it, and her discretion relieved him.

The rest of him?

His senses were hyper aware of her. He focused on her face, her hair, her skin. He wracked his brain for something to say. There weren't even any ants he could rescue her from here.

Around him, voices rose as everyone talked and laughed. The voices melded together. Except for hers. He could identify hers without effort, and he listened while she joined in about the latest celebrity gossip. Everyone expected his silence. He preferred it, and he wasn't about to change his habits because of her presence. Even if he had a strange desire niggling him to be part of the conversation, or at least to grab her attention.

"Fiona, I just love your site," Lexie's friend Anne, said, shading her eyes from the sun, blonde hair blowing in the soft breeze. "It's like shopping and talking with my best friend."

"Thanks, Anne. That means a lot to me." Fiona's face turned rosy, and her toes curled in the sand.

"You should team with Caleb," Steve said.

Caleb froze, his throat thick. Before he could put together a response, Anne did. "No, don't! Sorry, Caleb. But no."

The other women agreed with her, their heads bobbing in unison over their vibrant suits.

What the hell?

"Anne's right, Fiona," Lucy said. A coworker of Lexie's at the crisis center, she sported a crew cut and a nose piercing. "Your site works because it has the small, personal feel to it. No way you're going to be able to keep your vibe with a multi-million-dollar corporation behind it."

34

Lexie nodded. Even his sister? His stomach muscles clenched.

Fiona remained silent, but emotions played across her face—humor, embarrassment, acceptance. She'd make a terrible negotiator.

"I love your loyalty to my site, ladies," Fiona said. "And, Steve, while I appreciate your suggestion, I'm comfortable where I am."

Just as Caleb was about to speak—about what he wasn't sure—Steve rose and walked over to the fire pit, calling for Caleb to join him. Relieved, Caleb rose.

"Sorry, Caleb. I tried to help you."

Steve had no idea, especially since he didn't know about this morning's disaster of a phone call, or the previous breakfast meeting. "It's fine."

"You coming to poker tomorrow night?" Steve asked.

"Don't I always?"

Steve shrugged. "Just checking." He turned toward the umbrella. "Who wants burgers, who wants dogs and who wants Caleb's famous ribs?"

Caleb counted the requests and helped Steve cook on the fire. The smell of the seasoned meat combined with the burning wood and the salty air. Fat dripped and sizzled when it contacted the flames.

When the first round of food finished grilling, he brought a platter to the group, as well as drinks—bottles of beer and water, and cans of soda. Everyone ate in silence. He settled into his chair, put mustard and ketchup on his burger, snagged a rib, helped himself to chips and potato salad, and ate. After a few bites, he looked around and wiped his hands.

"Anyone want drinks?" he asked.

"Can you pass me a bottle of water?" Fiona asked

He nodded. When he gave Fiona her water bottle, their fingers touched, and electricity shot along his arm. He pulled his hand away. What the hell just happened?

After everyone finished eating and spent time relaxing and talking, they rose to go into the water. Everyone except Fiona, who stretched her legs and reclined in her chair. The waves rolled onto the shore. Usually, he was one of the first to race into the ocean, past the surf and into the deeper water, where he could float and stare at the sky. It was peaceful and relaxing and didn't require the dreaded small talk. But for some reason, he was reluctant to leave Fiona alone on the beach, unless she wanted it.

His blood heated at this unwanted chivalric urge.

"I'm sorry about earlier."

He retreated a pace. She apologized when he was rude. Why? He frowned, his blood cooling as he focused on what happened this morning. He rolled his shoulders. Had to give her credit, apologies took guts.

"I forgive you," he said. "It was the heat of the moment."

She frowned and an adorable wrinkle appeared between her brows. "Heat of the moment?"

"You'd just opened the envelope. You hadn't had time to review my proposal. I think you'll like what you see when you do."

"You think I'm apologizing for this morning?"

"Aren't you?"

"I'm not interested in your proposal, nor will I ever be. As you should have been able to hear this evening, those who like my website don't like the idea either." Her voice had risen, no longer the smoky sound that tied his insides into knots. Now the hoarse grating reverberated against his eardrums. He wanted to wince, but he wouldn't show her his discomfort.

She tossed her sunglasses onto her beach chair and pulled her cover up over her head.

He sucked in his stomach. The curves she'd half-hidden were displayed in their full-blown glory. He tried not to notice the amount of her skin showing— he'd seen plenty of women in bikinis before. But he couldn't look away. Tawny skin beneath a bright blue bikini, long legs, and a perfect ass. He followed her toward the shoreline.

"What were you apologizing for?" His impromptu question broke the silence.

She turned before she reached the water. "For the awkwardness of discussing business in front of your friends."

His breath hitched, and he didn't know what to do or say. He must have taken too long to respond because she stalked into the water. He didn't know how to deal with someone who cared about his feelings.

He wasn't supposed to have any.

****

From the surf, Fiona stared in awe as Caleb removed his shirt. For the first time, she glimpsed the black tattoos covering his shoulders, arms, chest, and upper back. He strode toward the water, powerful muscles bunching, bald head gleaming in the early evening light. He looked like a cross between a Roman god and a biker dude—awesome, powerful, and foreboding. She didn't know whether to be intrigued or put off—she'd never been attracted to the tatted look, but Caleb pulled it off.

She started as the water lapped her feet, pulling the sand away from her. Why did she care whether he had tattoos? He wasn't her type. He was arrogant and high-handed, and he wanted to buy her company. Still, she couldn't keep her gaze off him as she ignored her stomach flutters. And he had gotten rid of her ants. He swam to what had to be the middle of the ocean. Okay, maybe not the middle of the ocean, but far enough from the shore no one could get to him unless they were a strong swimmer. She suspected he'd escaped on purpose.

She frowned as she splashed in the water and hopped the waves.

"Is everything okay?"

Fiona looked at Lexie, who'd splashed over to her, and nodded. "Sorry, just thinking." *About work, about your brother…*

"So what's going on with you and my brother?"

"Nothing." He was nothing like the man she would fall for.

"You two looked like you were in deep conversation."

Lexie was her new friend, and her business rival's sister. She couldn't put her in the middle. "Not deep. We were just talking about business."

Lexie laughed. "He's never a big talker. I'm glad the two of you are both here, though."

Oh no. Not this. "I don't think so, Lexie. Besides, I don't want to ruin my friendship with you."

"He saved you from the ant invasion!" Lexie gave her a knowing glance.

Right place, right time. Speaking of time, it was time to change the subject. "You never told me he was the CEO of WW Media." Beneath the Pacific blue water, she crossed her fingers, hoping Lexie would respond.

"He's my brother. I don't think of him in terms of what he does for a living."

Fiona looked to where Caleb bobbed alone in the water. "Does he always isolate himself from everyone?"

Lexie shrugged. "He's quiet. He keeps his thoughts and feelings to himself. But he's the most caring person I've ever known."

Fiona refrained from commenting. *Caleb, caring? Ha!* When she fell for a man, he would never hesitate to show her his devotion.

Out of the corner of her eye, she saw him swim toward shore. He emerged from the ocean like the damn Roman god, Poseidon, water sloughing off, making his tattoos glisten.

"What's with all the tats?" she asked when she was sure her voice would be steady.

"Crazy, isn't it? He's this big, powerful corporate executive and underneath it all he's tatted like a biker."

"Secret identity?"

Lexie laughed. "I love it! Hey, Caleb!"

Fiona grabbed her arm and shook her head. "No, wait, I was joking."

She held her breath. When Caleb glanced toward them and approached, goose bumps formed on her arms and neck. It was like her dream all over again.

Lexie waved, he nodded, and Fiona sank into the ocean ready to douse her embarrassment.

"Think about it, Fiona. I bet I could set the two of you up if you're interested."

"There's nothing to think about, Lexie. Caleb and I are total opposites."

Chapter Five

Caleb's cell phone rang late the next afternoon. He ignored it. Instead, he focused on advertiser subscriptions, ratings numbers, and the proposed lineup for the next season. Numbers and charts and dollars ran through his head. After three rings, the phone stopped. Ten seconds later, it started again. With a muttered curse, he looked at his phone screen.

Lexie.

He squeezed his stress ball—no matter how much he loved her, he'd never been able to get rid of the fear deep in his gut anytime he dealt with family—and answered the phone.

"Lex."

"That's what I love about you, brother, dear. No greetings, no small talk."

He squeezed the ball harder—this time, due to sibling annoyance—and waited. When she sighed, he smiled to himself. The business tactic even worked on his sister, and while he never liked to do anything to make her suffer, sometimes silence worked better than arguing.

"Fiona tells me you don't like her."

This time, he squeezed the stress ball so hard he'd swear it was about to pop. "What are you talking about?"

"You heard me."

"How is it your business?"

"Simple. She's my friend, you're my brother. I'd like the two of you to get along."

"We get along fine." He'd known Fiona for a few days, yet she forced him to lie to his sister. Wonderful.

"Not according to her you don't. Please, Caleb. She lives across the hall from me, and I like her. I want to be able to socialize with the two of you together without it being uncomfortable."

When she paused, memories of their traumatic childhood flashed through his mind. Of family dinners so painful and awkward his neck hurt just thinking about how they might start fine but dissolved into a screaming match. Of his sister's wide gaze begging him to make things easier when his father threatened them. Of his mother's exaggerated politeness and pretended happiness, all to create an image of a perfect family. Meanwhile, his father sat stone-faced, waiting for the slightest mistake to occur and send him into a rage. Caleb shook his head to banish the memories, but the pit in his stomach remained.

"Please, Caleb." Her soft voice hinted she remembered those times too.

"Do you have any idea how awkward it would be for me to ask her out? We're business associates." Rivals more like, but he kept her separate from his business dealings.

"So, you have something in common already," she said. "You won't have to worry about all the small talk you hate."

Like he'd ever discuss business with…come to think of it, it might not be a bad idea. "What do you want me to do, Lexie?"

"Take her out. Show her how nice you can be. Show her the side I see."

He looked at the pile of paperwork sitting on his glass desk. He had a CAST call tomorrow to prepare for, and three meetings beforehand. The gods were conspiring against him today, but he could never deny his sister anything.

"Fine," he said. He'd come at his buyout proposal head on. Maybe if he buttered Fiona up a little, she'd be more willing to listen to his idea.

****

"I need to double check the dates when you want to advertise your private consultation business." Patricia handed her tablet to Fiona and pointed to the appropriate line on the ad form.

Fiona nodded.

"Okay," Patricia said. "I'll submit the form." She returned to her desk and the phone rang.

"Love, Laugh, Live, Patricia speaking." She glanced over at Fiona as she worked on her latest blog post. "Just a minute, please." She pressed hold. "It's Caleb Zeno."

Fiona swung around; her post forgotten for the moment. "What is with that man?" She pushed off the chair and paced in front of her desk. "Why won't he leave this alone?"

"Do you want me to tell him you're busy?"

She ran a hand through her hair and blew the wisps away from her face. "No, I'll take it." She plunked herself on her chair and grabbed her phone. Counting to five, she spoke. "Hello, Caleb."

He cleared his throat. "I thought you were in a meeting."

"Why?" She shouldn't be encouraging conversation with him.

"Because you didn't answer right away."

The nerve of the man. "I have work to do, Caleb. I can't brush everything else aside just because you call me."

He huffed. "This was a bad idea."

Had she entered the conversation in the middle? "What was a bad idea?"

"Calling you."

She frowned. "Well, I didn't ask you to."

"No, Lexie did."

Although she'd only known Lexie a few months, the two women had grown close. So why did Lexie ask her brother to call? "What about Lexie?"

"Not *about* her. I'm calling *because* of her."

She groaned. "Caleb, I don't have time to talk in circles right now. Is there something you wanted, other than for me to sell my company to you, which is still a no, by the way?"

"I called to invite you out."

"Out?"

"Yes."

Her body went cold. "I told you I'm not interested in selling my company to you. No in-person meeting is going to change my mind."

"This isn't a meeting. Lexie wants us to go out."

"Like as in a date?" Images of deep brown irises, muscular arms and those tattoos flitted through her mind, and her heart fluttered. "Why?"

A sound halfway between a cough and a laugh came through the phone before a long silence. Her heartbeat returned to normal. He wanted her company bad enough to date her to get it. So far, all their interactions had been somewhere on a scale between rude and uncomfortable. No matter how gorgeous he was, he was not the kind of man she should date, even if her friend suggested it. No matter how much a part of her wanted to know more about those tattoos...

"No, not like a date. She wants us to settle our differences, get along for her sake," he said, breaking the silence.

Her cheeks heated in embarrassment at her misunderstanding. "And we can't do it over the phone?" She swallowed. This had to be the strangest conversation she'd ever had.

"She says we need to see each other's faces."

He didn't sound anymore pleased about this than she was. *Give me a break.* She remembered the tingles of electricity skittering along her arm each time their hands touched. Had he felt them too? Maybe he was attracted to her and used his sister as an excuse to ask her out.

She couldn't reconcile the alpha personality he presented with someone who hesitated to invite her on a date. She had to be wrong. Meanwhile, this was the longest stretch of time she'd spent thinking about him without being annoyed.

"Do you always do whatever your sister wants?" The question fell from her mouth before she had the chance to evaluate whether she should ask it. She swallowed.

Once again, he made a strangled noise over the phone. Except this time, silence didn't follow it. "I try to, although I shouldn't admit it."

She laughed. Whatever she thought about him

45

professionally, he cared about his sister. "Okay, let's say I go along with this…for Lexie's sake. What then?"

"Dinner."

She had to eat. Did she want to eat with him, though? Lexie had mentioned how great her brother was. She'd apparently talked to Caleb about her as well. Usually, she hated being fixed up. But maybe it would be better to grab a bite to eat with him and then tell Lexie they just hadn't clicked. And since she had no intention of selling him her company, it wasn't like she risked mixing business with pleasure.

"Is the thought of eating dinner with me that bad?" His voice rumbled across the phone line. How bad could it be? Besides, if the beach was any indication, she would be thrown into social situations with Caleb. At least this way, they could try to smooth things between them.

"How about the new Thai place around the corner from my apartment?" she asked. She'd been meaning to try it. It was low-key and didn't look like the type of place where you lingered. The perfect spot for a quick "satisfy Lexie" dinner.

"Do you like seafood?"

"Yes." The Thai place had seafood.

"I'll pick you up tonight at seven. Dress casually."

"Tonight? It's short notice. How do you know I'm free?"

"Are you?"

She gritted her teeth but got it over with. "Yes."

"Goodbye, Fiona."

He disconnected the phone before she had a chance to say anything else. Still, his high-handedness irked her as much as his voice saying her name made her insides melt. Dress casually? Did he think she didn't know how to dress for the restaurant she suggested? He knew what she did for a living, right? She fingered the light wool pants she wore. They would work as long as she didn't spill anything on them between now and then.

"So, are you going to tell me?" Patricia arched a pierced eyebrow at her.

"Lexie wants the two of us to get to know one another." She made air quotes to emphasize just how ludicrous the idea was.

"So, she's setting you two up."

Fiona rolled her eyes. "She's trying to, but I don't think either one of us is thrilled with the idea. We're grabbing a quick bite. We'll call a truce and make Lexie happy."

****

He rubbed sweaty palms against his jean-clad thighs before ringing Fiona's doorbell. Of all the favors his sister asked of him this was, by far, the most ridiculous. And he would have said no if he could. But he never could, and here he was. When Fiona opened the door, he reminded himself he never let others see his emotions.

Her brown hair kissed her bare shoulders. Her turquoise top clung to her breasts. Her gray pants hugged her hips and made him want to pull her against him to see if she felt as delightful as she smelled. What the hell? She was supposed to be a business associate. The only thing he wanted from her was her company.

"I told you casual."

She frowned. "I see we're starting off on the right foot again."

His heart rate increased, and he cursed to himself.

"Hello," he said.

"A little better. Hello to you, too. And this *is* casual. We're going for Thai food."

"No, we're not. You should change."

She scanned his body, and he suppressed the urge to fidget. When she folded her arms, he resisted staring at her breasts. Well, maybe a glance or two…

"I'm not doing anything or going anywhere until you tell me what the plan is. This 'do this, wear that' might work for others, but not me."

Why was he such a beast around her? He stuffed his hands in his pockets. "You're right, sor—" Noise from inside her apartment distracted him. "Am I interrupting something?"

She paused and then understanding dawned. "No, the racket is my TV. You might as well come inside. Seems like we're going to be a while."

He followed her inside and blinked. Color overwhelmed him. The last time he'd been inside her apartment, he'd rushed toward the hysterical female and the ant swarm, seeing nothing but Fiona's panic. This time, in desperation, he looked anywhere but at her.

She led him into her living room. Two walls were painted red, the other two a warm cream. Colorful modern art hung on the walls, multi-colored blankets draped a sofa, chair, and ottoman, and plants covered most surfaces. Some Spanish language program played on the television.

"You speak Spanish?" he asked.

"No."

He pointed to the TV, and she shrugged. "I love telenovelas. They're so dramatic and filled with emotion. Even without the subtitles turned on, I can understand what they mean."

She might not need to understand Spanish to understand the program, but he needed a Fiona translator to understand her.

"Now, tell me where we're going so I can decide what to wear, since you seem to have a problem with this," she said.

"We're going clamming. And you need to wear…clothes for clamming."

Her beauty captivated him. Shaking his head, he refocused on his task. This was a favor for his sister. Her beauty was irrelevant.

"We're going clamming?"

Why did she repeat everything he said and was this alarming trait a habit? And did she expect him to answer her every single time?

She said, "You said seafood."

This he could handle. "Clams come from the sea. Seafood."

"What am I supposed to wear clamming?"

Why did women everywhere ask men this question? He'd said casual clothes. He wore jeans and a shirt. How difficult was this? He looked at himself and spread his arms.

She shook her head. "You are less than helpful. Sit, make yourself comfortable, and I'll be back in a couple of minutes." She left the room.

He might not understand why women asked about clothes, but he sure as hell knew "back in a couple of minutes" meant at least a half hour. He settled into the sofa, which was comfortable enough for him to wish he could lie down on it and was still searching for the TV remote when she returned.

"Is this better?"

He didn't know what shocked him more—her return two minutes later, or her ability to look even sexier in jeans and a T-shirt than in her previous outfit. She'd pulled her hair into a ponytail. It swished against her neck as she walked. Instead of the turquoise shirt, she wore a red V-neck. The color emphasized the rosiness of her cheeks. Her distressed jeans were rolled at the ankles and hugged her hips like skin. She wore gray Converse sneakers, without socks and she smelled like flowers.

"Are you ready?" she asked.

With a nod—words crammed in his throat, but he didn't know what to say—he followed her from the apartment and led the way to his car.

"A Range Rover?"

"I don't like putting clamming equipment in Barbara."

She stopped; her face creased in a frown. "Barbara?"

He swallowed at his slip. "My Ferrari."

Her nose wrinkled. "You named your Ferrari Barbara?"

That's what he'd just said. He wasn't planning to repeat himself. And then she smiled, and he almost forgot what they were talking about.

"I like the name. It reminds me of Bárbara Mori."

Her smile must have addled his wits because he had no idea what she meant. "I bought her in Santa Barbara. Who is Bárbara Mori?"

"A character from my favorite telenovela. It's a romance about a poor, beautiful, woman who improved her life by seducing a millionaire doctor."

She thought this was romantic. "Sounds manipulative to me."

Putting a hand over her heart, she sighed. When she reached for the door handle, he opened it and waited for her to settle before jogging around to the driver's side.

"I suppose you named this too," she said.

"Victoria. I visited Victoria Falls in Africa the first time I drove a Range Rover."

She ran her hand over the leather seat. "The vacation must have been incredible. I've never left the country."

She'd never been outside the US? He wondered why. He'd traveled all over the world for business and pleasure. "It was."

"Where are we going?" she asked as she buckled herself in.

"Pismo Beach."

He gripped the steering wheel, maneuvered through traffic, and tapped the touchscreen for the satellite radio. Usually, driving soothed him. But with her in the car, his senses were on high alert. The flowers he'd smelled earlier filled his nostrils. Every move she made distracted him. He scoured his brain for something to say.

"Here, let me." Her hand met his on the touchscreen, and his skin burned from the contact. He returned his hand to the steering wheel—not because he didn't want the skin-to-skin contact to last, but because he didn't want her to know how her touch affected him. The cool, hard steering wheel contrasted with her warm, soft skin.

She tuned the radio to a country song, and he shook his head at the image of his supercharged Range Rover playing music more appropriate for a ride in a pickup truck.

"What's wrong?" she asked.

"Interesting choice of music."

"My mom got me hooked when I was a child. Do you want me to change it?"

"No, you're welcome to play whatever you like."

The car idled in traffic, and he turned. Her eyebrow arched. He'd never seen anything so sexy.

"Did Lexie force you to let me have my way with the music?"

"My sister doesn't force me to do anything."

Fiona coughed. "Other than taking me to dinner."

He almost smiled. She did. Her gaze brightened, her cheeks dimpled, and her mouth...he looked away and she laughed. But unlike when she laughed at his business proposal, this time he didn't mind. The cars on the freeway moved again, and he tapped along to the almost catchy tune on the radio.

"I love Carrie Underwood," Fiona said.

"Why?"

"Her lyrics are so emotional."

He stopped tapping to the music and listened to the lyrics. Storms, wind, and mean men. He swallowed. Not what he wanted to dwell on. "As long as you like it."

"What about you? What music do you like?"

He preferred music without lyrics. "Jazz. Miles Davis." He could indulge his own emotions with it, without advertising his feelings to everyone.

She gave him a half smile, as if she'd read his

thoughts. But that was impossible. Her scent must be messing with his head. He wondered if the leather would retain the light smell after she left the car. He wondered why he cared.

At the beach, he parked and opened the door. The car was high off the ground, and she reached for his hand to exit. Once again, tingles ran along his arm when they touched. He glanced down to see what he stood on to cause such electricity between them.

Pavement.

Clearing his throat, he let go of her hand and opened the rear door. He removed a shovel, bucket, two rakes, and a dowel, as well as two pairs of rubber boots.

"Here, you'll need these," he said, and handed her a pair of boots.

"You could have just told me to bring rain boots," she said, removing her sneakers and stepping into the black rubber boots he gave her. They were the same ones Lexie used when the two of them went clamming together, and the calves gapped on Fiona just as much as they did on Lexie.

He'd been distracted by her. He hadn't considered whether or not she owned rain boots. "These are insulated."

He led the way to the beach. There were other people there, and he walked away from them, scouring the sand for the U-shaped holes that indicated where clams were buried. Seagulls squawked and circled overhead. Waves lapped against the sand. When he found what looked like a good spot, he turned. "Ever done this before?"

She shook her head, her ponytail swinging back and forth. What would her hair feel like if he caught the ponytail and let the strands glide through his fingers? He swallowed. He had no business being attracted to her.

"I'll dig, and when I find the clams, you'll rake gently to pry them from the sand."

He dug, conscious of her watching him. Or maybe she searched for clams. Either way, he wasn't used to having an audience, and he gripped the shovel handle tighter. A couple inches below the surface, he found a clam. "Take the rake and pry it loose."

For someone who'd never clammed before, she got the hang of it, and in fifteen minutes they reached their legal limit.

He stood to stretch before bending to grab the shovel. Water splashed his scalp. He brushed his hand over his head and reached down again. Once more, his head got wet. He glanced at Fiona. She looked innocent. Too innocent.

"Was that you?"

"Was what me?" she asked. Her foot tapped the sand, making a slapping sound in the water and wet sand.

She'd relaxed, which, for some reason, gave him satisfaction. "Never mind."

When he bent a third time, his cheek got wet. Straightening, he suppressed a smile at her giggle. "You're going to regret this."

"I don't know what you're talking about." She blinked, but he wasn't fooled by her fake innocence. Entertained? Maybe. But not fooled.

He continued to clean their equipment, palming an empty clamshell as he went.

"You're not planning to put the clams in your car,

are you?" She scrunched her face at the briny smell.

"No." He suppressed a shudder—he'd never remove the smell. He began walking to the car, shortening his stride so she didn't have to run. Just as she stepped in front of him, he dropped the extra clamshell down her back.

She shrieked, hopping and pulling her shirt away from her back. Amusement filled him as she found the cold, damp shell and held it in her palm.

Her nostrils flared, and despite her best attempts to hide her enjoyment, her irises sparkled, and her voice lilted. She was terrible at hiding her emotions.

"Retribution."

"I guess I should be glad you slipped it down my back, rather than my front." Her laugh warmed his insides, and he turned his face away, bending over his open trunk.

She pointed to the bucket of clams. "So…now what?" she asked.

"I assume you're talking about dinner, rather than continuing this game you started?"

He pointed to a shack at the other end of the beach. "We give them our clams, and they cook them for us. Then we picnic on the beach."

Her face lit up, and he had to remind himself not to stare. "We're done with the messy part." He removed his boots.

She did the same, hopping to keep her balance. Caleb reached to steady her and once again, an electric charge pulsed where his hand touched her elbow. He had to come up with a way to stop it from happening. She glanced at him, her gaze traveling from his fingers on her elbow, to his arm, and finally to his face. If he were the type who blushed, he'd swear his face heated. But he'd long ago taught himself not to. It was hot, even at sunset.

"If you're ready, we should go," he said.

She nodded. "How often do you come here?"

Shrugging, he slowed his pace to match hers. "I've been here a few times."

"Wow!" She stopped and he turned to her.

"What?"

"The sunset is gorgeous."

Purple and orange streaked the sky, turning the clouds a deep gray. The fading light glinted on the ocean waves that crashed along the shore. He nodded. With a sigh, she continued walking. The line of people at the clam shack waited with their buckets, and they stood behind them. Fiona kept turning to watch the sky.

"Tell me how you like your clams. I'll place our order, and you can go watch the sunset."

She shrugged. "I've never eaten them before. To be honest, they're so slimy…"

"Go find a table. I'll take care of the food." When she looked skeptical, he added, "Trust me."

She walked away, and he tried not to admire her ass. After ordering steamed clams with butter and garlic, French fries, coleslaw, and beer, he searched the tables for Fiona. He found her sitting with her back toward him at the table farthest away from the clam shack, with an unobstructed view of the sunset.

Caleb arranged the food, keeping an eye on the sky and trying not to notice the graceful slope of Fiona's neck. The beautiful sunset would give way to a clear night, perfect for stargazing. With any luck, he could finish his dinner with Fiona and spend time with his telescope.

She turned around. "This place is beautiful."

He nodded. "I like coming here during the summer."

"Does Lexie come with you?"

He shook his head. "She did once or twice, but she's not into foraging for food."

Fiona laughed. This was the second time today she'd laughed with him, and he wondered what he could do to make her laugh a third time.

Fiona took a taste of one of the clams, and Caleb waited. For some reason, he wanted her to like it. She chewed with care. "Okay, I have to admit, this is good."

"You doubted me?"

"Like I said, they're kind of gross looking. But Lexie doesn't know what she's missing."

"She eats them. She just doesn't hunt for them."

"She should try it sometime." Fiona tasted another clam and swallowed. "It's fun."

"So you're not going to hold my making you forage for food against me?"

"As long as you don't hold my splashing you against me."

"Deal."

Fiona wiped her mouth with her napkin before returning it to her lap. "So, tell me why we're here."

He leaned forward, elbows on the table. "You know why."

"You want to buy my company."

"Lexie hates conflict, and she likes both of us. I'm willing to try for a truce for her sake."

She raised an eyebrow. "And nothing else?"

If getting to know her made it easier for him to

discuss purchasing her company, it was a bonus, but one he didn't plan to discuss tonight. "Nothing else."

"So you always do what your sister wants."

"She deserves to be happy." Hell, she deserved way more than happiness—safety, security, and anything else he could do. He'd vowed to protect her, and he always would. But he couldn't tell Fiona.

Watching Fiona's face was like reading a map of her innermost thoughts. Disbelief and admiration filtered across it. Did she realize what she gave away?

"You should be more careful with your expressions," he said. The words surprised him. He didn't give advice to anyone, much less his adversaries. But someone like her, who wore her feelings for all to see, needed to be careful.

"What expressions?"

"The ones that show me what you're thinking."

She rose, snatched her garbage from the table, and went in search of a trashcan. He followed.

She stalked away, the heels of her sneakers making deep impressions in the sand, as if she were stamping her anger with them. Anger?

"Why do you seem angry with me?" He raced to her side. His legs were longer, but he touched her arm to get her to stop.

She spun around. "You tell me, Mr. Mind Reader."

Her gaze snapped in the setting sun, her skin taking on a rosy glow.

"I'm trying to help you," he said.

"Help me?"

"You're a businesswoman. You can't negotiate to your advantage if the other person can read on your face everything you're thinking."

She folded her arms across her chest, and he forced himself to ignore the cleavage her action emphasized. "So, this *is* a business dinner. I thought we were here because of your sister." She escaped his grasp and marched along the beach, away from the clammers and the parking lot.

"It isn't. We are." He jogged ahead of her, turned, and faced her, forcing her to stop. "I was just giving you advice."

"I don't need your advice. Robots show no emotion. And I'm not a robot."

He raised his arms. "Okay, no more advice. And I agree, you're not a robot." He scanned her body, and heat warmed him. Needing to change the subject, he looked at the horizon. The sun was almost below the water line. "Want to take a walk on the beach before we leave?"

"Is this your idea of an apology?"

She wanted him to apologize for protecting her? He swallowed. From her perspective, maybe he overstepped. He nodded. "I didn't mean to be bossy."

She looked over the water, and her face softened. "Yes, I'd like to take a walk."

In silence, they walked on the sand. He looked at the sky and stopped. "Wait," he said, reaching for her arm to stop her. Ignoring the electricity shooting along his arm, he pointed to the sky. "If you look right there, you can see Jupiter."

She stared.

His gaze shifted between the planet and her lips.

"How do you recognize Jupiter?" she asked.

"I like star gazing." He stuffed his hands in his pockets. "I have a telescope at home I use on clear nights."

She looked at him, her gaze softening. "My dad showed me Orion's Belt when I was a kid, but I don't think I can find anything else on my own."

He had no idea why he cared so much about her enjoyment, but it put him at ease. Warmth from her body floated toward him. An invisible pull made him want to get closer to her, to teach her about the stars. But they were together for the sake of his sister. No other reason. Even if he did like her.

"Do you ever mention astronomy on your site?"

Fiona stilled and looked at him askance. "No. I'm not sure how stars relate to a lifestyle site."

"It can relate on lots of levels—best star-gazing spots, folklore around constellations, eclipses, how to buy the perfect telescope...you should consider it."

"I don't think astronomy plays to my target audience."

"It could."

She faced him, shoulders thrown back, hands on hips. "I know what my audience likes and doesn't like. Thanks for the suggestion, though."

The sign of a good leader—whether political or corporate—was the ability take advice. But it went both ways, and she knew what her audience wanted. He watched the tide coming in. The waves provided a gentle background purr. "Okay, but you might want to think about it for the future."

"The future." She tapped her foot on the sand. "As in, the future when you are running my company?"

"I never said anything about running your company. In fact, I said it was negotiable, on page eight I think."

She opened her mouth, closed it, turned away, and turned back. Fiona wrapped her arms around her waist and stared at the water. "This isn't working," she said, her voice soft.

"What isn't?"

She pointed from herself to him. "This. Us. Getting along for Lexie's sake."

"No, it doesn't seem to be." His stomach dropped. He'd promised his sister he'd try to get along with Fiona. And for a short time, he'd enjoyed himself.

"Lexie's going to be disappointed," Fiona said.

He couldn't disappoint his sister. "Not if we don't tell her."

Fiona swung around. "Are you suggesting we lie?"

"Never. I'm suggesting we pretend, for her sake, to get along."

"I would never forgive someone who tricked me," she said.

"Then at least give me time to break it to her."

Fiona made a face. "Why are you afraid of your sister?"

He stiffened before making a concerted effort to relax. "I'm not afraid of her. But she's had a rough time, and I need to be careful with her."

"Careful with her? I know I haven't known her long, but she's never seemed fragile to me. Emotional maybe, but…"

"You don't know her as well as I do. I'm asking for time."

He held his breath and waited for her answer. Lexie had had too many disappointments in her life. And even though she was married to a man who adored her, she deserved anything he could do to make things easier on her.

Fiona stared at the waves, her arms wrapped around her waist. "Fine, I'll give you time."

Tension seeped from him, and his spine loosened. "Thank you."

"But I'm not lying. If she asks me a direct question, I'm giving her an honest answer."

"Fair enough."

"And to be clear," she added, "under no circumstances am I willing to consider any type of business deal with you. My company is not for sale."

She'd moved closer to him, so the toes of her Converse almost touched the toes of his Nikes. In the dark, it was difficult to see her features. But he smelled flowers, which mixed with the salty brine of the sea and floated around him. He could hear her choppy breathing mingle with the swish of the waves. And his entire body tingled.

She was clear, all right.

"Crystal."

Chapter Six

"So, tell me about your date," Lexie exclaimed on the phone the next day.

Fiona lowered the volume of the TV, sighing at missing her favorite telenovela episode. She double-checked it recorded before focusing on her friend's demand. She remembered her agreement with Caleb.

"We went clamming."

"Oh, my God! My brother took you clamming. What is wrong with him? The last time he took me, I got filthy, I sliced my fingers on the shells, and the sliminess made me gag."

Fiona shook her head. "It was kind of fun." And it had been, at least the clamming part. When he wasn't trying to convince her to sell her company, she had enjoyed the evening. She'd splashed him, trying to get him to relax, and it had worked. He'd been a good sport. He'd also taken care of everything so she could enjoy the sunset and had pointed out Jupiter. Had it been a date, and had it ended then, she would have counted it a success. *Not a "sweep me off my feet" success, but a success.*

"I never would have pictured you as someone who likes clamming."

Fiona leaned into the sofa. "Well, your brother dug for them, and all I had to do was rake them into the pail. And the clam shack was delicious!"

Even now, her mouth watered thinking about all the buttery goodness.

"And my brother?"

The ass. The enigma. The protector. She shivered.

"What did you think of him? Come on, he's growing on you."

Yeah, like a barnacle. "He was...fine." Fine was a good word, right? It could mean anything, depending on inflection. And maybe Lexie would take it in the sexy way people said it, even if she meant it as a synonym for "nice" or "okay." Because she didn't know how to answer Lexie's question without outright lying.

On the one hand, he was a cold automaton who showed no emotion and kept trying to sneak in ways to get her to sell her company. On the other hand, he was solicitous and gave away glimpses of himself—like when his gaze lightened, and she glimpsed the humor he hid—something she had a feeling he never meant to do. And when he did, she almost...liked him.

Since she had agreed less than twelve hours ago to give Caleb time to let Lexie adjust to the idea, she couldn't tell her the truth. *I hope he does it soon.*

"Oh, I'm so glad," Lexie gushed. "You must get to know what's beneath his exterior. I'm so happy you discovered the real him."

The real him? She didn't think she had enough upper body strength to chip away at his armor to find "the real him." But if Lexie thought so, all the better. It would make their friendship easier. She didn't have to date him. They just needed to get along in social situations, which, if she had her way, would be few and far between.

Fiona disconnected the call, shaking her head. What would it be like to have someone who cared so much about your feelings he went to such great lengths not to hurt you? Her chest ached with longing.

Grabbing her laptop, she logged onto Caleb's website, and checked the competition. She'd been meaning to study it and learn why he wanted to buy hers. But a bright purple coupon for new subscribers to the members-only portion of the website flashed in front of her on the screen. Just for kicks, she clicked on the pop-up. And her jaw dropped. Because an offer for new subscribers who "had tried smaller, overly cheerful competitors and wanted the experience of wide-ranging experts" to get fifty percent off their membership fee and first month's purchases through this site, stared at her in black and white.

He should have just said Love, Laugh, Live's customers and be done with it.

She squinted. Okay, maybe he hadn't mentioned her site specifically, but come on! There were very few sites like hers providing personal service that competed with Caleb's.

She pushed her laptop to one side and paced her apartment. No way. Of all the underhanded things to do, trying to befriend her and steal her customers at the same time was the worst. She didn't care if it was business. She didn't care if he was her friend's brother. He was a worm. Except worms were soft, and he wasn't. He was…he was…an armadillo. Sure, he might have armor protecting him, but she would find the slits in between those plates, and skewer him.

But first, she needed to enlist Patricia's help. And then they were going to fight.

****

Caleb stared at his computer screen, waiting for the videoconference to start. His three college friends and CAST business partners—Alex, Simon, and Ted—were due to sign on at any moment. Caleb looked forward to discussing their next investment. All of them had more money than they needed and pooling their resources had enabled them to help causes near and dear to their hearts. It made him feel good. Or at least, it did in the past.

This time, he had no idea who he wanted to benefit or how, and the typical list of charities and organizations didn't inspire him. He should suggest creating something. But he didn't know what. Well, not quite. He always wanted to help battered women's shelters. With his background, it was dear to his heart. The problem was he wanted something…different.

"Hello!"

His screen squawked, and Caleb smiled. Simon's icon appeared—he would rarely allow himself to be seen on video, even with his three best friends.

"Si. How are you?"

"Doing well. Working on landscaping ideas. You?"

Caleb shrugged. "Trying to convince someone to let me buy her company."

"Her?"

Caleb shook his head, and Simon laughed. "We'll talk more about this in private."

Caleb started to argue, but Ted and Alex logged on almost at the same time.

"Hey, guys," Alex said.

"Hello," Ted said. "So, who are we swooping in to save today?"

"Funny, Ted," Simon said. "I emailed you all a few ideas. What do you think?"

"I liked the arts in the schools project," Alex said. "Did you get my suggestions about which markets to target?"

"Yes," Caleb said. "How much are we talking about spending?" Caleb asked.

"It's going to vary, depending on location, size of the school system, etc." Simon answered. After another forty minutes of discussing possible geographical locations, as well as the progress of their current investments, they all signed off. Caleb stretched. None of the potential charities in their choice of cities inspired him. They were worthy, just…ordinary. And there were at least two other local arts-in-the-schools programs. As worthy a cause as it was, he wished they could create something more unique. With a sigh, he shut his computer down and got ready to go home. He'd reconsider the list later and maybe research local battered women's shelters. He called for his car.

Five minutes later, he exited his office and climbed into Barbara, thinking about Fiona's reaction to his Ferrari's name. The revving engine centered him, and he eased onto the road, putting aside thoughts of the infuriating woman. Jazz played on his Spotify app and Caleb hummed along. Would Fiona like his choice of music? He groaned and let the changing colors of sunset in LA distract him. The light from the setting sun gleamed off the steel and glass buildings. The harsh beauty made his shoulders loosen. At the traffic light, he slowed and opened his sunroof. A cool breeze wafted in, and he inhaled. What would Fiona say about the range of colors? He groaned.

His phone rang, and he depressed the "answer call" button on his steering wheel, thankful for the interruption.

"Hello?"

"Caleb, it's Lexie. Fiona was in an accident."

His heart thudded, then he made a U-turn and floored the pedal.

****

The pickup truck plowed into Fiona's passenger side. Her body jerked. Her head rocked side to side. The seatbelt dug into her chest. She gripped the steering wheel. Her car spun to a halt in the middle of the intersection.

She blinked. Her heart pounded in her chest, and the acrid smell of the side airbag filled her nostrils. The light had turned green, and she'd stepped on the gas. And then, wham. She looked around. She needed to move her car to the side of the road so she wouldn't get hit by anyone else, but knowing, and getting her body to obey her brain, were two different things.

"Crap."

She shook her head to clear her foggy mind, wincing at the neck pain. Raising her right hand, she ran it over her body and across her face. No blood. She inhaled. Her chest didn't hurt. She needed to call Lexie. She wasn't making it to movie night. Reaching for her phone that was somehow still attached to the dashboard, she dialed her friend.

"Lex, it's Fi. I was in a car accident."

"Oh my God, are you okay?"

Fiona shifted. "I think so. But I'm not going to make tonight."

"Where are you? I'll come right over."

She looked around. Only a few blocks from home, but Lexie and her hysterical attempts to help made Fiona shudder. "No, don't. I'll be okay."

Before Lexie protested, Fiona disconnected the call. She closed her eyes a minute, hoping she'd imagined everything. When she opened them, she still sat in the middle of the intersection, cars swerving to avoid her. She needed to get to the side of the road. Before she could do anything, pounding on her window made her jump.

"What the hell were you doing?" A man shouted. He had a dark beard and mustache, which trembled as he spoke.

She flinched. Behind him, a dented pickup truck parked at an angle. He must be the driver. A wave of dizziness rolled over her.

She rolled her window a crack. "Me? You hit my car."

"Because you were in the middle of the road!" The irate man screamed, and his spittle landed on her window. Her pulse raced.

"My light was green." She gripped the steering wheel. "You plowed into me."

He paced next to her car. He was large, with a beer belly. He opened his mouth, foul breath pouring from it, but a hand on his shoulder spun him around. Caleb.

Fiona gasped.

Caleb remained silent, his massive hand on the other guy's shoulder. His button-down shirt stretched across his wide chest and shoulder span. Tension rolled off him in almost visible waves. His blank face conveyed fury. And she didn't know why. He didn't frown or snarl or even glare. But her blood ran cold at his calmness. His only tell was a slight tic of his jaw muscle.

Her pulse pounded.

"The police are on their way," he said to the other driver in a low voice. So low, in fact, she strained to hear him through the cracked open window. "If you're smart, you'll wait in your truck."

The other guy tipped his head to meet Caleb's stare. He swallowed and rushed to his truck.

Caleb turned to her, and his attitude transformed. She couldn't point to anything specific to account for the change. But this man was the opposite of the man who had menaced the other driver. He was just as calm as he had been moments ago. The tic in his jaw was gone, and his gaze softened. Once again, he was Lexie's brother. He infuriated her, but he awed her with his presence. And he'd protected her. She didn't know what to make of him, except she felt safe.

Safe? Well, as safe as she could be around someone intent on luring away her clients. Why was Caleb here? Did he plan to get her to sell her company now, in the middle of an intersection?

She rolled open the window. His spicy aftershave wafted into the car.

Caleb leaned forward, resting his arms on the window jam. "Are you all right? Are you hurt?" His voice surrounded her, filling all her empty places. His pale face strained with worry. His voice was deep and rich, making her think of dark chocolate. She must be hungry.

"What are you doing here?"

"Lexie called me. I'm checking to make sure you're okay."

"I think so." Fiona stared at Caleb's hand, which dangled close to her shoulder. The hint of a tattoo peeked from beneath his cuff. She wanted to know what it was.

She reached for her seatbelt and unbuckled it. As she opened the door, he placed his hand on top of hers. It was warm and solid and sent tingles along her arm.

"Where are you going?" he asked.

"I need to get out."

"Stay in your car until the EMTs arrive. I don't know if you're hurt or not."

Fiona moved around inside the car. She bent and straightened her legs, raised and lowered her shoulders. "I think I'm fine." Once again she started to open the door and once again, he stopped her.

"How about you let the EMTs decide?"

In the distance, sirens sounded.

Before she could respond to Caleb, the cops arrived, and for the next half hour, questions about the accident, inquiries into her health, and the exchange of insurance information overwhelmed her. The EMTs checked her and instructed her to go to the hospital if her pain worsened later. And then the tow trucks appeared. Only when they'd loaded her car onto one bed, the dented pickup truck on another, did she realize she had no way of getting home.

"You getting in?" the one tow driver asked.

"I'll take her home," Caleb said.

She looked between the two of them, like she was a spectator at a tennis match. She hated watching sports. Especially now since her neck was sore.

The tow driver was a stranger. Caleb was her adversary.

It was time to Uber. "No, thanks," she said, addressing the two of them. "I'll call a ride share."

"I said I'll take you home."

The tow truck pulled away, but Caleb leaned against his car, arms crossed. His biceps were massive.

"I'm not selling my company to you."

A ghost of a smile graced his lips before it disappeared.

This was new.

"I'm not trying to buy your company," he said.

"Oh? Well, the coupon was a low blow." She scowled and grabbed her phone.

"Are you calling a cab or 911?"

A laugh escaped. "It's a toss-up right now."

His gaze lightened, even though his mouth didn't curve in a smile. "If I promise not to talk about business, will you let me drive you home?"

She shifted from one foot to the other. It was dark and cold. And the muscles in her shoulders and neck were getting tight.

"Lexie wouldn't like it if I left you here."

"So, your kindness is all an act?"

At his blank look, she continued. "You're pretending to be concerned for my well-being because of the agreement you made with your sister?"

He stood straight, his hand in a fist at his side. "My concern for you is real and has been since I heard about the accident."

Her stomach plummeted. "Sorry, I was mean."

His hand relaxed at his side. "If you'd rather call someone else to get you, I'll wait with you until they arrive."

He'd come to her rescue, had dealt with the angry truck driver, and offered her a ride. No matter what his other intentions were, he'd been nothing but kind. "No, thank you. I'd like a ride if you're still offering."

Chapter Seven

The expression on her face gave every thought away. Annoyance transformed to confusion to embarrassment and ultimately, to acceptance. Once again, he thought about how she must be a terrible negotiator, but he didn't want to anger her, like last time. Not while injured. Besides, he was relieved knowing what someone thought at any given time. He pointed across the intersection.

"I have Barbara. Come on, she's waiting."

As they walked, he wondered about his concern for her. Lexie had called him, begged him to check on her. Once he had, he couldn't walk away. The blood had frozen in his veins and time had slowed when he learned the victim's identity. He'd imagined any one of multiple horrible scenarios and his chest had tightened, making it difficult to breathe.

When the truck's driver started menacing Fiona, a desire to protect her had overwhelmed him. His vision had gone red when the man had raised his voice. Guys like the truck driver didn't respond to anything but intimidation. His father had taught the lesson well. And now, looking at her, alone, without a ride, he needed to make sure she got home safe.

Fiona's laugh brought him to the present. The sound warmed him, made him want to make her laugh more often. It almost made him want to join in.

"You call your car a 'she?' " Fiona snorted.

"All cars are 'she's'. You already know this, though." He enjoyed watching her reactions, although he'd never tell her.

She rolled her eyes. "I didn't realize how serious you were about car nomenclature."

She amused him. "Let's get in so I can drive you home to rest."

She held up a finger. Few people told him to wait. Of those who did, he listened to even fewer. However, she was one of them. He folded his arms and leaned against Barbara while Fiona made a phone call.

"Lexie, it's me. I'm fine. A little sore, and I have no idea what's going on with my car, but I didn't want you to worry about me." She nodded, before glancing his way. "She wants to talk to you."

He took the phone from her outstretched hand before opening the car door to let her in. Only when she was settled did he speak. "Lex?"

"Caleb? Are you sure she's okay?"

His sister was calm, compared to her usual temperament. He glanced at Fiona. Somehow, this woman handled Lexie. "She seems so. The EMTs examined her. The accident could have been worse. It was the other guy's fault."

"As long as Fiona is okay, I don't care whose fault it was."

"Lex, I have to go. I'm giving her a ride home. Are you home now?"

"No, I'm with Steve. Fiona was supposed to meet us at the movies. Do you think we should check on her?"

He looked over again at Fiona. She rested her head

against the back of the seat. He had a strange desire to brush her cheek. "I'm sure she'll be okay. Enjoy the movie."

"She was just in an accident, Caleb. Don't leave her alone, please."

He swallowed. "I'll stay until you return. Have fun." He climbed inside the car and handed the phone to Fiona. "I didn't realize you had plans with her."

"I didn't know I had to clear my social calendar with you." She winced. "Sorry, I was rude." She rubbed her neck.

"Is your neck okay? Do you want me to take you to the hospital?" He hadn't intended to be responsible for her, but he couldn't let her suffer if he could help it.

"No, don't worry. I'm just not good at keeping myself from saying every thought in my brain right now. But you didn't deserve it."

She gave a half smile, and he paused. She had a beautiful smile, even if her manners were a little lacking right now. He started the engine, but her hand on his arm made him pause.

"Um…" she said. She raked her gaze over him.

His skin prickled beneath her examination. He was off his game, since he let a woman who disliked him affect him physically. He waited for her to continue. When she didn't, he spoke. "Do you need something?"

She shook her head. "Never mind."

He gunned the engine.

She gripped his forearm. Maybe she was nervous about riding in a car so soon after the accident?

She looked around. "Your car doesn't look like a 'Barbara.' "

"What does she look like?"

"A super expensive boy toy."

Laughter rumbled in his chest, but he repressed it. "I work hard. I deserve a reward."

"You sure you want me here? The last car I was in, well, you know what happened."

His hand brushed her bare shoulder. Her skin was velvety soft, and he clenched his fist. She was injured. "I said you could have a ride. I never said anything about letting you drive her."

****

Fiona groaned. Her body protested the position required to sit in Caleb's car. She would be sore tomorrow.

"Okay?" Caleb asked.

Despite the lack of words, his voice oozed concern. Normally, his concern focused on Lexie. But since he arrived at the scene of the accident, his entire being had focused on her. Did she want this man concerned about her?

"I'm okay."

Leaning her head against the butter leather headrest, she inhaled. Like the last time she'd ridden in it, the car—she refused to call it "Barbara"—drove like a dream, although the noise of the engine gave her headache.

"I hate to ask, but do you mind if we make a stop? I know you need to get home, but I have to retrieve an important file from my office. If it's a problem, I can get it later, though."

His low voice made her stomach quiver. Unless she was hungry. She wanted to go home and go to bed, but it would be rude for her to argue. "No, it's okay."

He kept his gaze trained on the road. She thought

she'd be nervous being in a car, but it handled so well she didn't mind. Or maybe it was the way he drove—controlled. If she had a car like this, she'd screech around turns, zoom along the road, open the windows, and yell. Caleb drove like the car was an extension of himself. He'd done it the first time she rode with him too. Maybe he was different on his own or with other people, but with her he was more vigilant and reserved.

They approached a high-rise office building she'd last seen in the news. Over the entrance in large silver lettering was WW Media Group.

"Before you say anything, I'm not trying to convince you to sell your company to me." Caleb passed the entrance and pulled around the corner, driving into the underground garage.

"You're parking this here?"

He descended to the lowest level, eased into a spot, and turned off the engine. "Where else would you have me park?"

She unbuckled her seatbelt. "I don't know. Somewhere with armed security, maybe? Or bubble-wrapped garage walls with censors when you get closer than six feet away?"

His eyes glowed, adding gold flecks to the brown irises. It was the only signal he found her comment funny.

"Nothing will happen to my car. Why don't you wait here?"

"No, I think moving will keep my muscles from stiffening."

With a nod, he climbed from the car, walked around to her side, and opened her door. Taking her hand, he helped her. When he dropped it, she resisted the urge to grab it. Instead, she followed him to the elevator bank. At their approach, the doors opened, and he stepped inside. "Are you coming?"

Despite his comment to the contrary, if this was an attempt to convince her to sell her company—when she was injured—she'd kill him.

He waited, like he had all the time in the world. She wanted to go home. She entered the metal box. He took a key card and inserted it into a slot on the control panel. The elevator rose with a minor whirring, and her ears popped. The numbers on the digital readout climbed higher until they reached the highest number. Instead of stopping, the elevator continued. In alarm, she glanced at Caleb, but he remained stoic. When the door opened, he braced his arm against it as if to keep it from closing on her and motioned her to exit. She stepped into an office, with a glass-topped desk at one end, glass and curly maple conference table and chairs at the other, and floor-to-ceiling windows on two of the walls. A silver and red carpet deadened her steps. Fiona walked to the middle of the room and turned in a circle, taking in the expensive, but lifeless, office.

Caleb headed toward the desk.

"You're—"

"Getting something from my desk," he said. He sat in the chair and turned on his computer screen. Behind him, four large TV screens displayed logos of news and entertainment stations.

"But—"

"I planned on working in the office tonight." He focused his gaze on her.

"Stop interrupting me!"

Caleb stilled.

She shouldn't have yelled at him. But his constant interruptions and misunderstanding frustrated her. Now, she paused. The way he held himself told her he was on guard. She didn't know why, but she lowered her voice.

"I'm sorry for yelling. You had no other motive for bringing me here?"

He shook his head.

"Would your work have anything to do with my company?"

His gaze bored into hers. "My success is predicated on my knowing when to keep my mouth shut," he said. "But I have more issues to deal with than just your company."

She sank into a chair across from his desk, if you could call it a desk. All the glass made her itchy—there was no privacy.

He cleared his throat, and Fiona refocused on him. His set face reminded her of a stone statue—bland, blank. He often seemed heartless. Nothing at all like the stars of her telenovelas. A shiver of guilt ran along her spine. Someone heartless wouldn't have helped her today. Maybe she should give him a break.

She walked over to the window. Behind her, shuffling came from Caleb's desk. A gentle wind ruffled the boats on the water below, making their lights dance. White and red lights from the cars moved in a continuous line on the road. Fiona winced. How he could stand working in here was an anathema.

She rubbed her neck and arched her back.

"Sore?"

The shuffling noise stopped, and his voice was close. Too close. She turned and almost bumped her nose into his chest. Oxygen fled, and she resisted the urge to open her mouth and gulp air. Raising her head, she met his gaze. He didn't smile, but his expression showed concern. She nodded. "Getting there. I think it will be worse tomorrow."

He took a step back. "I'll take you home now."

"I can wait if you need to do anything else." Her gaze flitted past him, and she shuddered at the hard angles in the room. It needed color and soft textures.

"What's wrong?"

How to tell your rescuer you hated his décor? You didn't. "Nothing. Just...I guess I'm cold."

Although his expression remained the same, the slight narrowing of his gaze indicated he didn't believe her. Who would? It was June. "Air conditioning," she said.

He stopped on the way across the room. "I didn't say anything."

"You didn't have to."

He stiffened but continued across the room. He remained silent as the elevator descended. He ushered her into his car and once again drove in silence. Unlike the time they'd gone clamming, he didn't offer her the chance to pick the music, and she wasn't sure she should ask. During the drive home, she wracked her brain for something to say, but the silence wasn't awkward. Small talk might be. So, she stopped worrying and studied him from the corner of her eye.

Everything about this man was different from his sister. She wore soft colors and layers. His shirt hugged every muscle in his chest and arms. Well-cut jeans molded his ass and thighs. Lexie never stopped talking. Even when Caleb did speak, it was spare, every word taking on added meaning. Lexie was small and delicate, but feisty. He was large and powerful and…deliberate. At least those were his decent qualities, which she realized were buried, but strong. Highway lamplight glinted off his bald head in a steady pattern, and Fiona wondered about the texture of his skin. Memories of her dream flooded her, and she gripped the hemline of her top to keep her hand from feeling it. A trace of a tattoo peeked from above his shirt collar.

"What kind of tattoo do you have?" she asked before she could stop herself.

He straightened his spine. "Which one?"

So he had multiple ones. *Interesting.* "The one on your neck."

"It's a quote by Octavia Butler."

"The science fiction writer?"

He glanced at her, and Fiona got the impression he hadn't expected her to know the name. "Yes."

Getting information from him was impossible. Before she could ask which quote, he approached her building.

"I'll be all right on my own. You don't have to stay."

"I told Lexie I'd wait with you."

"She worries too much. Thanks for the ride. And for…everything."

He exited the car and opened her door. When he reached for her hand to help her, her skin warmed at the contact and her eyelids widened. His grip was powerful, yet at the same time, gentle. She met his gaze and froze, half in, half out of the car. Brown irises stared at her, and while his face remained expressionless and his voice silent, his eyes spoke volumes. Before she could determine what they said, he pulled her upright and let go of her hand. She missed the contact until he rested his palm on the small of her back.

"Let me see you inside and settled," he said. "Lexie will be here soon and then I'll leave and let her take care of you."

Fiona wanted to send him away, but she was tired of their constant arguments, and her head ached.

"Thank you," she said. "I appreciate it."

****

The doorbell rang an hour later. Despite Caleb's attempt to make her go to bed, she'd stretched on the sofa. Before she had a chance to hobble to the door, Caleb crossed the living room and ushered his sister inside.

"I needed to see how you were." Lexie rushed forward to hug Fiona. She pulled away at the last minute. "Wait, I don't want to hurt you. Are you okay?"

"I'm pretty sore."

"You poor thing. What can I do for you? Can I get you anything?"

"No, I'm good." Fiona turned to Caleb. Between the awkward stretches of silence, Caleb's jumping to get her what he thought she might need, and now Lexie hovering, Fiona had a strong desire to be alone.

But her friends meant well.

She paused. Friends? Was Caleb her friend? She looked at him, his large body perched in a too-small chair nearby. Who else would sacrifice their time to make sure she was okay? Yes, despite their business adversity, he was her friend. At least right now.

"You can go," she said. "Thank you for everything."

He rose from the chair, but Lexie's voice stopped him. "But what if you need something?"

"I'm going to bed, Lex. I can't imagine needing anything tonight. And if I do, I'll call you."

With a nod to her, and a brief hug for his sister, Caleb left.

Lexie sighed. "Are you sure you're okay alone? Do you promise to call me?"

"I promise." She squeezed her friend's hand. "Don't worry about me. I'll be okay."

With a concerned last look, Lexie left, pulling the door shut behind her. The quiet click reverberated through the empty apartment, emphasizing how alone Fiona was. She frowned. She liked being alone. And for the last hour, even though Caleb hadn't moved from her side, he'd been quiet.

So why did his absence unnerve her?

Chapter Eight

The next morning, after a deep sleep, Fiona awoke, stiff and aching. She hobbled into the kitchen to make coffee. It wouldn't help her muscles, but it would help her function. She was pouring coffee as the doorbell rang. *Who the heck is here now?* She peered through the peephole and smiled.

She opened the door. "Hi, Lexie. You're awake early!"

Lexie strode inside with a paper bag smelling of fresh sourdough bread. She followed her into the kitchen, frowning when Lexie shooed her out of the way.

"Don't you need to get to work?" Fiona asked.

"Not until I get you settled for the day."

The small kitchen forced Fiona to step out of the way as Lexie rummaged in cabinets to arrange breakfast, as well as stacking first aid supplies on the counter.

"You don't have to do this," she said, touching the bottle of aspirin, heating pad, and peroxide.

"Shush," Lexie said. "Go sit."

Lexie was on a mission, and it was easier to go along with it than fight. Fiona eased herself into the dining room chair and waited. Three minutes later, Lexie placed bread, fruit, juice, and coffee on the table, along with three place settings.

The doorbell rang again before Fiona could ask about the extra place setting. Before she could rise, the door opened.

"Hello?" A masculine voice called from the hallway.

Lexie called, "Caleb! You're here! It's about time."

Fiona frowned. *Again?* "I didn't realize you were joining us."

"How are you feeling?" he asked. He sat where Lexie pointed but focused his gaze on Fiona.

"Sore, as I expected." She shifted in her chair, uncomfortable at being the center of attention, and looked between brother and sister. "As much as I love the company for breakfast, don't you two have things to do today?"

Lexie patted her arm. "Don't worry. I'm leaving in five minutes. Caleb's going to stay with you."

Fiona swallowed the bite of bread she'd taken. "Hold on. I'm going to take it easy today. Caleb doesn't need to stay with me."

"And leave you alone?" Lexie's voice rose. "You were just in an accident."

Fiona winced. Lexie's excitement grew. Caleb stiffened. As Lexie continued with all the reasons she shouldn't be alone, Fiona observed Caleb getting more tense. His hand tightened around his cup of coffee, his jaw clenched, and although he stared at his sister, he was miles away.

****

It was stupid. Caleb's sister was a more excitable person than he was, and he shouldn't let her set him off. But the combination of her rising pitch and Fiona's pained look brought him right back to his childhood. As much as he tried, he couldn't stop the memories. Like photos in an extra fast slideshow, images of his mother, deflated by his father's verbal abuse, flashed through his brain. Sounds of his sister begging their father to stop, only to cry and shriek when he turned his taunts on her, battered his eardrums. Dizzy, he reached for Fiona.

He grasped the tabletop instead. With effort, he brought his focus to the present. Lexie had paused, her face wrinkled with concern. Fiona stared at him.

Shit.

"Are you okay?"

Fiona's voice penetrated the last of his fog, its smoky texture filtering through and filling the gaping chasms where old memories threatened to take over. His breath returned in a whoosh. Neither Lexie nor Fiona needed saving. He nodded once.

When Lexie returned to the kitchen, Fiona spoke. "Don't let Lexie's comments upset you," she said. "I don't need you to stay."

Upset him? How did she know? Had he shown anything in his expression while the flashback filtered through his brain? He couldn't have. He was too experienced at hiding his emotions.

But then how could she tell?

"How are you this morning?" His voice sounded like it came from far away.

"Sore," she said. "But I expected as much."

"You should take extra care of yourself," he said. "Get rest. Maybe stay home from work today."

He kept his voice detached. He didn't want her to hear the emotions he tried so hard to bury. She wouldn't understand. Even if something about her made him want to confess everything. He searched for a distraction, and his gaze landed on the spaghetti strap of her bright pink shirt.

Color. There were always colors around her. Despite their brightness, he found it…right.

"I can take care of myself."

Despite her gentle tone, her words hit their mark. He didn't need anyone else to take care of, either. He adored his mother and sister and had spent all his life taking care of them. He didn't begrudge the responsibility, but he didn't have room for anyone else. Fiona didn't need him.

He wasn't as relieved as he expected to be. "Do what you think best."

"Are you patronizing me?" she asked. "Even after your company's attempts to steal my customers?"

Before he had a chance to react, Lexie returned to the table with extra napkins. "Oh no, are you two fighting? Caleb, you can't fight with Fiona, she's injured. And Fiona, he's trying to help you."

Fiona opened her mouth to respond, and Caleb squeezed his hands into fists. The business discussion would have to wait. He kept business separate from his family, and especially his company's attempts to purchase Fiona's. The last thing he needed was Lexie's opinion. He needed to stop Fiona from saying anything, but how?

"We're not fighting," she said. "It's just a business disagreement." She turned to Caleb. "Although I do appreciate all the time you've spent helping me after the accident."

Caleb's posture loosened. She'd handled it without betraying anything. He nodded a silent thank you for not giving away his secret. She stared at him, and he got the distinct impression this conversation wasn't over.

Fiona winced and shifted in her chair. He scanned her living room and brought her a royal blue and red throw pillow. Placing it behind her, he asked, "Better?"

"Yes, thanks."

"Well, no more business talk," Lexie said. "Fiona, what are you doing today?" Lexie asked. "You should take it easy."

Fiona finished chewing the warm, sourdough bread with butter before answering. "I have a date with the telenovelas I recorded this week."

Caleb shook his head.

"What?" She looked at him over her fork with a piece of mango on it. "Don't knock them 'til you try them."

Lexie jumped. "Perfect!"

"What's perfect?" Fiona asked, sipping her coffee.

"Caleb can stay here with you to make sure you're okay, and you can introduce him to your favorites."

Fiona coughed. "I don't need a babysitter."

"No, but you need a butler."

****

Caleb turned toward Lexie so fast, Fiona was convinced he'd have whiplash. Along with her injuries, they'd make quite a pair.

"Excuse me?" His quiet voice sent shivers along Fiona's spine.

Lexie smiled. "You know, someone to fetch and carry for her."

"Someone…to fetch…and…" His voice drifted. Lexie's hazel gaze sparkled. Danced, even.

She was brave.

Caleb was…well, Fiona was torn between a healthy wariness and snarky laughter. Because who suggested a big, bald, tatted man be a butler?

More of his tattoos showed today. His V-necked T-shirt, which stretched across his chest, gave a glimpse of the tattoos on his chest—leaves and maybe branches? And the short sleeves showed off the bottom of the ink on his biceps, ink that wound its way around his arm to his wrist and formed a tree. The traces of black ink intrigued her, and if he didn't look like he might murder the next person to speak, she'd ask him about them. Instead, she focused on her food and left the siblings to their conversation.

"Carry." Lexie finished the phrase for Caleb.

With a screech of oak chairs against hardwood floors—Fiona wondered how many scratches he dug into her floor—Caleb pushed back his chair and towered over his sister. He held his hand to her, as if he were a nineteenth century gentleman asking a lady to dance.

"Come with me, please," he said. Lexie placed her hand in his and rose. He led her to Fiona's front door. Opening it, he held his arm, pointing to her apartment across the hall. "Steve needs you."

"He does? Funny, I didn't hear my phone ping."

"Guy's intuition."

With a laugh, Lexie stepped into the hallway. "Bye, Fiona!" Her singsong voice made Fiona swallow her sip of coffee carefully, trying not to choke.

"Bye, Lexie. Thanks for breakfast!" She wiped her mouth to hide her smile.

The door shut on just the two of them, and Caleb

cleared the table.

"What did you mean earlier, about my company trying to steal your customers?" Caleb crossed his arms over his chest. His muscles flexed.

Fiona's mouth dried. It took a moment for her to follow his train of thought.

"Your website is offering incentives for new customers to join your lifestyle club."

"Incentives are not stealing."

"No, but coming on the heels of me refusing to sell you my company, and the wording of the coupon, it sure looks like it."

He stilled, his face a mask except for his eyes. They narrowed; two brown orbs backlit with an amber glow. "I'll look into it."

"You sound like you're not sure what I'm talking about."

He uncrossed his arms and leaned against the couch. "Believe it or not, I don't have my hands on every single piece of business we do. But Amanda, my head of marketing, will know what's going on. So, I'll look into it. Because stealing, or even giving the impression of stealing, isn't what we do."

Sincerity oozed from his vocal cords, and his posture dared her to disbelieve him.

"Thank you."

He nodded. "What telenovela are you watching?"

Her heart beat faster. "Oh, there are a few. I'm so behind I need to catch up."

Caleb walked around the couch and sat. "Show me."

She joined him as fast as she was able, groaning in relief when she settled into the cushions.

He handed her the remote. "Do you need painkillers?"

"No, I took some earlier." She pointed the remote at the TV and found the latest episode. She hit "play." The screen drew her attention, and her pain faded into the background. The Spanish music grew more romantic. The man with the sexy mustache and the woman with the beautiful jewelry embraced. The woman's cheeks glistened with tears, and the man caressed her cheek.

"—Spanish?"

Caleb's voice pulled her into reality. "What?"

"Do you understand Spanish?"

"No, why?" She paused the TV so she could focus on him.

"Why don't you turn on the subtitles? How do you know what's going on?"

She shrugged. "And take away all the fun?"

"Are you serious?"

"Yeah. It's so much better without the English. For instance, I'm pretty sure Jorgé and Maria are in love, but they can't be together because Maria's father won't let them. This other woman, Sonia, has been trying to get together with him, but Jorgé only has eyes for Maria. Sonia's been trying to sabotage Maria so she can have Jorgé for herself. Meanwhile, Ricardo has been giving Sonia advice, all the while being secretly in love with her, but he's too shy to say anything to her."

"You can tell all this without knowing Spanish? Maybe you've got it all wrong. Maybe if you have the English subtitles on, you'd learn Jorgé and Maria hate each other, and Sonia's having his baby."

She laughed while shaking her head. "No way.

And based on their body language, it's what I think is happening. I prefer it my way."

He sat against the sofa cushions. After waiting a moment to make sure he wasn't going to talk again, she hit "play." Her throat clogged as Jorgé and Maria kissed. Two minutes later, Caleb said, "Wouldn't you enjoy this more if it were in English?"

She paused and shifted so she faced him, one leg bent under her, the other dangling off the edge. "Absolutely not! Telenovelas are so much more emotional than American TV."

"Why don't you at least research online to find a plot summary?"

"I'm happy with the way things are," she said. "I don't need to hear the words to feel the story."

"But…you're crying."

She smiled through her tears and wiped her cheeks. "I know."

****

Staring at her, his heart rate increased, and he tamped the panic from her tears. At first, he thought pain caused her tears, but her rapt attention to the screen made him realize otherwise.

Why would she want to do this to herself? And how could she enjoy a show she couldn't understand?

He should leave, before she recognized his complete lack of comprehension. But her rapt attention to the screen fascinated him. She was smart—his business dealings with her had proven it. Yet she focused as if she understood her show.

She stared at the TV screen, but he couldn't take his gaze off her. Her skin, despite its bruising, was luminous. Her lips were parted, and she gripped the edges of the sofa cushions until her knuckles turned white. This close to her, heat radiated from her body. He could hear a faint sigh.

If she were this passionate about a television show, how passionate would she be if he kissed her?

His whole body jerked in reaction, and she turned to him.

"Are you okay?"

Caleb nodded, unable to formulate a reason for his reaction. After a brief moment when she stared at him as if trying to read his soul, she turned back to her TV show.

He needed to leave before he followed through on his fantasy. He rose, and she gasped.

"Don't go. You're going to miss the best part!"

"Have you seen this episode?" he asked, folding himself back into the sofa.

She shook her head no.

"Then how do you know what I'm going to miss?"

Without looking at him, she grabbed his forearm. "Can't you tell by the music?"

Music? The whooshing sound in his ears prevented him from hearing it. All his attention focused on her hand on his arm. Her soft skin. Her firm grasp. And tingles of electricity zipped along his arm like speed demons on a raceway. It almost made him want to slap it away. He took his other hand, but instead of slapping, he rested it on top of hers and stifled a groan. Her mouth quirked in a hint of a smile, but otherwise she gave no indication she noticed. The drama on the screen transfixed her attention.

Despite his complete lack of Spanish comprehension, the on-screen drama was nothing compared to that inside his head. Because just like at the beach, as soon as she touched him, all his broken pieces settled. It was as if her hand and his were meant for each other. But the idea was absurd.

Her deep sigh interrupted his thoughts, and he looked at the screen. The credits were rolling.

"Oh, this episode was wonderful," she said, withdrawing her hand and wincing as she rose.

"Sit. You shouldn't be moving around."

She laughed. "I have to move around. I'll get stiff if I stay in one place too long."

He stood and put his hands on her shoulders, jerking his head toward the sofa. "I'm here. Tell me what needs doing and I'll take care of it. As far as getting stiff, go soak in the tub."

He swallowed at the image of her naked in water as it flitted across his mind. *Not helping.*

"I need to do laundry."

"I said I'll take care of everything."

Her eyelids widened. "You're not doing my laundry!"

"How about you put your clothes in the basket, and I'll carry it for you?"

"This is ridiculous." She turned toward her bedroom.

"A lot less ridiculous than your dropping everything halfway between here and there and being forced to get me to help you."

She opened and closed her mouth. After a few beats, she grimaced. "You're right." Her voice was filled with dismay.

Caleb swallowed a laugh. Telling him he was right had cost her. Was it because it was him, or did she not like admitting she was wrong? He wanted to know, but he wasn't sure how to go about it, since they were supposed to tolerate each other for his sister's sake.

She walked toward her bedroom, but when he made to follow her, she held out her hand. "No way. You can wait here until I call you."

Humoring her, he let her pile laundry into the basket and cover it with a towel. She nodded, and he entered her bedroom, being careful not to look left or right. When he lifted the basket, the towel slid over the side of the basket, and he readjusted it. Her squawk made him pause.

"Don't move the towel!" She pushed his hand away and readjusted it.

"Why not? It was falling over."

"Because it's covering my clothes. There's no need for you to see my dirty clothing."

He stifled his disbelief, waited for her to finish, and followed her from the bedroom to her washer and dryer, on the other side of her apartment. What kind of person was embarrassed by laundry? Once she got the laundry started, she stretched her back, her face crumpling in pain. Without thinking, he scooped her into his arms.

"What are you doing?" she asked, her body stiffening.

"Carrying you to the sofa."

"I don't—"

"—Don't start," he said.

Perhaps realizing the futility of protesting while she ached, her body softened in his arms. Her floral scent filled his nostrils. His steps slowed—the sooner they reached the sofa, the sooner he'd have to let her go, and he didn't want to. But he had no excuse. He deposited her with care on the sofa.

"No more talk about stretching or doing laundry," he said. "You need to rest if you expect to be able to get to work on Monday."

"I can't just lie here doing nothing."

"You'll tell me what needs to be done and I'll do it, blindfolded if necessary." At her grin, he nodded and pointed to the TV. "Now tell me more about these crazy telenovelas of yours."

Chapter Nine

By the time Monday rolled around, Fiona's muscles were sore but improving. Letting Caleb wait on her yesterday had done more good than she'd admit. Know what else she wouldn't admit? A softening toward him. His attempt to understand her telenovelas and his willingness to help her despite their adversarial business relationship gave her a glimpse into the man behind the façade. Not to mention how he'd swept her off her feet. Literally.

What she'd seen intrigued her. He might think he hid his emotions and feelings from her, but his actions demonstrated them better than most people's facial features. Lexie was right, there was more to him than met the eye.

She sank with care into her desk chair and turned toward her assistant. "What did you find about the coupon, Patricia?"

"WW Media isn't doing anything illegal. They're trying to draw people to their site. They're not mentioning us by name. They're making use of marketing techniques."

"Which means we need to counteract them," Fiona said.

"I put together a few marketing ideas," Patricia said. "Let me grab them."

While Patricia went to her office, Fiona opened her

email. Caleb had sent her a message. Wrinkling her forehead, she opened it.

Fiona,

The discount wasn't initiated by Amanda. I'm tracking leads now. I'll get back to you as soon as I know anything concrete. In the meantime, you might want to consider a varied pricing structure for your private clients, so you can offer your own discounts.

Hope you're feeling better.

Caleb

Then again…was he ever going to stop giving her unsolicited advice? "Patricia?"

Her assistant returned, a tablet in her hand. "Yes?"

"Caleb is looking into the coupon. I'm forwarding his email to you. Don't delete it."

She nodded. "Sure thing. Here are the marketing ideas."

Fiona examined Patricia's proposal, nodded her head, and checked her watch. "Go for it. And maybe investigate varying our pricing structures." Her throat tightened. "I have an appointment at a shelter downtown. The director is interested in advertising on our site. I'll be back around lunchtime."

As she made her way downtown in her rental car, she prepared herself for the shelter. It was for abused women and their children. Their experiences filled her with sympathy. She shook her head. She needed to get ahold of herself. She also needed to make sure her own bruises didn't show. At the next stoplight, she looked at herself in the mirror. She was fine.

The director met her at the door.

"Hi, I'm Melanie. I'm so glad you could meet with me today." She led Fiona through the waiting area, more like a comfy living room, into her office, and gestured for her to sit. "Welcome to Gretchen's Sanctuary."

"Thank you. I was a little surprised when you called to ask about advertising. I didn't think places like this wanted to publicize their existence."

The director crossed her legs. "We are very careful about our security and have a variety of methods we use to communicate without compromising anyone's safety. But we need to let women know we are available to them if they need us. It's why I'd like to include our logo and contact information— just a phone number— on your website in a variety of spots."

"I'd be happy to help you in any way I can."

"Wonderful, can you show me what options are available and how much they cost?"

"No," Fiona said.

Melanie frowned.

"I won't charge a place like this for advertising on my site. You need to spend your money on the women and children who need you. So, tell me what you have in mind, and I'll make sure it happens."

The emotion on the director's face almost made Fiona cry. "I don't know how to thank you."

"Just keep doing what you're doing." Fiona rose and grasped the woman's outstretched hand. "I don't need any other thanks."

Melanie's phone buzzed, and she held up a finger to Fiona. "Yes. Let him in and have him sit in the waiting room. I'll be there in a minute." She said goodbye and turned to Fiona. "I'm sorry. I have a meeting with a donor, and he's early."

Fiona shook her head. "Don't worry. Email me

what you want, and I'll take care of everything."

As Melanie held open her office door for Fiona, the door to the waiting area burst open. A small, tow-headed boy raced into the room.

"Marcus!" A feminine voice from the hallway cried.

The boy announced, "I went potty!"

Fiona smiled, but movement to her left made her gasp.

****

The little boy ran over to Caleb and jumped up and down. His wide grin brightened his face, and in his exuberance, he touched Caleb's knee. Caleb's heart melted. He leaned forward in the upholstered chair and rested his elbows on his thighs. "You did?" He kept his voice gentle. The last thing Caleb wanted was to scare him.

The boy nodded. "Aw by myself."

"Marcus, come here!" His mother came to a halt in the doorway, a look of terror on her face. But whether it was from her son's escape, or Caleb's presence, he wasn't sure. He allowed himself to smile. "Great job," he said. He wanted to give him a high five, but raising his hand might not be appreciated, given his size and the way he looked to others. He nodded at the trembling mother, who grabbed her son and raced to the residents' area.

"Mr. Zeno, you're early," the director said.

Caleb glanced at the director and froze. Fiona. Her mouth froze in an "oh." He blinked, and she came to life.

"Caleb, I didn't expect to see you here."

His features readjusted into the mask he wore, and

he nodded. "Nor I, you." *And I never expected you to see me like this.*

"I'm meeting with the director about advertising." When he remained silent, she continued. "And you?"

"Donor opportunities."

Her gaze sparkled. "That's wonderful."

Air left his lungs, and spots danced across his vision. He couldn't speak. She thought it was wonderful.

Caleb swallowed. He didn't know how to get back the easiness, the relaxed attitude. Not in front of Fiona. But he had to.

She glanced at him, and his knees weakened. Her smile lit her face. He wanted to smile right at her without wondering what would happen if he let his emotions show.

She touched his shoulder. "Good luck." Her soft voice encouraged him, and before he could list the forty-seven reasons why doing so was a bad idea, his body overruled his brain, and he touched the back of her hand and allowed a smile to escape.

This was not part of the plan.

"I should go and leave you two to your discussion. It was nice to meet you, Melanie. Caleb." She nodded at him, a soft smile illuminating her face. Only when the room emptied did Caleb realize he'd held his breath.

****

Caleb had smiled. He'd actually smiled. It made Fiona's stomach all fluttery. And that was before he turned to her. She could imagine her reaction if he ever smiled at her and meant it.

Fiona's heart thudded in her chest. She could not fall for Caleb. He was her adversary, and she never mixed her business and her personal life. Besides, he wasn't her type at all. It didn't matter how jaw dropping his smile was. It didn't matter he was a potential donor at a shelter for battered women. They were pretending to get along for Lexie's sake.

Caleb was the exact opposite of the man of her dreams. Her dream man would sweep her off her feet with romantic gestures and an intense emotional connection, like the heroes in her telenovelas. *Even if his smile…nope, never mind. Not happening.*

She sat in her rental car outside the shelter, trying to calm her breathing and excise these thoughts of Caleb. However, as she glanced in her rearview mirror to check for traffic before she exited the space, he left the building as well. At the intersection, she glanced at his Ferrari behind her. In fact, he followed her all the way to her office building. When she opened her door to exit the car, he approached.

"Why did you follow me?" she asked, craning her neck to see him.

He gestured toward her head. "I wanted to make sure you got here okay."

This man…"I did. Thank you."

Instead of walking away, he rested his forearm on the roof of her car. "How are you feeling?"

She gave a half laugh. "Better, just sore muscles."

He leaned down. "Would you like a hand?"

This wasn't a good idea. After his heart-stopping smile, being this close to him did funny things to her insides. She needed space and time to readjust. "Yes, please."

So much for space and time.

She placed her hand in his and intense heat shot

along her arm. She searched for some recognition of a similar phenomenon. His gaze darkened, pupils large.

He blinked and pulled her from the car, his other hand protecting her so she wouldn't bang the car doorframe. When she stood, the top of her head came to his shoulder, but instead of a disadvantage, he offered protection.

"Thank you."

"You okay going inside?"

She nodded, finding it hard to breathe. "It wasn't necessary for you to waste your time." Should she try to elicit a smile? Part of her wanted to; the other wanted him to leave. It was safer with him gone.

He pulled his hand away and jammed it into his pocket. His jeans were worn and tight. How had she not noticed them before?

"It's not a waste of time." He looked off into the distance, and she caught a glimpse of the tattoo at his neck. Never in her life had she been so interested in one man's tattoos. He cleared his throat. "About the shelter." He paused, and the muscles in his jaw tensed.

"I think it's wonderful you want to support them."

"They do good work." His voice had softened.

Fiona touched his arm. His muscles jumped beneath her fingers. "As do you."

His face went blank, and the two inches between them stretched like two miles. Fiona's stomach dropped. He readjusted his gaze and looked past her shoulder. "Will you come to my office to discuss my proposal?"

She dropped her hand to her side as if she'd been burned. "I've already told you there's nothing to discuss. And I wish you'd stop giving me pointers about how to run my business. I don't need them."

"Have you even taken a look at the proposal?"

She shook her head.

"Then how do you know there's nothing to discuss?"

She leaned against the car. He was right. "Fine. Tomorrow."

His gaze pierced hers, and she couldn't look away. Her traitorous body reacted to him in ways it shouldn't.

"Ten thirty," he said.

Twenty-four hours was long enough for her to create a logical list of reasons why she couldn't allow him to buy her company. It would also have to be long enough to douse the heat of her desire.

Chapter Ten

The twenty-four hours between seeing Fiona and waiting for her to arrive increased Caleb's desire. He'd done nothing but think about *her*, not about buying her company. Her eyelashes were thick and curled at the ends. The texture of her skin against his lips would be smooth. Her tongue in his mouth would be warm and erotic. She'd destroyed his equilibrium from the moment she walked into the shelter, and he'd yet to recover it.

An almost magnetic current bypassed his brain and had made him follow her from the shelter. She'd seen his loss of emotional control, and she hadn't criticized him for it. He wasn't sure what to make of it. When her movements made her wince, he'd forgotten to worry about himself and looked after her wellbeing. Yearning seared him the second her hand touched his arm. It had taken all his self-control not to react to her touch. And more importantly, not to ask her why she'd touched him. Comfort? Because it would mean she understood his emotions.

Impossible.

She made him feel things, and she almost made him think it might be possible to show those feelings. It wasn't true, of course. Showing one's emotions let others know your weaknesses. And once they knew, they could destroy you. He asked her to meet with him as much to distract himself as to pursue their business arrangement. Hopefully, the logic required in a business meeting would get rid of this off-kilter feeling she created in him.

Feeling. He wasn't supposed to feel anything in business.

He propped his elbows on his desk and groaned.

His secretary alerted him to Fiona's arrival. His office door opened and the woman he'd fantasized about stepped over the threshold. Her floral perfume wafted into his office. "Are you okay?" she asked, voice low with concern.

No. "Yes."

"You groaned." She approached his desk and sat in the chair across from him.

Shit. "Let's discuss my proposal," he said.

Her smile, one he hadn't seen before, reminded him of a spider on a web, waiting to swallow him whole.

He leaned in his chair, laced his fingers on his chest, and waited.

For the first time in his dealings with her, she waited, too. The whir of his computer's fan kept the silence from being oppressive. The faint hum of traffic far below filtered in as well. But she didn't speak. It must have been the effect of her floral perfume, because rather than wait for her, he spoke. "And?"

"My answer is the same. No."

"Why?"

She grabbed the folder with his proposal. "You list the benefits of selling my company to you as affiliation with your name brand, enhanced reach, and financial backing. I don't need any of those."

"Of course, you do."

"No, I don't. Even though your lifestyle section is like my company, my numbers are better than yours. I have no limits to my reach now, but I will if you buy my company, because I'll lose what makes me unique—the personal touch can only exist with a small, boutique company, rather than a corporate conglomerate like yours. And I have all the financial backing I need right now."

"But think of how you could expand with more money backing you, especially if you stay on and run it."

"I don't want to expand. This deal would be great for you, but meaningless for me, despite your generous financial package. Not to mention, I'd lose my independence."

"I'd give you the freedom to do what you want."

She shook her head. "Someone 'giving me freedom' isn't the same as being my own boss. I'd still be reporting to you and your shareholders. I want what I currently have. So, thank you for the opportunity, but my final answer is no." Her stance relaxed. "Did you ever learn about the coupons you're offering on your site?"

He concentrated on her change in subject. "I'm told it's just a normal offering we do once in a while. It has nothing to do with you."

She looked skeptical as she headed toward the door, but his brain skipped over to her refusal. He should argue with her, convince her of her error, coerce her into selling her company. Except the logical part of his brain knew she was right. Unfortunately, his newly awakened emotional side overruled his logical part. He didn't want to let her leave.

Damn floral perfume. "Wait."

She paused, halfway to the door and spun on her heel. A strand of hair escaped its constraints, and he wanted to wind it through his fingers.

He lost his edge.

"There's nothing left to say, Caleb."

Not his edge, his mind. "Go out with me."

Her mouth dropped open. "What?"

"On a date."

"Why?"

Good question. "It'll be fun." So would a game of chicken, but he'd never risk his Ferrari. Or his Land Rover. Or any of his other cars either.

"No, it won't."

"Why not?"

"Caleb, we already tried. And neither one of us enjoyed it."

His stomach clenched. Her words hurt more than he'd like to admit. "Not true."

She walked toward him. "We got in an argument and decided we'd pretend to get along for Lexie's sake, in her presence. Which, by the way, you still need to confess."

"Not if we like seeing each other."

She squinted. "I think you might want to cover your head the next time you're in the sun. The heat has addled your brains. We're not meant to be together. You're not my knight in shining armor."

If he'd allowed himself to show his feelings, he would have burst into laughter. "Your knight in shining armor?" Instead, he stood and folded his arms across his chest.

Her face reddened, but she didn't change her mind. "Yeah, the one who is going to come sweep me off my feet, ply me with poetic words, and woo me. You're not him. Trust me. Although your head is quite shiny." She winked at him.

Did she wink at him? The head of a multi-million-dollar media conglomerate, who could annihilate her business by lifting his little finger? He waited for the insult to offend him. For the challenge to gird him to do…something. But he wanted to convince her she was wrong.

"I didn't think you needed a knight in shining armor to have one drink."

"You have no idea what I need." Her gentle tone somehow issued a challenge. One he wanted to meet.

"So have a drink with me tomorrow night and we can discuss your needs."

"Discuss my needs?"

He nodded at his attempt to knock her off kilter. And from her deep shade of red, his attempt worked. Good. If he couldn't get her company, he was going to get her.

****

Staring into her mirror, Fiona wondered why Caleb invited her. She'd already convinced him she wasn't going to sell her company. Lexie hadn't been around when he'd invited her for drinks. She didn't understand his motivation.

He couldn't be attracted to her, could he? She scrutinized herself in the mirror. Sure, she was attractive in an average sort of way, but after all their encounters, did he think they were suited to each other?

And his desire to discuss "her needs?" She needed

a man unrelated to her professional life who showed his emotions. She had to show him they weren't right for each other.

Except he was sexy as sin. Her mouth dried. Her insides clenched and her body ached. Her fingers trembled with the desire to touch him.

To hell with her body. The alcohol would dampen those needs, right?

She clasped a diamond hoop in her ear, wrapped a paisley scarf around her neck and hurried to the lobby as fast as her red stilettos would allow. Fiona made it outside at the same time Caleb arrived in his bright blue Ferrari.

"I would have come upstairs." He opened the car door for her.

She slid into the seat. "I know. But I was ready." Fetching her at her door had been part of his plan; therefore, she met him downstairs.

He got in the car and raked his gaze over her entire body, a trail of warmth tracking it. "You look pretty."

She smiled and took in his black button-down open at the neck and gray slacks. It hadn't escaped her notice how well they showed off his ass. The hint of a tattoo showed at his neck. Tonight, if nothing else, she'd learn about it. "Thank you. You do too."

He quirked an eyebrow. "I look pretty?"

She didn't know what flustered her more—his eyebrow quirk or her use of the word "pretty" to describe him. "Uh...sorry, not pretty...good. You look good." So much for smooth.

"Mm hmm." He merged into traffic.

Determined to keep the upper hand, she waited until he stopped at a light. "Nice eyebrow lift, by the way," she said.

He froze, and his hands clenched the steering wheel so tight his knuckles whitened. She refrained from smoothing her hand over his, even though she wanted to. Was showing one reaction so bad? Why? He glanced sideways at her, and she smiled. His hands loosened against the steering wheel. What would those hands be like on her body? Gentle? Firm?

She cleared her throat. "So, where are we going?" she asked as the light turned green.

He turned the wheel and drove down the road, the tendons in his arms and hands rippling from the movement. He resembled a panther—sleek, powerful, and predatory.

"My apartment."

Her mouth dried. She swallowed. "Your apartment?" Her voice sounded like a croak. She hoped he didn't notice. This was not the way to retain the upper hand. "You said we were going for a drink."

He tilted his head. "I know. But trust me, you'll like the view."

For the first time since she met him, Fiona wished she hid her emotions as well as he did. Had this been anyone else, she would have demanded he turn around and take her home, ending the game before it started. But this was Lexie's brother. While she might be playing with fire, he wouldn't hurt her. So, she enjoyed the ride. And it meant staring at him.

Passing under streetlamps, the light shone off his head, making the skin glow. What would it feel like to touch it? She smoothed her hands on her black pants to keep them by her side. His hard profile looked like it was carved of granite—aquiline nose, firm jaw, high cheekbones. The woman who could soften him…

The car stopped, and Caleb turned. "Are you finished staring?'

"For now."

A slight disturbance drew her attention, as if he'd huffed, but she couldn't be sure, and he exited the car almost immediately.

He led her from the car, which he'd parked in what looked to be a private garage, and into the elevator. Punching the uppermost button, he rode in silence. The doors opened into the foyer of the penthouse apartment—a loft-like space with floor-to-ceiling windows on all sides. Lights from below twinkled. She approached the glass. Her reflection shone in the window, and behind hers was Caleb's.

"You're right, the view is spectacular. It must be beautiful during the day, too," she said. "If I lived here, I'd never tire of it."

He nodded, not even willing to admit his feelings about scenery. She wasn't going to let him off the hook, though.

"Do you like it?"

"It's my apartment." He walked toward the middle of the room, where a black marble bar served as a divider between the living and dining areas.

She followed him. "We all have our own things. It doesn't mean we feel anything toward them. I had a bedroom during childhood, but I didn't like it."

"Why not?"

She fingered the edge of her top. Somehow, she'd allowed this conversation to get more personal than she'd intended. She licked her lips, her mouth dry. "Because it meant my parents had to sleep in the living room. We didn't have much money, and there was one bedroom. They gave it to me."

He stared at her, unblinking. "What do you want?" He pointed toward bottles of top-shelf alcohol.

She shook her head and folded her arms. "I want you to answer my original question."

"Anyone ever tell you you're stubborn?" he asked.

She smiled. "Anyone ever tell you this is a lousy way to convince me we're good together?"

He pinned her with his gaze, his irises darkening. She remained silent, waiting for him, even as his stare did fluttery things to her insides. Seconds ticked by, and the faint hum of appliances came into the foreground. He flared his nostrils, taking a deep breath. "Yes, I like the view. It's the reason I bought this apartment. I find it soothing after a long day at the office."

She smiled and walked toward him. "See, not so hard." She nodded toward the bottles. "I'll take a gin and tonic, please."

His grip loosened on the counter. "Make yourself comfortable."

Here? She looked around. A seating area surrounded a central fireplace—gray leather and black marble, sharp corners, and hard edges. Nothing offered comfort, no color or texture provided warmth. She sat on the sofa, waiting for him to bring her drink.

Caleb handed it to her in a crystal tumbler with a slice of lime.

"Wow, fancy," she said.

His gaze glowed, as if he smiled on the inside. She wanted him to smile. He sat on the other end of the couch and rested his elbows on his knees. "I believe we were going to discuss your needs." He spoke without looking at her, staring instead into his scotch.

She almost choked on her gin and tonic, but she hid her shock. "Good. I need to know about your tattoos." Gauntlet thrown.

He set his whiskey on the table and angled his powerful body toward her. "Do you, now?" Despite his impassive face, she would swear he rose to her challenge. He also closed in on her personal space. The air around her thickened.

She nodded.

"You saw me at the beach."

"From a distance. I couldn't tell what the tattoos were, other than a tree."

"So you want to get me naked."

Now she did choke on her drink, and he closed the distance between them, pulled her toward him, and patted her back. The heat from his hand scalded her, his sudden proximity made her aware of his size and power, and the oxygen in the room evaporated. She was in over her head.

"I'm sure there are ways to show me your tattoos without getting naked." Even as she said this, a part of her wished he'd remove his clothes anyway. She shook her head.

He rolled his sleeves, exposing strong wrists and muscular forearms, covered with black vines and leaves. The black ink stopped at each wrist. Hidden amongst the foliage were words: strong, proud, brave. Like his apartment, there was no color. There didn't need to be.

"Those are stunning." Her fingers itched to trace the lines. Her hands hovered over his arms as she wondered what his skin would feel like. Her heart thundered in her chest. Her hand descended. His skin twitched at her touch; his muscles rippled beneath her finger moving in slow motion from his wrist to his forearm. He bent his head to watch her, his breath loud near her ear, a strange hitch sounding the closer she moved to his rolled cuff. The edge of the fabric caressed her fingertip, and she stopped.

"What do the words symbolize?" she asked.

When his gaze met hers—brown eyes almost black—naked need shone from its depth, and she forgot her question. Her pulse pounded. She licked her dry lips, his gaze narrowed, and everything slowed. They sat as if suspended until he inched closer and brushed her mouth with his. She sighed. The single sound acted like a catalyst. He ran his hands through her hair almost in slow motion, making needles of desire prickle through her. He cupped her neck and brought her in close. The air between them hummed with electricity, and she couldn't have pulled away even if she wanted to, which she didn't. He licked the seam of her lips, as if asking for entry, and she complied. Their tongues danced, and a soft groan escaped from him. The sound echoed in her head. His mouth covered hers, and she wrapped her arms around his neck, her fingers stroking the base of his skull. His skin was smooth as she'd suspected, and she memorized him by touch.

His mouth devoured hers, and their teeth clicked. She huffed at the disturbance, and their breath mingled. Tilting her head, she deepened the kiss, and her nose bumped his. A laugh bubbled from her chest, and he tipped his forehead against hers and smiled. His cheeks rounded, his lips stretched, and his entire countenance changed. She gasped, chest heaving, at the unexpected sight.

Caleb crossed the room, his face once again a mask, before he turned his back to her. The air around her cooled, and she braced her hands on either side of her. She willed her heart rate to return to normal. His blurred reflection showed in the window, head bowed, hands folded on top of his head, like a marathon runner cooling off after a race.

He hadn't planned the smile. The moment had carried him away as much as it had her. But getting a glimpse of his smile—of letting down his guard—meant she didn't want to let him slip away.

She approached with care and stopped several feet away from his stiff form.

"We have a problem," she said.

He raised his head and met her gaze in the reflection.

"I can't decide if I want to share your beautiful smile with the world or keep it all to myself."

He blinked.

"On the one hand, it's heart-stopping and rare enough I want to be the sole recipient of it. On the other hand, it seems a shame to prevent the world from seeing it."

His body jerked, and he clenched and unclenched his hands. She waited, not understanding why smiling was such an issue, but knowing they stood on the precipice of...something. She'd intended to knock him off kilter tonight to prove they weren't right for each other. She'd done the first part, but it backfired. Because she wasn't ready to let him go.

****

"Maybe it should be our secret for now." He

clenched and unclenched his hand, until she slipped hers in his. Her hand was soft, but not fragile. It was capable and reassuring, and despite his initial horror at showing his emotions, he couldn't let go.

"For now?" she asked.

As if there was a future here. Kissing Fiona had shredded any fantasies he'd imagined. Her lips entranced him from the moment she climbed into his car. Watching them mold themselves around her glass tormented him. Sitting next to her, even separated by a sofa cushion, tortured him. The pressure, which built in her proximity, became unbearable. If he didn't kiss her, he would die.

"For now," he said.

He couldn't think of the future. He could barely think of the present. He'd never expected the rush of emotion the second his lips touched hers. In the past, he'd always kept entanglements with women free of emotion. But it was impossible with Fiona. Every time they were together, she swept away all his barriers and allowed emotion to flood him. He wasn't prepared. It terrified and amazed and disturbed him at the same time. But he hadn't been able to control it. And it was dangerous. When she'd gasped, he'd crashed back to reality, needing distance to replace his mask. If she didn't recognize his emotions, she couldn't hurt him. Only, she'd somehow found a way to normalize what he'd revealed.

"So, I guess I get your beautiful smile all to myself."

For an emotional woman, her calm was remarkable. He studied her face. Her pupils were dilated, and her cheeks were flushed, almost matching the ruby red of her top. Her pulse throbbed in her neck, and her hand in his warmed. But she gave him space. He'd wanted to prove they deserved another chance, and their chemistry was off the charts. He didn't know if he could handle the emotions along with it, though. He focused on her words.

"You have another problem," he said.

"I do?"

He rubbed his thumb across the back of her hand. "You need a thesaurus."

"Why?"

"Because you keep using girlie words to describe me."

She frowned. "What girlie words?"

"Pretty and beautiful. I'm not sure my masculinity can take it."

"Oh, I'll bet it can."

She stepped toward him, still holding his hand, and he pulled her close. His heart pounded, but whether from desire or fear, or a combination of both, he couldn't tell. She made him feel things, and when he slipped and showed his feelings?

She'd liked it.

She stroked the back of his neck, her hand roving toward the top of his head and to his nape. He let her explore—anything to keep her in his arms. The longer she stayed, the less he wanted to push her away, even though he should. Emotions were dangerous, because they let the other person see his vulnerabilities, gave them a map explaining how to hurt him. Fiona didn't seem to be using them against him…yet. He'd have to see what she did with the information, which meant he should make sure they continued to see each other.

It also meant he needed to do a better job of keeping his mask in place.

Chapter Eleven

The next morning, Robert Macintosh, Caleb's VP of mergers and acquisitions, knocked on the door and walked in, handing him a folder.

"What's this?" Caleb asked, pushing away from his computer. He'd had to concentrate extra hard today after his evening with Fiona. It had ended too soon, yet not soon enough. After their drinks, and fantasy-provoking kisses, he'd taken her home, thinking he'd forget all about her. But he couldn't get her from his mind.

"More information about Love, Laugh, Live and several different strategies to get the owner to buy into our purchase," Robert said. "I've also taken the liberty of including information for forcing her to sell."

Caleb froze, folder in midair. He shook his head. "It won't be necessary."

Robert settled into the chair across from Caleb's desk. "So, she agreed?"

"No. I'm thinking of getting rid of our lifestyle brand."

Bolting from the chair, Robert looked at Caleb like he'd lost his mind. More like his heart. But he'd never tell Robert.

"Are you kidding?" Robert asked.

"No."

Robert's mouth, already open, widened. "Are you

serious?"

Caleb nodded. "Keep it between us right now."

Without another word, Robert left the office.

****

Fiona's phone rang during her break for lunch. "Hello?"

"Fiona? It's Caleb."

His voice was deep and gruff. Her heart pounded in her chest. She hadn't been able to get his kiss, his smile, or the feel of his skin from her mind. Which, considering how not right for her he was, came as a huge shock. Because she wanted to get to know him better.

"H…hi," she croaked. *Great. Just great.*

"What are you doing this evening?"

"Working." She'd gotten nothing done this morning, so she had a lot to atone for.

"Wrong. I'll get you at seven."

"Oh, you will, huh?"

"See you later."

The phone clicked off before she had a chance to respond, and she stared at it in disbelief. Had he hung up on her? She returned his call, and he answered right away.

She grinned. "You've got a lot of nerve assuming I'll cancel my plans for you. Make it seven thirty." She dove into work, humming.

Four new reviews posted to her site made her heart sink. They all criticized her content, knowledge, and service. Swallowing, she looked at them from an objective point of view. Not everyone liked everything. This was a subjective business, and poor reviews were expected. Except she'd never received anything less than four stars and all her client satisfaction surveys were positive.

Her suspicions rose. "Patricia?"

"Yeah?" Her assistant glanced at her.

"Can you investigate who left the latest reviews on our site? See if you can determine a way to connect with them? I hate leaving customers unsatisfied."

"We got negative ones? Now? Seems a little suspicious timing-wise, don't you think?"

Yeah, it does. Fiona shrugged. She didn't want to be suspicious, but Patricia agreed... "Could just be a coincidence."

"I'll look into it."

She got to work, trying to shake off the bad feeling, and reminding herself Caleb had always been upfront about his desire for her business. Posting bad reviews wasn't like him. At seven, the buzzer rang, alerting her to someone at the front door of her building. Shaking her head, she let him into the office.

"Caleb. You're early."

He entered her office. The room shrank around him, and the oxygen evaporated. His slate blue silk button-down was tailor made for his expansive chest, as were his gray slacks. Despite his size and his muscles, he was smooth and sleek, and Fiona's mouth dried.

"I thought I'd see if I could hurry you along." He leaned against the doorframe, his gaze roving the room.

Not wanting to show him how much his presence threw her off kilter, she pointed to the multi-colored upholstered sofa across from Patricia's desk. "Make yourself comfortable. I'm not finished."

The chances of her regaining concentration with him in the room were nil, but she wouldn't let him think she was at his beck and call. Sitting at her desk, she focused on her computer. Usually, the office had a lavender scent, thanks to Patricia's electric candle on her desk. But Caleb's spicy aftershave overpowered its subtlety. His scent wafted around her and carried her to yesterday's kiss. She shivered.

"Cold?"

His deep voice curled around her, warming her insides like a glass of aged scotch. If she answered him, she'd prolong the conversation and the distraction. But the blog post she edited blurred in front of her.

With a sigh, she pushed away from her desk and looked at her watch. Great, she'd lasted a whole seven minutes. Retrieving her purse from beneath her desk, she rose, nodded to Caleb, and led the way out the door.

His shiny blue, ridiculously expensive man-toy sat in front of her office, and he opened the door for her to enter.

"Where are you taking me?" she asked.

"You'll see."

For a man who showed no emotion, he looked pleased with himself. "You're not going to tell me? What if I had plans?" She bit her lip to keep from laughing.

At the traffic light, he turned. "You do."

She wrinkled her brow in confusion. "Oh?"

"With me."

She faced him, eyebrow raised. "Nice of you to ask me. I'm impressed by your moves."

His lips twitched, and he turned toward the road, gunning the engine when the light turned green. She gasped. Caleb slowed the car before he pulled onto the side of the road.

"Are you all right? I didn't mean to frighten you." His unease echoed in the tone of his voice.

She shook her head, as much to banish her fright as to assure him. "It's fine. You startled me. Not a big deal."

He gripped the steering wheel. "I should have remembered you'd be sensitive because of your accident."

This stoic man had let down his guard from worry over her. Pleasure surged through her. "Please don't worry. My reaction had nothing to do with my accident."

Tenderness swept through her. She reached for his arm and squeezed. The muscles and tendons in his forearm rippled beneath her hand and made his tattooed vines sway. She still didn't know the significance of the words hidden among the leaves. Right now, she didn't care. She was too preoccupied with the heat and texture of his skin, the restrained power in the sinew, the raw sexiness he oozed. The silence stretched. Caleb watched her. Concern and surprise flashed. Unsure of the meaning, she withdrew her hand, clenching it on her lap. With a nod, he continued onto the road once again, leaving her to puzzle over her feelings and his reaction.

Ten minutes later—no clearer than she'd been before—he stopped in front of a row of shops—an ice cream parlor, a clothing boutique, a bookstore, and a cell phone store.

"You're leaving your car here?" she asked, exiting, looking around at the non-descript cars parked in the metered spaces. "On the street, where anyone could scratch it or dent it?"

"It's the only place to park." He deposited his coins

and joined her on the sidewalk.

"Doesn't it bother you, risking a car like this?"

"It's a risk I'm willing to take. This is important." He took her arm and led her to the bookstore.

I'm important. She looked at him with a quizzical frown, but he shook his head. Instead, he held open the door and ushered her inside.

The bell jingled, and a sales associate wearing a chunky turquoise necklace rose from behind the sales desk. "May I help you?"

"I need your reference section," Caleb said, his hand still grasping her upper arm.

The sales associate motioned toward the back of the cluttered store, and Caleb led Fiona in the same direction.

She craned her neck to get a better look at the bestsellers and romances they passed, but Caleb wouldn't let her stop until they were surrounded by reference books—dictionaries and study guides as far as the eye could see.

"What are we doing here?" she asked.

"Just wait." He scanned the top shelf.

Tapping her toe on the carpeted floor, she asked, "Did you drag me here to do errands?"

"Nope." He bent to scan the second shelf.

"Well, you look for whatever it is you need, I'm going to look at the romance section."

"Wait, here it is." He handed a book to her.

"Roget's Thesaurus?"

He rose to his full height and folded his arms across his chest. "I told you that you needed one."

She glanced between the book and the man. He looked serious. Formidable even. And the book? The book was hilarious—all because she'd called him "pretty" and "beautiful." Okay then.

She flipped through the pages. "You think you're so…ingenious?"

He nodded. His eyes glowed. "I do."

Anyone else would have cracked a smile, but not Caleb. She took it as a challenge.

"Fascinating establishment to court me."

His lips twitched. "I try never to be boring."

"You must be quite the lothario."

This time, he ran a hand down his face, but not before she spotted the humor in his gaze.

"Let it out, big guy."

He strode away from her. She followed, using the opportunity to admire the way his gray pants hugged his ass.

"Oh, being chased through a bookstore by a female." She laughed. "Scary."

He stopped short, and she almost plowed right into him. His shoulders shook. Had she pushed him far enough yet? She peeked around him, assembling her expression into one of false innocence.

"What's the matter?" she asked. "Cat got your tongue?"

"No, but you do have the thesaurus."

She handed it to him, and he laughed. The laugh didn't start in the toes and work its way out the mouth. It wasn't loud enough to shake the walls or long enough for people to turn and stare. If she had the thesaurus open, it would be classified more like a chuckle or a snicker. Maybe even a chuff.

But from Caleb? It was the equivalent of an earthshattering, window rattling, category five hurricane.

Satisfaction warmed her, and a thrill of excitement raced along her spine. She rose on tiptoe, moved his arm with the thesaurus out of the way, and kissed him, right in the middle of the bookstore.

****

As her soft lips slammed into his, her body pressed against him, and Caleb dropped the thesaurus. It thumped when it hit the carpeted floor and in the back of his mind, he considered retrieving it—it was a shame to damage a good book—but then his senses, and his sense, kicked in. His pulse raced, and her delicious scent enveloped him. She was all warmth and light, and he gave into her kiss.

He dragged her breath into his mouth, as if he required her oxygen to breathe. This time, they didn't laugh while they kissed. Just pure bliss. He ran his hands through her hair, its silky strands tangling in his fingers. He pulled her even closer, and she wrapped her arms around him, stroking his back and sending shivers of desire along his spine.

Slowly, her gaze came into focus. Her pupils were dilated, her mouth reddened from their kisses, and the sales associate cleared her throat.

He straightened and nodded to the girl behind the counter, who turned beet red. Grabbing the thesaurus, he brushed it off, trying to regain his equilibrium. Fiona took it from him, and their fingers touched.

"Wow," he said, his voice husky to his own ears.

"Yeah, wow," she whispered. She traced her lips with her finger, and Caleb hardened, wishing he were the one touching her lips. "We should put this book back now."

He shook his head. "It's my gift to you."

Her lips rose in a smile. "Cute."

They walked toward the front of the store. "Wait," she said, and reached for a romance displayed on a table.

He stood there, watching while she studied the back of the book before replacing it where she'd found it.

"Don't you want it?" he asked.

"I already read it. She's my favorite author. I started reading her, as well as others, when I was a teenager. My mom used to take me to the library every week. I think I read their entire romance section."

"Romance. Why am I not surprised?"

"Don't knock it, mister. Guaranteed happily ever after. Lots of emotion. Strong women. Next to telenovelas, they're my favorite thing for a rainy weekend afternoon."

He retreated a step. "I wasn't knocking it. It makes perfect sense. In fact, I'd expect nothing else from you."

She frowned, and he waited for her to argue or comment or…something. But they were in the middle of a bookstore, which, while not crowded, was public—although it hadn't stopped him from kissing her—and he didn't want to encourage a showdown here. So, he took the thesaurus from her and walked straight to the counter, paid for it and ushered her outside.

She stopped and folded her arms, eyebrow raised. She looked adorable annoyed. This could be fun.

"You 'expect nothing else' from me?"

"Is it a problem?" He held out the bag.

She glanced from him to the bag and to him again.

Emotions roiled in her expressive gaze—annoyance, confusion, lust. Lust? Good, it was mutual. He could drown in all her feelings. Whereas before he'd thought they put her at a disadvantage, now he liked knowing he caused her to feel things, because she caused him to feel things too.

It scared the hell out of him. He wouldn't think about it right now, though. Right now, he wanted to know why what he said made her annoyed.

"Thank you." She took the bag and stuck it under her arm. "I feel like you're belittling my taste in reading, and therefore, me."

"Not at all." He stepped closer to her, noticing the way the setting sun glinted off her hair, creating a bright outline around her. Should he? Against his better judgment, he reached for her shoulder and stroked her upper arm. "I think your taste in reading fits with your personality. And if I had a problem with your personality, I never would have asked you out tonight or kissed you."

She blushed. Did her skin feel as hot as it looked? She was warm beneath her cottony sleeve. Her mouth moved.

"What?"

"I kissed *you*," she said. "*You* just kissed me back."

This woman killed him. "Guess I should remedy this." He maneuvered her against the brick outer wall of the bookstore, cushioned her head with his hand, and pressed his lips to hers.

****

Lord could this man kiss. And if repetition proved anything, he liked kissing her. She didn't object. Oh no. His smooth skin, restrained power, and spicy scent made her want to disappear into him and his kiss. All sounds from outside—cars, birds, people—were a soft buzz in the background. Or maybe blood rushed in her ears. Did he know he poured all his hidden emotions into his kisses? If she told him, he'd stop, and she didn't want him to stop. But he should. Because there were things to talk about. She pushed against his shoulders.

He pulled away, his chest rising and falling, pupils large and black with desire. "What?" His voice was hoarse, like all the polish had been put into his kiss and there was none left for his voice.

"As much as I love this…" Her face heated. "…we need to talk."

His body blocked her from the view of the passersby on the sidewalk and the street. Heat rolled off him, cocooning her into a bubble of protection and desire. It was impossible to think.

"What do you want to talk about?"

She looked around. "Was this your plan?"

"Was what my plan?"

"You said we were going out, and you took me to a bookstore. Don't get me wrong, I love bookstores. I could spend entire days in bookstores. But was there something else? Because we do need to talk, and I'd rather not do so pressed against a wall."

He retreated two paces.

Better.

"I wanted to take you to dinner afterward. We can talk on the way." He pointed down the block, and they walked, their bodies next to each other but not touching. If there were a way to see energy, Fiona would bet you could see the sparks of attraction zinging between them, like fireflies on a July night.

"So, what did you want to talk about?" Caleb asked.

"What are we doing?"

His step hitched, the only clue he knew what she meant. "Walking to dinner."

She play punched him on the arm. "You're not this dense."

"I thought we were giving ourselves another chance to see if we enjoyed each other's company."

"No," she said. "That was last time."

He stopped and faced her. "Last time?"

"Yes, when I came to your apartment, and we had drinks."

"We had more than drinks."

She swallowed. She wondered if he made this difficult for her on purpose. "True, there was kissing involved."

He nodded and thrust his hands in his pockets. Following his movements, her gaze travelled down...there and she jerked her head to meet his gaze, which looked amused even though the rest of his face showed nothing.

"So I ask again," she said. "What are we doing?"

He rocked on his heels. "I think we're moving along the 'getting to know you' stage."

"What stage would we be at now?"

"Well, I'd hoped we'd moved away from the 'pretending to get along for my sister's sake' stage."

She nodded and gave him a sly look. "I hope you're not planning to move toward 'softening my resolve so you can go after my company again' stage?"

Every muscle in his body froze, and she'd swear

the air between them dropped twenty degrees. She wouldn't have been surprised if frost poured from his mouth. She retreated a step.

"I would never, ever, take advantage of you." He took a step toward her.

She took another step back.

"My desire to work with you is unrelated to my desire to get to know you better. I don't mix business with pleasure." Somehow, she found herself against the wall of another building. He needed to stop doing this.

"Because you squash them all against the wall beforehand?"

His body loosened, and his gaze brightened. "No." Stepping away from her, he held out his hand, and she took it. The wall he'd backed her against fronted the restaurant where they planned to eat. The unassuming storefront gave way to tables covered with navy tablecloths; the silverware gleamed and the white tea candles on each table added intimacy. He gave his name to the maître d', who led them to a corner table and left them alone.

He reached for her hand, and she grasped his, staring at their fingers entwined. Her stomach rumbled, and he huffed. Her gaze flew to his in surprise, and he looked away. Deciding not to push, she looked around the restaurant. Most tables were filled with couples.

"So, what kind of restaurant is this?" she asked. The pressure of him trying to pull his hand away lessened, and he cleared his throat.

"Northern Italian. I know the chef, and he always makes off-menu meals for me when I come here."

As if on cue, the waiter brought a black truffle salad to the table, along with steaming, fresh-baked bread. Caleb waited while she tasted the salad, and she groaned in delight. "Oh my gosh, this is amazing."

He nodded. "It is."

She dropped her fork. "That's all you're going to say?"

Tilting his head, he handed her the breadbasket. "What would you rather I say?"

"Something befitting the exquisite taste we're experiencing."

Laughter made her turn. "Ah, my dear, the challenge of Caleb." The man came around from behind her. "I'm Paolo, the chef. I'm glad you like my salad."

She gave him a broad grin. "It almost seems a shame to call it a salad. It should be a work of art."

Paolo turned to Caleb. "She. Is. Mine."

Caleb shook his head. "Nice try. If you're lucky, we'll come again another time."

"I'd love to come and talk to you about your recipes for my website," Fiona said.

After giving him a brief explanation of what she wanted to do, Paolo agreed, and they arranged for a time to meet. He returned to the kitchen, and Fiona dug into the salad.

Caleb shook his head. "I should be upset."

"But you're not."

"Nope."

"Why not?"

"Because I'm starting to understand why you're so good at what you do. And I can't get upset at talent. I don't think it would have occurred to my website people to interview the chef."

She smiled. "As to my being good at what I do, it's

because to me, it's about relationships. When I go to a restaurant I love, I want others to know about it. And they tell me about their likes and dislikes as well. But we're not talking about jobs any more tonight, are we?"

"No, I'll give you a night off. However, I've already told my mergers and acquisitions people to forget about your company. Which is why I'd like to go down this personal road and see what develops between us."

She stared at him across the table. He surrendered. Why? Could he be falling for her? She thought about his not mixing business with pleasure, took in his broad shoulders and chiseled jaw, remembered his bone-melting kisses, and warmed at the concern he showed for those around him. She wanted to believe him, but she had one last question. "I don't suppose you know anything about bad reviews being posted to my site?"

His brows rose, and she had her answer. "I didn't think so," she added. "Which means I'm interested in seeing what develops between us."

Chapter Twelve

He refused to talk about jobs tonight. Not with Fiona, whose brown wavy hair fell to one side, flowed over her shoulder, and rested at the top of what had to be perfect breasts. His hands twitched, but whether from a desire to run his fingers through her hair, or touch her breasts, he couldn't be sure. Maybe he'd just been gripping his fork too long.

She spooned chocolate mousse into her mouth. The curve of the silver touched her lower lip, and her tongue licked the mousse before she slid the spoon inside. He stifled a groan. Her pink lips were plump, and he remembered their softness against his own. What would they feel like against other parts of his body? He gripped his fork tighter, the silver edges digging into his palm. She licked her lips and swallowed; nostrils flared. He wouldn't survive the rest of this meal.

If someone pressed a gun to his head, he wouldn't be able to tell them what he ate or what they talked about after the truffle salad arrived. As with everything else, dining was an emotional experience for her, and every impression she had of the food danced across her face. He could watch her for hours.

His heart stuttered. He wasn't testing her emotions from a "how can I use this to my advantage" standpoint. He examined them from a "what do I have to do to make her look at me that way" standpoint.

When had he made the transition? And it scared the hell out of him because he suspected she'd require him to reciprocate. His pulse increased.

"Earth to Caleb!"

He jumped, swore at himself for doing so, and focused on Fiona. "I'm sorry, what were you saying?"

She smiled. "Does it matter? I think you found something else to occupy your thoughts."

If she only knew. He shook his head. "It was rude of me. I apologize."

"Care to share?"

You scare the hell out of me. "I admire your smile."

She blushed, and Caleb's heart almost stopped beating.

He nodded. "It makes your eyes sparkle."

She placed her spoon on the plate, so the rounded dome was in the exact center and the handle at three o'clock, before meeting his gaze once again...and smiling. "Thank you."

They had to leave now. He rose, walked around behind her, and placed his hand on the back of her chair. "Are you ready to go?"

"Um..." She looked around. "Shouldn't we ask for a check or something?"

"I took care of it ahead of time."

He pulled out her chair and she stood. "So, I'll start calling you 'Mr. Take Care of Everything?' "

He placed his hand between her shoulder blades and walked with her toward the exit. "Caleb will be just fine."

Her laugh vibrated beneath his palm, and his lips twitched. By now they were outside, and it was dark, so no one could see. His car was parked right on the street.

She could find her way walking beside him. His hand at her back wasn't necessary, but it was comfortable. His fingers caressed the silky fabric of her top. The contact warmed his skin. They reached his car too soon; he contemplated continuing to walk down the block, but that was the drawback of having such an identifiable car. She'd never believe he'd walked past it. He opened the door and drew his hand back so she could get into his car.

She remained silent until he pulled onto the road. "Dinner was amazing," she said. "Thank you."

"You're welcome."

"And the thesaurus was funny."

He nodded.

"What are we doing?" she asked.

"I'm driving you home." *Even though I don't want to.*

"It's not what I meant."

"What do you mean?" he asked.

She turned her body to face him, her outlines shadowy. "Well, we've now gone out a couple of times…"

He nodded. What had started as a favor had morphed into an experiment and progressed to a need.

"And are we going to continue?"

"I think things have gone well," he said.

" 'Gone well' is how you're going to describe spending time with me?" She withdrew her hand and wrapped both arms around her stomach. He wanted to take her hand back.

Instead, as they passed a deserted a park, he gripped the steering wheel. Shadows of slides and climbing equipment hulked, taking on shapes a more creative person like her would be able to reshape into monsters and fear.

He didn't fear monsters that went bump in the night. He feared letting Fiona see who he was. Moonlight glinted off the hood of his car, and he squeezed the wheel tighter. She touched his hand, and he loosened his grasp. He turned to her. The traffic light turned red.

Words caught in the back of his throat, and he struggled to speak. "I'm not an emotional person." He searched in vain for better words. "I don't describe things like you do. It doesn't mean I don't enjoy them, though."

"And if I need emotion? What then?"

He clenched his jaw. There were some things he could never do.

She sighed. "So?"

"I like spending time with you, more than I thought I would."

She snorted. "Whoa, you sure know how to give compliments."

This wasn't working. He took her hand in his, caressing her palm with his thumb. Her skin was smooth and warm. The light turned green, and he let go of her, although he wished he didn't have to. "I didn't know you were looking for a compliment. I thought we were talking about how we were getting along."

"Based on how you kissed me—and on how I kissed you back—I would describe our relationship in a different way," she said.

"How would you describe it?"

She rested her hand on his knee, leaning forward until they were inches apart.

He could barely concentrate on the road ahead.

"I'd say we have bone-melting chemistry. I'd say our conversations are interesting, and we share excellent taste in food. If we stay away from talking about business, your sister is right—we are very good together."

He wanted to pull her onto his lap and kiss her senseless. Next time he'd make her drive.

"But we have a big problem," she continued.

He focused once again on her words. "What is it?"

"I have no idea how you feel. I don't know if you think of me as a sexy lay to scratch an itch or as someone you want to have a relationship with. And I don't like not knowing. It makes me self-conscious."

He counted to ten before speaking. "I've never wanted to make you feel self-conscious. Just because I don't show my emotions doesn't mean I don't have them, though."

"I've figured you out," she said. "I've even uncovered some of those emotions you try to hide so well. But if you and I are going to have a relationship, I need you to show me a little more of yourself. An occasional smile or laugh or even a frown. You know, markers along the side of the Caleb road, so I know where I am and where I'm going."

She was funny, he had to admit. Maybe a small smile wouldn't be awful. She'd liked his smile before. He let himself relax, and the corners of his mouth curved.

"See! There you go. I knew you could do it if you tried."

She touched his cheek, and his smile grew, before he grew serious once again. "It's safer to keep my feelings to myself." He couldn't bring himself to tell her why.

"It might be safer, but it keeps people away. Now, if you want to keep me away, fine. But if you want us to have a relationship, keeping me away doesn't work."

He approached her building, put the car in park, let go of the steering wheel, and traced his fingers from her arm to her jaw. She trembled.

"I don't want to push you away." He ran his hand around the back of her neck to the base of her skull. "I haven't wanted to push you away since the first time we argued after clamming."

He tipped his head until their lips met. Once again, he lost himself in her kiss. Their tongues danced, and her moan vibrated against the back of his throat. Her hands wrapped around his neck, and his skin burned at her touch. He moved away from her lips, trailing kisses to the hollow at her collarbone. She tipped her head and made a mewling sound. His damn car was too small. He'd have to remember to drive his Land Rover next time. Or maybe buy an RV. Instead, he took her by the shoulders and pushed her into her seat, his touch gentle.

"We have a terrible habit of kissing in the worst places," he said. This time, he grinned at her, taking away any sting his words might cause. "Change of plans. We're going to do this right this time. Buckle up."

Fiona clicked her seatbelt. "If you smile at me, I'll do anything you say."

"I'll keep it in mind." He revved the engine. "Come to my place? I'd like to avoid running into my sister right now."

She nodded.

He pushed every speed limit on the way.

****

Being with Caleb was surreal. It was the only way to describe it. He was the epitome of an alpha male—stern, commanding, and hot as Hades. However, she'd been the one to carry most of the conversation tonight while he stared at her, including their "relationship conversation." Granted, his gaze on her made her skin go hot, cold, and tingly. And his smiles, hard earned and rare, made her forget her name. But if she thought about what she wanted in a man before right this minute, she would have listed any number of telenovela heroes.

But now? She couldn't string three words together in a coherent sentence. Not while Caleb had his large hand around hers, rushing her to his penthouse apartment. Not while he undressed her with his gaze. And not while he led her into a room dominated by the most massive, masculine-looking bed she'd ever seen.

The bed and headboard were black tufted leather. A gray and black paisley print throw blanket lay diagonally across the silver duvet cover, which folded to reveal black silk sheets.

Her gaze darted around the room. One windowed wall faced the water in the distance. Moonlight glinted off buildings below, and she could see how, at another time, the view would be blinding. Right now, it sparkled from the lights of the surrounding buildings. White walls made it unnecessary to turn on the lights, since the light from the moon reflected off them. A dresser and two night tables featured harsh angles and silver accents. The floor was bare.

And Caleb was close.

He stood in front of her, their toes almost touching. His broad shoulders and chest loomed over her. Such a commanding presence could have frightened her. But somehow, after their conversation in the car, he was hers to do with what she wanted.

And she wanted.

She wanted him, and she wanted to make him react.

In the V of his shirt, his skin begged to be touched. Slowly, she raised a hand and traced the space between the fabric. He hissed.

Stepping even closer, shivers ran along her spine, but she maintained the contact of her finger against his chest. She opened a button of his gray silk shirt and trailed her finger lower. With each button, his muscles jumped, and desire pooled in her belly.

He didn't pull away, and he didn't touch her. He let her lead. When she reached his black leather belt, she pulled his shirt from the waistband, spreading the sides wide and admiring his sculpted chest and abdomen. With both hands, she caressed him, tracing each muscle and rib. When she pushed the shirt over his shoulders, the tattoo on his back, which wound its way around both arms, became visible.

"You have to explain this to me later," she whispered, and licked along the inked lines. His biceps flexed as she tasted his salty skin. She ran her hands along his arms and clasped his hands, both as an anchor and as an unspoken reminder for him not to do anything. Rising on tiptoe, she brushed her body against his. Her breasts ached, and she did it again. She wanted to feel his skin against hers, but she'd have to step away, and losing contact with him was too terrible to contemplate. So, she continued moving against him.

And then she raised her head to taste his lips.

His hands tightened on hers, and he shuddered. "You're killing me," he whispered, his voice ragged.

Letting go of his hands, she wrapped her arms around him and held him close, as much to anchor herself as to revel in him. He buried his head against her neck and nipped. She let her head fall to the side to give him better access and he growled. Her skin heated and she could no longer bear to be covered in anything but him.

"Undress me," she begged.

She moved her hips against him. With shaking hands, he pulled at her turquoise silk blouse. The friction of the silk moving against her skin left burning trails of heat in its wake and she squirmed, trying to free herself of the garment. His skin was so close. She wanted to feel him against her.

Once he'd removed her blouse, his hands danced along her spine and unclasped her black lace bra. He slid it off her, inch by slow inch until it landed on the floor with a faint tap. And then his hands were on her breasts, his thumbs rubbing the tips, and she lost all ability to think. She was no longer in charge of the situation, and she surrendered to him.

He lowered his head and mouthed each breast until her knees weakened. Gripping his shoulders, she let her head fall back. He pulled away and she moaned, but the separation didn't last. Just as the cool air tickled her stomach, he lifted her, dragging her against his body with exquisite friction. She wrapped her legs around his waist, and her moan turned into a gasp. He covered her mouth with his and strode across the room, his movement creating jolts of desire deep inside her. The room tilted as he laid her across the bed, and a second later he joined her.

Their bodies aligned and touching as they lay side by side, she stared deep into his brown eyes. His desire matched her own. She stroked his cheek, and uncertainty flashed in the chocolate depths before disappearing.

His vulnerability touched her. "I've wanted this for so long," she whispered.

"All night." He kissed along her jaw.

"Days." Her hands moved along his head, feeling his skull beneath her fingertips.

"Weeks." He kissed her neck, behind her ear and she shivered.

She needed his mouth. Now. Tilting her head, she found it, covering it with her own. Mouths open, their tongues battled for control and her body strained against his. She needed to be closer. He wrapped his arms around her and held her tight.

He might not show his emotions with words or even facial expressions, but he poured his heart and soul into his kisses and his touch.

Her hands slipped to his waist, and she fumbled with his waistband. He moved, and she stifled a scream as desire rushed through her.

"Off. Please. Now." She couldn't form words, much less a sentence, and she bucked her hips against him.

He swore and held her body away from him, still joined at the mouth while he removed his clothes. Using the space, she removed her skirt, shimmied out of her underwear, and slammed her body against his, needing the feel of skin against skin.

He was hard and rubbed against her. Shock waves raced through her.

"Condom," he groand against her lips. The cold air made her gasp. He pulled away. A drawer glided open, the sound rasping in her eardrums. She reached for his hand and took the foil packet. She needed to feel him, touch him.

Every part of him shook as she took the condom from him and slid it over his hard length. His eyelids were squeezed shut, his face in almost a grimace of pain. She stroked the length of him and cupped him in her hands.

"Fiona," he rasped.

She squeezed gently, and his eyelids flew open.

"Fiona!"

Before she had a chance to react, he grabbed her and rolled them over on the bed, so he was on top. He rose above her, straining for control. "I need you right now," he said.

She nodded, unable to form words, and spread her legs. He entered her, and she whispered a long "ohhh." His arms braced on either side of her head. She raised herself to meet him, to force him deeper. She ran her hands from his back to his butt. His muscles rippled beneath her palms, and she clenched. Their bodies moved in tandem, a primal rhythm both sensual and powerful. She rode wave after wave of pleasure.

Each time Caleb increased the pace, she met him. Each ragged exhale she met with one of her own. They reached the crest at the same time. Lights exploded behind her lids, blood rushed in her ears and her body turned to liquid as she climaxed. Caleb shouted her name, pumped into her, and collapsed. He buried his head against her neck.

Warmth and peace washed over her. As her heartbeat slowed, unexpected joy filled her. Lying cradled in his arms, Fiona stroked his neck, reveling in the warm afterglow. She'd never felt so safe, protected, or cherished as she did right now. After a few minutes, he turned his head toward her, and she kissed him. His expression was soft.

"That was amazing." She smiled.

He returned it, and it once again stunned her. This man had the most beautiful smile she'd ever seen, made even more so by the scarcity with which he bestowed it. She nuzzled her nose against his and he froze.

Frowning, she pulled away. "Caleb, what's wrong?"

He didn't move or pull away, but his body hardened, his muscles tightened, and his face went blank.

"Caleb?" She stroked his face. "Talk to me."

He swallowed; fear, confusion, and wonder crossing his face.

"I've never...I...Forget it."

Fiona pushed against him until he moved off her. She sat, pulling the sheet over herself. "No, don't tell me to forget it. I've just had the most amazing sex of my life with you. I want to know what you're thinking."

He rolled away from her and sat against the ebony headboard. His bare chest glistened with sweat. Instead of looking at her, he looked across the room. "I've never had a problem finding women to have sex with, but I've never had this kind of experience."

Fiona stiffened. She hadn't expected to be his only

sex partner but hearing him talk about it so soon after what they had done hurt. However, the second part of his sentence prevented her from freaking out.

"What kind of experience?"

"I've never had trouble hiding how I feel. It's habit. I don't have to think about it. Or I never used to have to. But with you, it takes effort. The emotions slip through."

"Like your smile."

For the first time in the conversation, he looked at her. "Yes."

She took his hand and he squeezed.

"I thought it was some weird, one-off thing. But all these emotions started crowding in as we were having sex. And I've never had such a mind-blowing climax before either."

She grinned. "Think there's a relationship between those two factors?"

He huffed. "I don't know. Maybe."

She elbowed him in the ribs. He grunted and pulled her close. Snuggling against him, she rested her cheek against his chest. His hands brushed her back, making her sleepy. "I don't know who taught you to hide your emotions, but nothing bad will happen if you show me yours," she whispered.

His hand stopped for a few seconds, not losing contact but not moving, before continuing the soothing motion.

Baby steps.

****

Morning light streamed in from the bare windows across from Caleb's bed and glinted off Fiona's dark hair, turning it various shades of brown, red and gold. It draped across her bare shoulders and even across his chest. He ran his fingers through it, watching the play of colors, careful not to disturb her sleep.

They'd had sex twice more last night. All three times, emotions had rocked him, making his chest tighten. The experience terrified him, and at the same time satisfied him more than any sexual encounter. And although one part of him urged him to keep himself away from Fiona and her emotions and find sexual release with some random woman like he used to do, another part challenged him to stay.

Wanted to stay.

He'd faced billion-dollar mergers with less fear than the idea of a relationship with this woman. But he'd grown tired of mindless sex, interchangeable partners, and no joy. It was time to change things.

Starting with breakfast, something he'd never made for any of his partners.

Sliding from bed, careful not to wake Fiona, he drew on his boxers from the night before—shocked thinking about the frenzy Fiona had been in to remove them—and padded into the kitchen. His stomach growled, and he headed to the Subzero refrigerator, removed eggs, butter, milk, cheese, and mushrooms, and set them on the concrete countertop. Five minutes later, omelets sizzled on the Viking range, Colombian coffee brewed, and artisan whole-grain bread toasted.

"Something smells good." Fiona walked into the kitchen wearing the shirt she'd stripped off Caleb last night.

He stared at her, admiring how her breasts filled his gray button-down in ways he'd never imagined.

She blushed. "I hope you don't mind…"

He cut off any other words with a kiss. "Nope, looks better on you than it ever did on me."

She laughed, and his heart squeezed. "I don't know," she said, following him over to the stove and wrapping her arms around him from behind. "You filled this nicely last night. Until I ripped it off you."

Her compliment, mixed with her touching him and her heady, morning-after-sex scent filled him. There it was again, the catch in his throat that short circuited his ability to speak.

She placed a kiss between his shoulder blades before letting him go. "Where are your plates?"

He pointed with the spatula, and she set the table outside, while he put the finishing touches on breakfast. Three minutes later, they were seated at the glass table on his balcony overlooking the water.

She swallowed a bite of the mushroom omelet and sipped her coffee. "I can't decide what I like better. Your breakfast or your view."

He hadn't taken his gaze off her since she sat. "My view is gorgeous," he said. Her cheeks deepened to a dark pink. The flush covered her neck and disappeared into the V of his shirt. He wondered how far the pink went and if he could strip her right here.

"Don't even think about it," she said.

He raised his head in surprise. She laughed. Had she just read his mind, or had he spoken out loud? Why didn't her laughing at him bother him? His head pounded with questions. It was too early for this. Shaking his head, he dug into his omelet.

"I've learned to read you," she said in between bites. "You're not as adept at hiding your feelings as you think."

"God help me."

She reached for his hand and entwined her fingers with his. Her grasp was warm. It grounded him, connected him to her, and made him feel a part of something—someone—like he hadn't in a long time. He raised her hand to his lips and kissed her knuckles.

"What are your plans for today?" he asked.

"I need to write articles for the website and blog and put together proposals for clients. And connect with Patricia about those reviews. You?"

"Can you do it here? I have reports to go over and a conference call, but we could go to the beach later." The sea air drifted across the balcony. "It's a perfect day for it."

"I think I'll concentrate better if I go to my office," she said. "Besides, I don't have my computer with me. Or my bathing suit. But we can still go to the beach this afternoon."

A sliver of disappointment sliced through him, but she was right. He'd concentrate better without her here as well. "Call me when you're done."

She nodded. "You know, you never told me about your tattoos."

He swallowed with care as the piece of egg threatened to choke him. Taking a swig of orange juice, which tasted sour now, he looked off at the horizon. "What do you want to know?"

"It's such a distinctive tattoo—a massive oak tree across your entire back in excruciating detail, winds around your arms and has 'hope,' 'light up the darkness,' and other words hidden within the leaves. What's the significance?"

This was not how he wanted to spend the morning

after the best sex of his life, but he shouldn't be surprised. He'd known the subject would arise. She'd warned him. It was a matter of time, and there was only so much distraction he could cause.

"The tree represents strength. My roots gave me strength. And the words hidden within the leaves and branches are reminders of what I've gone through, lessons learned, and where I'm going." He hoped she wouldn't pry beyond his explanation. Not now.

"It's stunning." She smiled. "That word okay for you, or should I check the thesaurus?"

He laughed, startled he could do so in front of her, but realizing he enjoyed it. "It's better than pretty."

Her fingers followed the lines of ink on his forearms as far as she could reach. Her touch tickled him, making goose bumps appear. "Pretty isn't the right word for artwork like this."

"You're right. The reason I don't show my emotions to people is in business, it makes more sense to keep them to myself. And in my personal life, well, it's always been safer."

She frowned. "Safer?"

He stiffened. "My father…he was…it's complicated."

He didn't know how to give her more without telling her everything. And he wasn't ready yet. When she remained silent, he relaxed.

"Lexie and I didn't have the best childhood. The tattoos remind me I can get through anything. No matter how bad."

She traced the word "brave" hidden on the inside of his forearm. Frowning, she met his gaze. "Did this hurt?"

He shrugged. "I don't know if hurt is the right word." When she rolled her eyes, he continued. "I'm not trying to be difficult. Yes, there were needles. A large image like this can be painful. But you do it in stages, so I'd say it was more uncomfortable than painful. But there was a purpose, so..." He shrugged again.

"I could never suffer through it."

Rising, he took her empty plate and stacked it on top of his own. "I'm glad." He led the way into the kitchen. "I like your skin just the way it is."

Chapter Thirteen

Fiona raced around her apartment, throwing beach things in her bag, trying to make sure she wasn't forgetting anything. She was supposed to meet Caleb at the beach in a half hour, and at this rate, she was going to be late. A knock on her door interrupted her. She groaned.

Peeking through the peephole, she spotted Lexie and opened the door.

"Hey, Lex."

"Just saying hi. I haven't seen you in, like, forever."

Fiona swallowed. Lexie was her friend, and she'd share news about a guy, especially since Lexie wanted her and Caleb to date. But he was Lexie's brother. How much could she tell her?

Lexie walked in and pointed to the beach bag. "What a fabulous idea. It's a perfect beach day. If Steve and I weren't going to meet with friends of his, I'd join you. Are you going by yourself?"

"I'm meeting your brother."

The squeal made Fiona wince and her ribs ached when Lexie squeezed her in a hug. "Oh yay! I'm so glad! You like him! I can see you do. Aw, you're blushing!"

Fiona would never understand how two siblings could be more different. Lexie expressed more emotions in five sentences than Caleb had in the last five times she'd seen him. Well, maybe not. He expressed himself pretty well during sex. Heat flooded her body at the memories, and she turned away from her friend.

Lexie grabbed her arm. "No, no, no. You're not turning away. This is 'Sharing Time with Lexie.' "

A laugh burst from Fiona's throat. "I think I might need an official section of my website." She gave her a hug. "Okay, but this is one of those times I wish you weren't his sister."

She sat on the sofa, Lexie joined, and Fiona began, "I never expected to like him. I know he's your brother, but you've got to admit he's a little uptight and keeps himself walled off from everyone. Plus, he was after my company. But he kept showing up. And he is so damn gorgeous. And I guess he wore me down."

"If anyone can whittle away his defenses, it's you. Do you…" Lexi swallowed before she peered at Fiona through lowered lashes. "Do you think you want to move forward with this? With him?"

Fiona's neck heated. She shouldn't want to…but she did. She looked at her watch. "I'm going to be late to meet him at the beach."

"This is important. He can wait."

It was hard to admit it to herself. What was she supposed to tell Lexie? "We're seeing each other and getting to know each other better, I hope. And I'm starting to realize he does show emotion, I just have to pay attention."

"Give him time. He'll relax with you."

Fiona tapped Lexie's knee. "He's already smiled a few times and even laughed."

Lexie's mouth dropped. "Whoa. That's huge!"

"I know. Pinocchio is becoming a real boy."

"You might not want to tell him. Just some sisterly advice."

"Yeah, he's already on me for some of the words I use."

Lexie rose and turned toward the door. "I'm so glad the two of you are together. You're perfect for each other!"

Once Lexie left, Fiona finished getting ready and headed to the beach. Umbrellas dotted the sand and people frolicked in the water. Off to the side, away from the crowds, she spotted Caleb and with a wave, she ran over.

"Sorry I'm late. I ran behind and then your sister waylaid me."

He rose, sculpted and tan, and embraced her. "I'm just glad you're here now." He hadn't brought an umbrella, but he took her red one and stuffed it into the sand, then helped her spread her towel. He moved his chair next to her and linked hands as they stared at the ocean. A light breeze blew, smells of sand and sea and sunscreen wafted around her, and the waves lapped. Lexie was right—it was perfect.

Caleb rose. "Walk the beach with me."

"I think you meant, 'will you?' " She smirked.

Folding his arms across his chest, he stared at her until she nodded, and he lifted her to her feet. Holding hands, they walked on the wet, packed sand, the waves splashing against their toes. They headed away from the people and the farther away they got, the looser Caleb became. When she laughed and fidgeted at his hand tickling her side, he answered with a wicked gleam in his eye and chased her into the water. Her shrieks mingled with laughter—*his laughter!*—and they splashed in the sea.

"Come with me," he said, taking her hand and riding the waves. He headed deeper, and at her reluctance, he turned and lifted her. She pressed her chest to him and wrapped her arms and legs around him as he treaded water. "Trust me."

She held tight to his shoulders. They'd made it past the waves, into a calmer part of the ocean, where the water still wasn't too deep and the waves swelled, rather than crashed. Bobbing like a cork, she reveled in being this close to him, feeling the strength of his protection. She slid off him, and he held her in front of him, keeping her safe. His pupils dilated. His desire was palpable, but even though they were away from most people, they were still in public. They couldn't...

He reached for her head and brought her to meet his lips. One kiss, two, and she had to pull away. "We can't do this here," she said, even though she wanted to.

"I know," he said. "I just had to taste you."

She treaded water next to him, trying not to be jealous of the water touching him, lapping against him. The sun's heat warmed her, while the ocean cooled her, but flares of desire remained. She held Caleb's hand, floating. Gulls cried overhead and the breeze blew. In the distance, music played.

"Ice cream?" she asked, pointing to a truck on the ridge behind the beach.

Nodding, Caleb led her to their spot. He put on a T-shirt, and she wrapped a towel around her waist, and they walked to the ice cream truck.

"What kind do you want?" he asked, pointing to

the list of flavors.

"There is no flavor other than chocolate," she said.

"So, I suppose a list of flavors is—"

"Distraction," she interrupted. "Pure distraction, so those of us in the know can have as much as we want."

With a huff, he signed "two" to the man behind the counter.

"Smart man." Fiona slipped in front of him and handed the ice cream man money.

"Wait, I've got it," Caleb said.

She shook her head. "Nope, my treat today."

He stiffened.

She waited, watching him. In all the times she'd been with him, he'd never let anyone else take charge. Another lesson he'd have to learn if the two of them were going to work. She filed the information away for later and stroked his forearm. "It's just ice cream," she said.

His chest rose and fell. His muscles tensed, and Fiona anticipated his argument. But slowly, he relaxed. With a nod, he took his cone and put his money away. "Thank you."

"Did you get the work done you needed to?" he asked.

"Yeah, you?"

"Mostly." When she just looked at him, he continued. "I have an investment foundation with three guys—friends from college—and we're looking for a charity to support. So far, we're not happy with anything."

"There are an awful lot of worthy causes to choose from, so I can see why it would be difficult."

He licked his chocolate cone. "It's because there

are so many, we look for special cases. Organizations that don't draw funds from the public. Or sometimes we start our own."

"Your group must have a lot of capital."

He nodded. "The four of us have done very well for ourselves. So capital isn't a problem. We funded a park and therapy garden and outfitted a Boys & Girls Center with enough computers to teach the kids how to code. We tend to look for meaningful causes."

Fiona's throat thickened with emotion, and she hid behind her ice cream cone.

And then a thought clicked into place. "Does your investment group fund the shelter?"

He raised his head and stared at the horizon. His steps slowed, and his free hand made a fist. What nerve had she touched on? She reached for his fist and held it. Next to her, his body was stiff. She could feel it as they walked together—his smooth gait hitched. But the closer they got to their umbrella, the easier he breathed and at the last minute, he opened his hand and took hers in his.

He shook his head. "No. I know how badly they need money to expand. It's a good thought."

"You didn't seem to think so a few minutes ago when I first suggested it."

He whipped his head around. "How do you do this?"

"Do what?"

"Read me."

"Body language."

"No one else can."

"That you know of."

He stayed silent for a few minutes. "True."

She brushed her hand against his knee. "It's hard to do. I just happen to be good at it. My family was very emotional—we all wear our hearts on our sleeves. So it's easy for me to read people."

He nodded.

"I didn't mean to upset you," she said.

Taking her hand in his, he brought it to his lips. "You surprised me."

"Back to a few minutes ago. What was wrong?"

He dropped her hand. "Nothing. I was thinking about how my group would react to it."

He lied. She knew it as sure as if he held a blinking sign. Aversion oozed from him as easily as dishonesty did now.

She leaned forward to get out of her chair, to leave before things went any further with a guy who couldn't be honest. But she paused halfway. Caleb was unlike anyone she'd ever met. He had issues, with a capital I. Even if he didn't tell her what those issues were, she could see them shimmering around him. Lexie vouched for him.

So, if he were averse to the idea, and lying about it—which he was—there had to be a good reason for it. He hadn't done anything else to make her think he was dishonest. Even hiding his emotions—he wasn't very good at it around her. She remained in her chair.

"I know there's more," she said, looking sideways at him. "I hope someday you'll share it with me." She gave him a little leeway and would wait to see what happened.

****

"Simon." Caleb joined the group videoconference. He waved to Ted. "Alex," he added as their last partner joined. "I have an idea for our charity investment."

He wasn't sure why he hadn't thought of the idea himself, but Fiona had planted the idea in his head, and he hadn't been able to stop thinking about it. At first, he'd frozen, terrified she'd somehow seen into his reason for supporting the shelter, discovered his secret. But her hand on his arm brought him to reality. She could read his emotions, not his mind. His secret was safe. She reacted to his presence.

It didn't mean he liked talking about it or wanted to take his involvement further. But the more he considered Fiona's suggestion, the more comfortable he got with it. The problem was she asked questions, and she read him so damn well. He needed time to prepare his answers, his body language, and his emotional responses. The middle of a crowded beach wasn't the place. He should have just told her. Instead, he'd avoided answering her question.

Unlike most people, she hadn't given him a hard time, although he could tell from the set of her shoulders, she wasn't happy with his doing it. If she could give him a second chance, he had to meet her halfway.

He explained his volunteering at the shelter, told them about its mission and its fundraising goals. "Right now, their building is full and can't take in anymore families in need. There's an apartment building they've been eyeing but they need money to buy it, renovate it, and increase the security protocols."

"Can you get us a copy of their financials?" Simon asked.

"And their technology needs," added Ted, a cyber security expert. "I might be able to help there."

"And if you send me the specs of their current building, as well as the new one, I can see what can be done about renovating," Alex the architect said.

"Okay, I'll get the information and email it to all of you within the next week."

They disconnected, and Caleb dashed off an email to Melanie at the shelter. He was due to volunteer there again tomorrow, so he hoped she'd see his email before he arrived and have the information.

He shook his head. Not being open with Fiona didn't sit well with him. The rest of their time at the beach had been tainted in his mind by what he hadn't said. He hadn't been able to tell her about his experience as a kid, so he'd glossed over his initial reaction.

He'd done his best to bury that part of his life. When he'd first started volunteering at the shelter, he'd feared it would bring all his old memories and trauma back. Instead, he got so much from making the kids laugh, he found his wounds healing just by being there. If he'd had a place to go as a child, maybe things would have been different.

He dialed his sister's number.

"Hey, Caleb, how are you? I hear you and Fiona are together. I'm so excited for you!"

He squeezed the stress ball he kept on hand and always needed when he talked to his sister. "I'm fine, Lex. Thank you. But I wanted to ask you something."

"Sure. Is everything okay? Do you need me to come over?"

"There's nothing wrong. I just…have you told Fiona anything about our childhood. About Dad?" His mouth filled with a bitter taste just mentioning him, and he resisted the urge to throw the ball against the wall. The man wasn't worth the damage he might cause to the wall.

"She knows we didn't have the best family life, but I haven't said anything. Why?"

"Because we were talking about the shelter. I wasn't honest with her. I must fix things, but I needed to know what you've told her."

"Caleb, you can trust her. I know you haven't known her long, but she's trustworthy."

He closed his eyes against the moisture that formed every time his sister tried to take care of him. It was his job, not hers. He cleared his throat. "Thanks, Lex."

Hanging up the phone, he visualized talking to Fiona. It was not a conversation he wanted to have. But it was necessary. Especially if he wanted a relationship with her.

****

Fiona hurried across the outer office the next morning and unlocked her office door to answer the ringing telephone.

"Hello?"

"Fiona? This is Elaina Mathews."

"Elaina, how are you? Did you have a chance to look at the proposal I sent you?"

"It's why I'm calling, Fiona. I don't think I can work with you."

"What? Why not, Elaina?" Elaina was a prospective client; someone Fiona had been after for a long time. She'd built a rapport with her, yet her tone suggested otherwise.

"Please, Fiona, don't act like you don't know. You've been accumulating bad reviews and now you're working with WW Media."

"What are you talking about?"

"I'm sorry, Fiona. But I picked you because you're like working with a friend. If I wanted someone shilling for a large corporation, I would have found someone else."

Elaina disconnected before Fiona could respond. Fiona's heart beat faster, and she turned on her computer. Emails scrolled by, seven from clients. Each one she opened cancelled their contract with her.

"What is going on?" Her voice echoed in the empty office.

Patricia walked into the office, her face pale. "Did you see this?" She thrust a handful of papers at Fiona. They were printouts from the Internet—photos of her and Caleb together, business articles claiming their partnership was more than personal, screenshots of the business deals on Caleb's website. Rumors and innuendo.

"Oh my God." She turned to Patricia. "Where did this come from?"

Patricia rattled off sites just on this side of reliable but with a long reach.

"Get me the numbers of all our clients. I'll call them all and talk to them."

Three hours later, Fiona ended the call for the last time, shaking. Although not everyone left, and her longstanding clients who chose to remain had believed her, a slew of her newest clients and prospects believed she combined her business with Caleb's. And even if she pleaded her case, they didn't like the idea of a big corporate influence on her company. In addition to the articles, his website had deals targeted to her clients.

Combined with the bad reviews Patricia hadn't had any luck tracing, it sounded like she was expanding her business and working with him, losing the personal touch she was known for. She buried her head in her arms. This was why each time Caleb had suggested she join her business with his, she'd refused. What the heck happened?

Grabbing her phone once again, she made one last phone call. Caleb answered on the first ring. "Hey, you were on my mind. We need to talk."

"You're right, we do."

"That sounds ominous," Caleb said, his deep voice laced with concern. "Do you want me to come over?"

"No!" The last thing she needed was for someone to see him walking into her office.

"Do you want to talk at my office? I can send a car."

It would be even worse. "No, how about my apartment tonight?" It was plausible he could visit his sister. She needed deniability.

"I'll be over at eight."

Fiona paced her apartment waiting for Caleb to arrive that evening. She loved the size of her apartment—it was warm and inviting, and when she watched scary TV shows, it wasn't large enough to make her think the boogey man hid somewhere. But tonight, it crowded in on her, and every time she paced from one room to the other, she had to avoid crashing into her grandmother's antique rocker or the bookshelf filled with her favorite romance authors. Finally, her doorbell rang, and she raced to answer it. Her body ran hot and cold when Caleb stood in her doorway. His shoulders were wide enough to block the entire entranceway. Even in her anger, her body responded to him, and it made her blood boil. She retreated, and he entered.

His face showed concern, but he held his shoulders stiff, his posture erect. His steps were slow, measured. "Fiona, what's wrong?"

The sound of his gravelly voice pushed through her defenses and made her burst into tears. She covered her face as she regained control. Then she straightened. She wanted Caleb to rush to her side, dry her tears, croon it would be all right. But Caleb retreated, and all trace of emotion had disappeared from his face. He always rushed to help everyone. Why did he avoid her? She wiped her face and sat on the sofa. After another few seconds, Caleb sat on the edge of the rocker, as if he were afraid he'd break it. Or like he wanted to run.

"I walked into work this morning with seventeen private clients. I left my office this evening with eleven."

"What happened?"

"I hoped you could tell me." She thrust a folder she'd left on the coffee table at him and waited while he absorbed the information. She had to hand it to him, his control amazed her. She couldn't read a single thing from his face as he paged through the photos and articles. It was like watching a robot. But somehow, he calmed her.

"Who did you tell about us, Caleb?" Her chest tightened, and her stomach roiled. She hadn't been able to eat anything all day.

"What do you mean?" His voice was quiet. Too quiet. Why was he so distant?

"I haven't mentioned our relationship to anyone

other than your sister. So, it had to have come from you." Her face burned at the image of him talking about the two of them to someone who could do something like this.

The tone of his voice warned her of his anger. "I don't discuss my personal life with anyone. Ever. You're the one who appeared on television."

"Where I talked about my business, not my personal life." She wished he'd take her in his arms. "Besides, it was before we met."

"I know, but you appeared before thousands of people. Or maybe it's a dissatisfied former client."

"I don't have any."

His body jerked. "How is it possible?"

She got a small amount of satisfaction from his surprise. "Are you doubting me or calling me a liar?"

"I've never met anyone who didn't have at least one dissatisfied customer."

"Now you have. Or had." She would have laughed if any part of this situation was the least bit funny.

He shook his head. "I have no idea what is going on here."

"Have you looked at your website?" Her heart rate increased again as she pictured what he'd find.

Caleb tapped a few keys on his phone. His body stilled, and he swore. Rising, he continued the pacing Fiona had done just a few minutes before. He dialed and put the phone to his ear. "Robert, you and I need to meet tomorrow morning. Seven. My office." He returned to the rocker. "I'll take care of this. Trust me."

"Why?" This man, to whom she was head-over-heels attracted and growing to care for might be responsible for the partial collapse of her business. How was she supposed to trust him?

"Why what?"

"Why should I trust you're going to take care of this to my satisfaction?"

He paused mid-pace. "You're right. Come to my office, and you can sit in on the meeting."

Would a man who betrayed her show her this much trust? She started to speak, but he interrupted. "Understand this, Fiona. I *never* let outsiders sit in on my internal meetings. Ever. Until now, with you."

Fiona closed her mouth. Out of everything she'd imagined Caleb doing or saying, inviting her to an internal business meeting was not on the list. "What kind of meeting is this?"

"One where we're going to get answers."

Chapter Fourteen

After a sleepless night fueled by fury, Caleb stalked into his office at five thirty the next morning. He'd fumed. He hadn't allowed those emotions to take over since he was a child, trying to protect his family from his father, and failing. But Fiona set them free. When he'd realized how futile fuming was, he'd planned his strategy. And now he waited to implement it.

He suspected what happened and requested this meeting with Robert at seven this morning, but there was a big difference between him and Robert. He never mixed business with pleasure. As soon as he and Fiona started a relationship, he'd dropped the idea of buying her company. He had the internal memo to prove it.

Except she didn't know, his internal voice had whispered. And all the advice and suggestions of ways she could increase revenue had compounded the misunderstanding.

And then she'd cried. He'd never seen her cry before, not even when the ants invaded her kitchen. Not like this. He expected hysterics from his sister, not Fiona. Seeing those tears shut him down. He'd spent his life dealing with his sister and his mother, the two women in his life he loved most in the world. He didn't have it in him to do it again. As much as he wanted to, the sight of her tears threw him into his past, churned his stomach, and shredded his insides. He couldn't do it.

First, he'd address this professional transgression. She didn't deserve the damage to her reputation, and he planned to fix it and help Fiona get her business back. It was only fair.

And then he would end their relationship. No matter how much it killed him. No matter how attracted to her he was, no matter how much he enjoyed talking to her and being with her. He'd assumed he could handle her because she was calm and rational, even if she showed her emotions. But he misjudged the situation. Between last night and now, he'd been torn into pieces, tortured over what had happened, and he couldn't handle the emotions.

His phone buzzed at six forty-five and he told the security guard to let Fiona inside. She was early. He admired punctuality.

She walked into his office dressed in a charcoal pantsuit with a pale pink blouse. The color gave her cheeks a pretty hue and the suit showed off her slim waist. But he banked his attraction. This was not the time. It never would be.

"Fiona." He nodded to her and pointed to the conference table in his office, keeping the desk between him and her. "Robert will be here in fifteen minutes. Make yourself comfortable. There's coffee and tea on the sideboard."

"Want to give me a hint of what this meeting is about?" She fixed herself tea and sat with her back to the window. His chest ached at the distance between them, but he didn't have any other choice.

"Robert is my head of mergers and acquisitions."

"That doesn't tell me much."

"Just wait."

Her perfume distracted him, and her neck begged to be touched. He kept himself occupied at his desk, swiping through reports he needed to read, anything to keep him from staring. Finally, Robert knocked on the door.

"Robert," Caleb said. He pointed to the table. "Sit."

Robert let his shock show. "I see from Ms. Hamilton's presence it's an acquisition meeting. Excellent. Are we waiting for the lawyers?" He spoke, swaggering toward the sideboard, and Caleb resisted the urge to speak. He'd learned long ago people hung themselves on their own rope, if given enough of it.

Caleb glanced at Fiona, who frowned. He shook his head at her, and she smoothed her facial features. Her gaze shot daggers at him, and her cheeks were now red.

"No, for now it's just the three of us."

Caleb pressed a button beneath his desk and then joined Robert and Fiona at the conference table. "Robert, why don't we start this meeting with what you've been doing about Ms. Hamilton's company?"

"Are you sure you want me talking about it here, with her?"

Caleb nodded. "I find honesty does a lot to further my goals."

Robert crossed his ankle over his knee. "Well, we've all seen the numbers. Ms. Hamilton's business is worth around two million, which we can cover with ease. Our reach is greater and by automating a lot of what she's doing by hand—conducting surveys, outsourcing articles, corporate sponsorships—we can clear five million in the first two years."

"How do you know?" Caleb asked.

Robert puffed his chest, like a balloon filling with helium. For a moment, Caleb wondered if his voice would squeak. "I had my team do some preliminary research."

Caleb cut in. "Yes, I saw the research. But the numbers you're talking about now never made it into the report."

"Because it was preliminary. I had them look deeper after you and I met."

"The meeting where I told you I wasn't interested in acquiring Fiona's firm?"

Out of the corner of his eye, Fiona shifted. His stomach churned. He needed her not to say anything yet. This was why he never let emotions intrude in business. You got a lot further by keeping a cool head.

"Research is never a bad thing, Caleb."

"Except when it goes against my wishes."

Robert leaned forward. "It's a great business decision. I knew you'd see it with more numbers."

"But you never showed me those numbers, Robert."

"I planned to next week. Only…"

Caleb waited, as much to calm his pounding heart as to see what Robert would say. But Robert didn't say anything.

"Only?" Caleb asked.

"I started hearing rumors maybe your meetings weren't strictly professional."

"What business is it of yours?"

Robert folded his arms. "Look, I don't care who you bang. But this acquisition would be perfect for us.

And she'd just appeared on television and told however many millions of people her business thrived on her personal touch. If clients saw another side of her 'personal touch' "—he had the nerve to use air quotes—"she'd be more inclined to accept our offer."

"Were you responsible for the coupons on our website?" Caleb asked.

"It was marketing."

"At your suggestion?"

Robert nodded.

"You cost me tens of thousands of dollars in profits," Fiona said, her voice like steel.

Caleb turned toward her. She exuded a calmness he envied.

This was business. Terrible business, but business, nonetheless. Business deals weren't meant for emotions like envy.

"Which we'd triple by adding your business to ours."

Caleb redirected his focus to Robert. "But we're not acquiring Fiona's business. I've told you before, and I'm telling you again now."

"Caleb, it makes no sense."

"Who else in the company helped you target Fiona's business?" He slid his iPad to Robert, who typed in a list of six names. Caleb looked at them and nodded. Rising, he returned to his desk and buzzed his secretary.

"Kathy, I'm emailing you a list of six people. Would you send them to my office at ten? Also did you take care of the task I requested?"

"Yes, want me to send them in?"

"Please."

He grabbed his stress ball and returned to the conference table. "Robert, you're fired. Human resources and legal will talk with you later this morning. In the meantime, wait here until security…oh, here they are now."

Two security guards entered the office and stood next to the door. Robert's face turned beet red.

"Caleb, come on. You can't fire me."

"Yes, I can, and when legal hears the recording of this meeting, they'll support me. Go clean your desk. I won't have people working for me who disobey my instructions and sabotage other companies in my name." He nodded to the security guards, and they stepped forward. "We're done here."

The guards escorted Robert from the room and Caleb retreated to the wall of windows and stared at the ocean view. His emotional response during this meeting was foreign to him, and he needed to regain control. His back muscles ached, and his neck was taut.

"Thank you," Fiona said, her voice softer since she confronted him.

He turned toward her, squeezing the ball in his hand. "Don't thank me."

She walked toward him, her gaze alternating between his face and his hand. "Why not? You were quick to jump in." She reached for his hand holding the stress ball and stroked his knuckles. He swallowed. "I must admit, I was angry at first when you bossed me around, telling me to come to your meeting and not letting me speak. But I'm impressed with how you handled everything. You blindsided him."

Caleb nodded. "I needed him to admit what he did. I couldn't take the chance he'd hide his actions."

"Thank you."

"I still have to help you recover your clients."

She shook her head, her gaze bright.

Please don't let her cry again. Anxiety slithered along the back of his neck.

"I don't think it's possible." She turned to the table. "I've got to get going and see what other damage control I need to do."

"I'm taking care of it."

Her gaze flashed. "This is my company, Caleb. I can manage."

"I know you can. But your problem is my fault. I'll fix things."

She shook her head. "I don't think you can." As she headed toward the door, she paused. "Will I see you later?"

Longing streaked through him. She'd come to the meeting in control of her emotions. She hadn't dissolved into tears either before or after, even though she looked as if she might. Could he risk thinking she was different than he expected? "I'll call you tonight."

****

Fiona returned to her apartment that night and staggered inside. She'd spent all day trying to salvage her business and she had no idea if she'd been successful. She'd written a heartfelt piece for the blog, submitted to interviews by members of the media, and worked on an advertising campaign with Patricia. But it still looked like her word against the world, and she was bone tired.

And then there was Caleb.

She'd been furious when the first reports of her relationship with him had appeared. He'd angered her even more with his high-handed proposal to deal with things. But after sitting in on his meeting, she realized he'd been right, and she was grateful. It should have made her feel better, but it didn't. Because he'd frozen her out.

She didn't know why. Her chest ached to connect with him, to see him look at her with eyes glowing, to hear the rasp of her name come from his lips. Instead, he acted as if he didn't know her.

After changing from her work clothes and making herself a bowl of soup, she curled on the sofa with a romance novel. Her phone rang, and relief flooded through her.

"How are you?"

She appreciated Caleb's concerned tone. "Worn out." She ran a hand through her hair. "Thank you again for today."

"You need to stop thanking me."

"What's wrong, Caleb?"

"Nothing."

His flat voice alarmed her. A lump formed in her throat. "Don't lie to me. Something is wrong."

He sighed. "What do you want from me?"

"Honesty. Please." She whispered the last word. He'd berate her for showing her emotions, but she didn't care.

"I've never lied to you."

"Except by omission. What's going on?" His lack of comment on her emotions almost hurt her more.

"I destroyed your company." The rasp in his voice betrayed his pain.

"Not you personally, and you're trying to fix it. I was angry, furious, but I'm over it now."

"How?"

She leaned into the cushion and grabbed the soft, multicolored afghan her mother had made her. "Because emotions don't control me, not when their cause disappears. I thought you'd sabotaged my business. But you didn't. Someone in your company did and you're fixing it. So I'm disappointed and scared and exhausted, but I'm not angry at you any longer."

"But you were." His voice lost its iciness and became more modulated.

"I was."

"You thought I would sabotage you."

"I didn't know what to think," she said. "You wanted to buy my company, even when I said no."

"But I told you I'd stopped. I don't mix business and pleasure, Fiona. Once we kissed, it was over."

She ran a hand through her hair. "Caleb. You don't let people know how you're feeling. You can't also make decisions and not tell anyone. Like when you were giving me advice about increasing my revenue."

"I wanted to help you be even more successful than you already were."

"But I didn't ask you for it, and you didn't tell me it was your reason. You have to let people in, at least a little bit."

Silence stretched across the line. "I'm sorry."

"Is there anything else bothering you?" she asked. "Because you didn't seem yourself today."

"Like you, I have a lot on my mind," he said.

"Is there anything I can help with?"

His breathing hitched. "Don't you think you have enough to handle?"

"Like you, I can separate business and pleasure."

"I saw that today," he said. "I wasn't sure if you were going to interrupt me. You looked about to blow at one point."

She smiled at the memory. "But I didn't."

"But you didn't."

"Emotions aren't bad, Caleb."

This time his pause lengthened. "As long as you can control them."

****

Caleb checked the financial papers the next day. Thanks to the work of his public relations department, all the major papers ran stories about WW Media's withdrawal from acquiring Fiona's company. As expected, their stock took a brief hit, but recovered by midday. WW Media had survived the storm. But had Fiona's company? The answer wouldn't come for a while. In the meantime, he'd accomplished two of the three things on his list—he'd fired Robert and all the employees who had helped him. He was in the process of helping Fiona get her business back. A few well-placed publicity coups, with the help of his PR team, and she'd be back on her feet. Hopefully. But the third item, ending their relationship, left him in a cold sweat.

For a man who blocked all his emotions, this was not the place to be. He assumed his feelings for Fiona caused his cold sweat. The problem was he didn't know what to do. It was like he switched places with Fiona—his emotions had escaped into his business meetings, while hers had been reined in after a brief interlude.

What. The. Hell.

The old Caleb would go ahead and call it off. The reasons to do so were as obvious as black ink on white paper. She caused him to feel things, a dangerous predicament. His father had homed in on any display of emotion and twisted it to his advantage. Caleb had spent his life perfecting his mask and taking care of his mother and sister so they couldn't be hurt. He didn't have it in him to do it for another person.

But the new Caleb, the one Fiona had unwrapped, didn't want to lose her. She'd maneuvered beneath his armor and made him second guess himself. The few times he'd let his mask slip, she'd rewarded him with joy and compassion. She hadn't used his emotions against him. Even sex with her made him feel new things.

He'd witnessed firsthand how she lost control once in a while but regained it on her own. Except, he hadn't been able to comfort her when she'd cried. Instead, he'd retreated, closed himself off, and focused on the business at hand. He'd seen the disappointment in her expression. And he would continue to disappoint her.

Except, if he were honest, these new emotions Fiona evoked had enhanced his life. Sure, they terrified him, but he also found heightened enjoyment.

He needed to analyze his relationship with Fiona. It's what he did in business—he never made rash decisions and look how successful he was. He didn't have to rush into anything.

After evaluating the notion from every angle, he tore himself away and turned to his to-do list. He'd had to revise it since the fiasco with Fiona's company. Now, hiring a new mergers and acquisitions head moved to the top. With a groan, he called Lexie's husband, Steve.

"Hey, it's Caleb. Can we push dinner to seven-thirty tonight?"

"Sure. Everything okay?"

"Yeah, just a crisis I have to deal with." He didn't want to discuss it with his sister's husband. Not until he knew what Fiona had told Lexie.

"We can postpone if you want," Steve said.

"Nah, the game's on tonight. I'll meet you at the bar at seven thirty."

Caleb didn't rise for air again until right before he had to leave. He went straight from his office to his private garage and peeled onto the street. Parking around the corner from the bar, he stretched and inhaled the cool evening air.

Inside the sports bar, the lights were dim, but fifteen TV screens glowed, making it easy to spot Steve across the room. Caleb wove his way around tables of people eating and cheering until he arrived where Steve had saved him a seat at the bar. The scuffed wood, team pennants and memorabilia made this one of his favorite places to watch the baseball game. He perched on the stool, ordered a round and clapped Steve on the back.

"Thanks for waiting."

Steve passed him a bowl of nuts. "Lexie tells me you're in the doghouse. Something about forcing Fiona to sell her company?"

Tension returned to Caleb's shoulders. He swore. "It's not like that. At least, not now." Since Steve already knew part of the story, Caleb filled him in on the rest.

"And she doesn't hate you?"

"She was fine when she left yesterday." She was, wasn't she? He wracked his brain trying to determine if he'd missed any signals. Fiona didn't hide her emotions but remained more reserved than Lexie. Had he misjudged her?

"You should marry the woman."

Caleb jerked so hard he almost fell off his stool. When he recovered, he stared at the just-delivered a pile of wings. Marry Fiona? "What are you talking about?"

"Any woman who can almost lose her company and not want to kill you should be married right away."

Caleb pulled his phone from his pocket. It was too noisy to call, so he texted.

—hey, just wanted to check in and see how you're doing.—

"Proposing right now?" Steve asked with a chuckle. "Smart man."

"I'm just checking to see how she is. We didn't talk today."

"Maybe she's angrier than you thought."

Sweat formed along his spine. Maybe he should have checked on her this morning. Or this afternoon. But he'd been swamped, trying to help with her company's recovery. She'd understand, wouldn't she? *Dammit, this is why he hated emotions.*

Shaking his head as much at Steve as to dispel his thoughts, he focused on the game on the screen above them. The Angels were winning seven to three in the seventh inning. Every time a new player approached the mound, Caleb glanced at his phone, but Fiona didn't respond. Was she angry? Away from her phone? Hurt?

No longer able to ignore his own questions, he turned to Steve. "I'm gonna go. I've got an early morning tomorrow."

Steve gave him a knowing look but remained silent.

Just as Caleb reached for his wallet, a guy strode to

him.

"You bastard!" the man shouted and swung at him. "You ruined my life!"

Caleb ducked and within seconds, Steve jumped in, trying to help. But others joined the fight so wooden chairs crashed, glass shattered, and the last thing Caleb thought about before blacking out from an upper cut to his jaw was Fiona.

Chapter Fifteen

All Fiona wanted to do was get inside her apartment and go to bed. She'd spent the day fielding phone calls from the press and drafting another heartfelt statement she'd posted to the website. In it, she'd poured her heart and soul, describing who her company was, why she loved it and how she wasn't planning to sell it, no matter what other reports said. She hoped it would be enough to keep her afloat until she could find new private clients. Based on website clicks, she was still okay. Now she needed peace so she could deal with tomorrow.

She slipped her key in the lock, but before she had a chance to turn it, Lexie's door swung open.

"Fiona! Oh, my God, Fiona. I'm so glad you're home!"

Fiona turned. Lexie's tear-streaked face crumpled, and her entire body was shaking. Dropping her purse and briefcase, Fiona turned, and Lexie fell into her arms sobbing.

"Lexie, what's wrong?"

"It's Steve and Caleb! They were attacked in a bar fight and they're in the hospital."

Icy tendrils raced along Fiona's spine. "What happened?"

"I don't know! I just got the call now. I have to get to the hospital." She pulled from Fiona's arms, but

Fiona held tight.

"Wait, Lexie. Hold on, okay." She grabbed her phone from her purse and found a text from Caleb. "Caleb texted me. I didn't hear it. It must have been on vibrate."

She opened her texting app.

—hey, just wanted to check in and see how you're doing.—

"He sent this over an hour ago. It must have been before the fight." She searched her recent calls list and her voicemail, but there was nothing from him. Why hadn't he contacted her? She paused. Lexie was already hysterical.

"Lexie, you have to remain calm."

Lexie nodded and fumbled for her keys. Fiona held onto her arm. "Let me drive." The last thing they needed was to get into an accident.

Fiona fought for calm, navigating her newly repaired BMW through the busy Los Angeles streets, but her mind whirled in a million different directions. Why had they gotten into a fight? How bad were their injuries? Why hadn't Caleb called her?

The last question niggled at the back of her mind. They were close enough to have sex. They were close enough for him to start to let her see his feelings. Weren't they close enough for him to call her if he were hurt? Unless he was so badly injured, he couldn't call...

She groaned.

"I know," Lexie said. "It's awful!"

Fiona reached across and patted her shoulder. "I'm sure they'll be fine. I just wish Caleb had called me."

"My brother isn't one to let others take care of him. I'm sure it's not personal."

Pulling into the hospital, Fiona parked the car and she and Lexie rushed into the emergency room. They were directed to a curtained room. Lexie headed to Steve, while Fiona headed toward Caleb. She willed herself to stay calm for his sake.

Through the open doorway, she saw her big, strong, bald guy lay on a white gurney, his face a mass of harsh colors, his skin pale beneath the injuries. She swallowed. "Wow, I'd hate to see what the other guy looks like." She hoped she sounded nonchalant. Walking toward him, she stopped at the edge of the bed. "How do you feel?"

He gave a mirthless laugh, then turned away, but not before he winced. "I'm fine if you don't make me laugh. What are you doing here?"

"Oh, I don't know. My boyfriend gets in a bar fight, it might be a good idea to come to the hospital to check on him." She took his huge hand in hers. Still strong, the knuckles were bruised. He'd hit back. She cradled it and studied his face.

"Boyfriend?" he said.

Fiona met his gaze. "I'd say so, wouldn't you?"

He swallowed. "Steve thought you might be angry with me."

"I can be angry and still want you as my boyfriend." He didn't look like he believed her. Had no one ever taught him? "Where else are you hurt?"

"My ribs and back. They want to take x-rays. I'd rather go home."

"Let them do what they need to do—"

"Oh my God! Caleb! Are you all right?" Lexie ran over, her makeup streaked with tears. She jostled the bed trying to get close, and Caleb stiffened. Fiona wasn't sure if it was from pain or discomfort from his sister's emotion, so she stroked the side of his neck.

"How's Steve?" he asked once Lexie stopped moving.

Her eyes filled, and her voice shook. "He's battered and bruised, and his leg is broken, and the police are involved…They're keeping you overnight, right? I mean, you shouldn't go home until they make sure…"

The longer Lexie carried on; the more uncomfortable Caleb grew. He might not show his emotions to others, but Fiona had learned the signs. The corner of his eye twitched. The muscles in his jaw clenched. The neck muscles beneath her hand tightened. She stepped forward and put her arm around her friend.

"Lexie, Caleb and Steve are in good hands," Fiona said. "Why don't you go to the cafeteria and get some tea."

"Oh, good idea. Do you want something? You do, of course you do."

Fiona steered her toward the door. "I don't want any but thank you. Go wash your face, get your tea, and take care of Steve." She gave her friend a hug and waited while she trudged along the fluorescent hallway before she returned to Caleb.

He'd assumed his blank look again, the one she hated, which meant he was upset.

She took his hand. "Wow, listen to the silence."

His other hand fiddled with the blanket, and he turned his head away after meeting her gaze for the briefest of moments.

"What's going on?" she asked.

He didn't respond, but his Adam's apple bobbed as he swallowed.

"Hey," she whispered, leaning over, and brushing her hand over his bald head, being careful to avoid any of the bruised areas of his face. "Talk to me."

"It's my fault."

"What's your fault?"

"Steve getting injured. It's my fault."

"Did you start the bar fight?"

"No, one of my ex-employees did."

Her eyelids widened. "Ex-employees?"

He nodded and winced again. "One of the guys I fired for working with Robert was in the bar. I didn't see him, but he saw me. When he did, he took a swing at me."

"So, it's his fault, not yours."

Caleb shook his head. "If Steve hadn't gotten hurt, Lexie wouldn't be upset. I should have protected him."

"It's not your job to protect everyone."

He clenched his teeth and remained silent.

"Caleb, even if you fired the guy, he had to have been crazy. Who in his right mind picks on the big bald guy with the tats? Besides, if you want to get technical about it, you fired him because of me. So, it's *my* fault."

Caleb's face flushed. "No!"

Fiona leaned over and stroked his face. "Hey, easy there. I'm just trying to show how silly it is to go around blaming yourself. That guy is an adult. He made his own stupid decision. It's not your fault."

He stared at her, his expression unreadable. Until he blinked. "What the hell is taking them so long?" he asked. "I want to go home. This is unnecessary."

Just then, an orderly arrived. "Mr. Zeno? We're

ready to take you to X-ray now."

The orderly wheeled him away. When he left, she cried.

This man assumed he had to take care of everyone. And if he erred, she'd leave. Good lord, who had taught him this? She'd have to teach him he was too hard on himself if she wanted a relationship with him.

And she did.

Hurrying to the bathroom, she splashed cold water on her face and wiped it dry. She stared at her reflection in the mirror. She had to get control of herself before Caleb returned.

An hour later, the orderly wheeled him in, set the brake, and left.

"You're still here," Caleb said.

"Did you think I wouldn't be?"

He didn't answer, and he didn't meet her gaze. Regardless of his injuries, they needed to talk.

"I know this isn't the best time to discuss this, but I think we need to set some ground rules for our relationship," she said

"Ground rules?"

She smiled, dragged a chair close to his bed, and took his hand. She examined the scrapes and bruises. "You must have quite a right hook."

"When necessary."

"I'm glad it's not more damaged than this. I like what you do with this hand."

His face flushed. His mouth opened and closed. Then, as if realizing he'd given himself away, he made his expression neutral. She laughed, foiling his attempt. He turned away, and she moved to the other side of the bed to meet his gaze.

"Rule number one," she said. "No avoiding each other. It means we are each other's safe place. You can say or do anything with me, feel however you want, and I won't use it against you. Just like you won't use any of my emotions against me."

He stared at her, and she waited. "Then why were you avoiding me today?" he asked.

She frowned. "I wasn't…oh, your text. I'm sorry. I spent most of my day on the phone with reporters. When I finished my last call, I shut off my phone to work undisturbed. I didn't even see your text until I got home, and Lexie told me what happened to you." She leaned over and kissed him on the lips. "Just because I don't respond to you, doesn't mean I'm avoiding you."

His expression cleared. Had he been worried?

"Okay," he said. His voice was deep and sure. "I'm glad they talked to you."

"They? What do you mean?"

"The financial reporters. I contacted a bunch of them and suggested they talk to you…"

He did what?

"Fiona? What's wrong?"

She paused before speaking. "Why would you do this?"

"Because I wanted to fix things for you."

"Without asking me?"

"My employees tried to ruin your company. It's my job to fix things."

"No, Caleb, it isn't. Love, Laugh, Live is *my* company. Unless I ask you for help, I need you to back off and let me handle things."

Again, he stared. "Okay, I'm sorry."

She nodded. She'd let it go for now because of his

injuries, but later, when he healed, they'd have to talk further about it "That brings us to rule number two—"

"There's more?"

She leaned in her chair. "Well, it would be pretty dumb to number the rules if there were only one of them."

He shook his head but winced. "Continue," he said, as if he were enduring a hardship.

"Rule number two is we split the load. You're here for me and I'm here for you. We can depend on each other."

His muscles bunched, as if he were backing away from her. "It's not going to happen, Fiona."

"Why not?"

"Because I can take care of myself."

"I can, too. But sometimes, it's nice to be able to depend on another person. I'm just saying you're free to depend on me, and I'm free to depend on you. When it goes both ways, it makes life less burdensome."

"I don't understand the rule."

"You will. In the meantime, you're going to have to trust me. Rule number three."

He groaned.

"Honesty. No matter what. Rule number four. I can add more rules to this list later."

He laughed. The sound surprised him as much as it did her, and he paused. She kissed his lips. "Are we good?"

"Rule number three," he said. "Honesty."

"Always."

"You're not still mad at me?" he asked.

She swallowed. "I'm annoyed, but I know you were trying to help, so I'm not angry. But I'm serious.

Please don't make decisions for me again."

He reached for her, pulled her head toward him, and pressed her lips with his.

"I don't want to hurt you," she whispered, touching his split lip.

"It would be worth it."

"No." She pulled away. "It wouldn't."

****

The hospital discharged Caleb five hours later. Steve had to stay another day.

Caleb had balked at getting in the wheelchair, but Fiona had made a joke, and somehow he agreed. When it was time to go home, Lexie had begged him to stay at her apartment. He didn't need his sister's oppressive concern. He'd always taken care of her.

"You stay with Steve. I'll be fine."

"But you have bruised ribs and you're going to need help."

He squeezed the arm of the wheelchair so hard, he might still have imprints of it in his hand, hours later. And then Fiona stepped in.

"Lexie, you're going to have your hands full taking care of Steve." Bile had risen in his throat at the memory of his friend's injuries, but Fiona had stroked the side of his neck and put her arm around his shoulder. "How about you let me take care of Caleb?" And once again, she'd managed to placate his sister and make him feel better too.

The woman was magic.

They returned to his apartment, where Fiona made herself at home, prepared a light meal, and helped him get ready for bed.

"Come on, it's just like when you took care of me

after my car accident," she said. He was sore and moved gingerly. He wanted to grumble, but Fiona was so patient, he stopped himself.

Now they were in bed with the lights off, with Fiona snuggled against him, he released the breath he'd held all day. Fiona wasn't angry with him. Having her take care of him wasn't the worst thing in the world. Steve would be okay and somehow didn't blame him either.

He was an idiot for even considering ending his relationship with Fiona.

"What are you thinking?" she whispered next to him.

Rule number three, honesty. "How lucky I am to have found you."

She grinned against his skin. "You're right."

"Can I get it in writing?" he asked.

"Where should I write it? Here?" Her fingers tickled his stomach. "Here?" She drew on his knee. "Or maybe here?" She tapped on his head.

"You're going to kill me."

"Pretty good way to go," she said.

This time, *she* was right.

He slept late the next morning, groaning when he rose.

"Hey, don't move," she said. "At least not without me."

He would have laughed at the incongruity of someone her size helping someone his size but laughing hurt too much. His ribs were painful, as was his face. Once she'd helped him into a semi-upright position, he leaned against the pillows, panting.

She kissed the top of his head. "Stay here and rest

today. You'll feel better later." She handed him pain meds and a breakfast tray filled with eggs, bacon, and a buttered bagel.

"Are you joining me?"

She shook her head. "I already ate. I'm going to work from here. Eat, and I'll be finished with my shower by the time you're done."

She turned toward the bathroom. "Wait," he cried. "At least let me watch if I can't join you!"

Her gaze gleamed and for once, Caleb appreciated how her emotions showed on her face. She stood at the end of the bed and slid the strap of her light blue silk nightgown off her left shoulder. He stared. Her creamy skin beckoned. When she repeated the move with the strap on her right shoulder, his nostrils flared. And when she lowered the nightgown, exposing her breasts, his groin hardened, and he leaned forward. His injured ribs protested, and he leaned against the pillow. His breath was short. He didn't know if it was from the exertion of trying to move or from watching Fiona.

The silk slid along her ribs, exposing pale skin, and he stifled a groan. When it fell off her hips onto the floor, he couldn't stop staring at her pink silk panties. What he would give to remove them. His hands twitched. A throaty laugh escaped her, and he met her gaze before staring once again at her panties. In slow motion, she slipped her fingers between the skimpy fabric and her hips and slid them down her legs.

As she bent over, her breasts swung forward, and his mouth watered. The final straw occurred when she kicked the panties toward him. He raised his hand and caught them, damning the pain, and listened to her laughter as she sauntered into the bathroom.

The sound of water had never been an aphrodisiac before but listening to it spatter against the glass walls of the shower, imagining what she soaped and knowing if only he could get himself out of bed he'd have a front row seat, made sweat pop on his brow. His hips twitched and he imagined standing in the shower with Fiona, water and soap sluicing their bodies. His hands would stroke her skin, traveling from her delicate neck, over her breasts, around her waist to her bottom.

He groaned.

"Oh my," she said.

He drank in the vision of her standing at his bedside wrapped in a towel.

She caressed his cheek, and he turned his head to kiss her palm.

"We should make you more comfortable."

"I suggested it earlier," he rasped.

She moved close to him and helped him sit. "Let's get you into the shower."

"Oh, now you want me naked."

Laughing, she helped him off the bed. "I find it makes washing more successful."

Together they removed his shirt and she blanched. She traced the purple bruising across his ribs. "Oh, baby," she whispered, tears making her voice thick.

Her tears were more potent than Lexie's shrieks had ever been, and ice formed in the pit of his stomach. "No." He staggered until the bed prevented him from moving anywhere. "Don't cry over me. Ever."

She blinked away her tears, swallowed the lump in her throat, and reached for his face. "Your pain is my pain."

He fought against the swell of emotions battling

within him. He didn't know what to do with his own feelings. He couldn't handle hers too. "It can't be."

"Yes, it can," she whispered. Cool air surrounded him as she backed away. And then her lips, as soft as silk, touched his skin. He looked at her. She kissed her way across his ribs, stomach and back, as if to heal him with her touch.

He molded his hands around her shoulders, dragging her toward him. His lips sought hers and he buried his fear, loneliness, and need in the kiss.

"Shower," she whispered.

"Join me."

They stumbled toward the bathroom, connected by their mouths and hands.

"No." Fiona withdrew from him and leaned into the shower, turning on the water. "As much as I want to, you need to do this yourself."

Did she mean because if she joined him, she'd be turned on too? He wasn't sure, and he didn't want to ask the question. With a deep sigh, he removed the rest of his clothes and stepped into the shower, alone.

The water jets spewed water hot enough to loosen his tight muscles, and he groaned in relief. Everything hurt, but somehow, by the time he turned off the water and left the shower, the pain had eased. He reached for a towel and stopped.

"Let me," Fiona said, peeking her head in the door.

He wasn't a fan of being babied, but he let her dry him, wishing her hands rather than the Egyptian cotton ran over his skin. From the hunger in her gaze, he'd bet she wished it, too. By the time he dried and dressed—she helped him with that, too—he was turned on and exhausted.

"Why don't you relax until we have to go to the police station," Fiona said.

He wanted to refuse, to show her he was fine. But his body protested, and he suspected she was right. He wouldn't tell her—it would encourage her to take care of him.

Without a word, he stalked—or tried to—into the living room and eased onto the sofa. He turned on the TV. Fiona worked at his dining table. She smiled, and he didn't want to know why. He blinked. He scrolled through channels until he found one of his company's finance channels. He blinked again. His eyelids were growing heavy. After checking the markets and his company's performance in them, he leaned his head against the leather cushion. He'd just rest his eyes a minute…

"Caleb."

He stirred.

"Caleb. Wake up."

He blinked.

"Hey, sleepyhead," Fiona said. "We need to go see the police."

He leaned forward with a grimace. "Give me a minute." When she made a move as if to help him, he shook his head, and she straightened. "I can do it." He rose, washed his face, and returned to the living room. "I'll drive."

****

Caleb grabbed the keys to Fiona's BMW, and Fiona couldn't help but laugh. "I don't think that's the best idea," she said.

"I can drive just fine." His voice, like his mood, was grouchy. "We'll stop at the bar and get my

Ferrari."

"Forgetting, for a moment, those crazy logistics, I don't think your ribs are going to like being folded into your Italian shoebox."

His eyelids widened. "My *what*?"

"Italian shoebox."

"Barbara is not a cardboard container."

Oh Lord, he fixated on naming the car. "Nope, but your ribs are going to think you're in one and they are going to hurt."

Caleb squeezed the keys so hard his knuckles whitened. Without a word, he held the apartment door for her and pushed the elevator button for the garage.

She waited. If he climbed into the driver's seat of her car, he'd see what a bad idea this was. Following him, she walked toward her car. He stopped and glared at it. Then he cursed. He stalked around the car, as if hoping it would magically turn into his Italian sports car. When it didn't work, he opened the driver's side door. He started and stopped and winced and cursed several times. He slammed the door and walked around to the passenger side, where the extra space due to a lack of a steering wheel made it easier for him to ease himself inside.

A large part of her was glad he'd started showing his emotions. A small part reminded herself he hurt.

"I should have brought one of my other cars," he grumbled.

"Are they all blue?" she asked as she put hers into gear.

"Yes. It's my favorite color."

His favorite color? "Then why isn't there anything blue in your apartment?"

"What do you mean?"

"Everything in your apartment is black and white. There's no color."

He paused for a moment before he shrugged. "It's nobody else's business."

Nobody else's business? Why would he care whether anyone knew what color he liked, especially in his own home? Like her, her apartment was cheery and…she almost gasped. The colors she'd chosen reflected her personality. Caleb wanted to keep his hidden. Why?

Before she could question him further, they pulled into the police parking lot, and he had her wait while he exited and opened the door. He moved slower than usual, and she could see pain radiate from his eyes, but he insisted on being chivalrous. They walked together into the station house.

An hour later they were finished. Caleb had refused to press charges against his former employee, so the man received a warning.

"Why did you let him go?" Fiona asked as they left.

"Steve and I agreed not to press charges. Losing his job made him angry."

"But he hurt you both."

"And we'll recover," Caleb said. "He, on the other hand, will have to find a new job. Arresting him isn't going to solve his problem. He needs to learn healthy ways to deal with disappointment. I'd rather get him help than punish him."

"Caleb, it's not your job to take care of everyone."

"Yes," he said. "It is."

"Will you tell me why?"

He shook his head. "Steve and I know what we're doing. Better than you might think."

He spoke the last sentence under his breath, but still, Fiona heard it. "I never doubted you. I'm just surprised."

This time, they returned to Fiona's apartment. She kept an eye on Caleb, who rested most of the day, while she put together pitches for potential clients, and marketed her existing site to current clients. She wasn't sure what worried her more—his external injuries or his need to take care of everyone around him. By dinnertime, he'd thawed.

"I'm sorry I was such a bear today," he said, coming behind her and wrapping his arms around her. He kissed her neck and moved to rub her shoulders.

She dropped her head, letting him work out her kinks. "It's okay. I understand."

He stared at her, his face a rainbow of colors from the bruises. "Do you?"

She nodded. "Of course. And even if I didn't, everyone is allowed a bad day now and then."

His expression cleared. She remembered he still didn't show his emotions. Rising, she turned to him and hugged him. "Why don't we see how Steve is doing?"

"If my sister is taking care of him, he might need rescuing."

Chapter Sixteen

They went over to Lexie's apartment that evening. Steve, who looked as battered as Caleb, rested on the couch. Lexie hovered. The apartment smelled like a bakery and when Fiona walked into the kitchen, racks of cookies, brownies and three pies beckoned from the counter.

"Lex, what's all this?"

Lexie shrugged. "I bake when I'm nervous."

Fiona gave her friend a hug. "Steve and Caleb are going to be fine. They're bruised and a little battered, but they're healing."

"I know, but it was either bake or hover, and Steve hates when I hover."

Fiona took a bite of a brownie and groaned. "Oh my gosh, this is so good. You should open a bakery."

Lexie smiled. "Maybe someday. How's my brother doing?" She peeked into the living room where the two men were talking.

"About the same as Steve. He refuses to press charges against the guy who did it, though."

"I never expected Caleb to follow through," Lexie said. "Steve won't either."

Fiona leaned against the counter and wiped a stray crumb from the corner of her mouth. "I don't understand why he won't. The guy could have killed him." Even now, she shuddered thinking about what he'd gone through.

"Caleb is used to being the protector. He must see something redeeming in the guy. I sure don't."

"Me neither. I wish he wouldn't put the burden on himself. It's a lot for one person to bear." She could imagine the weight he must carry.

Lexie looked over the half wall separating the kitchen from the living room, where Steve and Caleb sat. "There are things you don't know, things I can't tell you. Get him to talk to you."

Fiona nodded. There were a lot of things she didn't know about Caleb. His gaze found her the second she walked into the room, and she joined him on the sofa.

"How about we all watch a movie?" Lexie asked. "We can order pizza, and I have plenty of dessert."

"No, really?" Steve asked.

Lexie rolled her eyes. "You're lucky you're injured."

"I'm not too injured to do this." Steve pulled her close and tickled her.

Caleb tracked his sister's every move. Fiona tapped his shoulder, and after a brief hesitation, he turned to her.

"What movie do you want to watch?"

His gaze slid to the side. "Whatever everyone else wants is fine," he said.

"You have to have an opinion." She needed to occupy him so he could stop trying to take care of everyone else. It had to be exhausting.

"I doubt you'd like what I suggest."

"Why not?"

"Because you like the emotional ones. I like action."

"Those involve emotions too, you know. I used to love watching them with my dad. It was our Saturday night tradition."

He looked at her like he didn't believe her. Fiona was just glad he no longer focused on his sister.

"Hey, guys," she said, raising her voice to be heard over Lexie's laughter. "Let's watch an action movie."

"Fiona, I think I love you!" Steve said.

"Ugh." Lexie asked. "Here, Caleb, you pick."

He looked around. "Why do I think you all are plotting something?"

Fiona snuggled against him, being careful to avoid any sensitive spots. "Believe me, honey, if I were plotting against you, you'd have no idea."

He swallowed and put his arm around her. "Your face would give you away."

He scrolled through Netflix until he came to one of the Fast and Furious movies. Steve applauded, and Caleb pressed "play."

"You think it would." The movie started. "Maybe it's part of my plan too."

He chuckled. "Okay, let's see what happens next time."

"Careful what you wish for," she said.

"I always am."

****

Caleb didn't relax until the third scene of the movie. Whenever he was around Lexie, his senses jumped to high alert, even when they shouldn't. This time, Steve compounded his tension. When they'd arrived at his sister's and the women had gone into the kitchen, he'd apologized to Steve for putting him in harm's way.

Steve would have none of it.

"Wasn't your fault, bro. Forget about it."

He wasn't sure he'd ever be able to forget. And then Fiona had entered the room—after Lexie—with a weird look on her face. She always had some look on her face, but this time he wasn't sure what it was. But having her next to him, her body warm and supple, went a long way toward helping him.

At some point, Fiona had run to her apartment, and his sister moved to his side. "You've told her how you feel about her, right?"

"How I feel?" Why did everyone press him about feelings?

"Oh, my God, Caleb, I know you act like a robot sometimes, but you aren't one. You must talk to her."

Why were they talking about his relationship? And why wasn't Steve helping him? He looked at his friend, who just shrugged and disappeared into his phone. Great. "I do talk to her."

"How do you feel about her?"

"I-I care about her." More than cared, to be honest, even if he didn't like to admit it to himself, much less anyone else.

"A lot?"

When his sister trained that gaze on him, he could never refuse to admit his thoughts. He nodded, his neck muscles tight, and every fiber of his being trying to resist this conversation.

"Like, as much as you do me?"

He glared at her and suppressed a shudder. "It's not the same."

She scrunched her face into an expression reminding him of when they were teenagers. "I know that, idiot. I'm trying to determine how much you like her."

He hated dealing with emotions, but it's all Lexie wanted to talk about. What did she want him to say? Fiona was never far from his mind, whether at work or at home. When they were apart, he missed her. She uncovered feelings he buried—like compassion and joy and…and love—and brought them to the surface. And when they were apart, he missed her. Christ.

His palms grew moist.

"Caleb?"

"I like her. A lot." *Please don't ask me for more.*

"What's more than a lot?"

"Lexie…"

"Caleb."

"Love. All right? Love is more than a lot." Goddamn it. He hadn't wanted to say it out loud, but she'd forced him to.

She squealed, making him wince. Fiona could probably hear it from wherever she'd disappeared to. His chest tightened, and he waited for Lexie to stop making the blasted noise.

"And the sex?"

Oh, my God, that topic was even worse. "I won't discuss this with you. Can't you be satisfied with what I've said and leave it be?" Even if their sex was the most amazing, mind-blowing, ultra-emotional experience he'd had in recent memory.

"Why not? If you can't discuss it with your sister, who can you discuss it with?"

A strangled sound from Steve indicated he listened. And was still no help. "Anyone else!" He never discussed sex. Why would he start now?

"So, have you told Steve?"

"No!" They both spoke at the same time.

"Hmm, so you have strong feelings for her and you're not willing to discuss your sex life. You don't just love her. You are crazy, head over heels in love!"

In love? What the hell was the difference? Love had never been anything other than another responsibility. Until Fiona. "Don't jump to any conclusions, Lexie."

Was he *in* love with Fiona? He should be uncomfortable, but he couldn't ignore the idea now. It felt right. Felt? Since when did he feel?

Since Fiona.

She'd entered his life, wormed her way inside of him, and laid bare all the emotions he'd buried.

Was it love? He loved his sister, but not the same way.

Was love never wanting to be far from someone? Always thinking of her? Having this overwhelming urge to protect her? He protected Lexie, hell, he protected everyone, but it didn't mean he loved them.

When he and Fiona left Lexie's, they returned to Fiona's apartment, his mind still whirling.

"It was awesome," she said. "I loved it."

He jerked at the word love and looked at her askance. Were his feelings for her the same as hers were for the movie? Rationally, there were different types of emotions. But the whole concept was new to him, and her ease at using the word threw him.

"Yeah?" he asked, after several moments had passed.

"Yeah. The car chases, the excitement. It was terrific."

She knew there was a difference, as did he. His feelings for her were much stronger. A band tightened around his chest, and he forced himself to relax. They were talking about the movie, about cars. "Now you know why I like Barbara."

"Somehow I don't think you'd allow your car to do half the stunts from the movie."

"True, but the power and the speed as I drive her is a little like the feeling you got from watching the movie."

Tension returned, and he contemplated his feelings. Fiona connected to her emotions—she ran her life with them. She'd understand, and maybe she'd be able to help him, too. But he couldn't tell her his feelings until he confessed everything. It wasn't fair to tell someone how they made you feel without their having all the information.

He had to tell her about his life before her. Only then could he be sure his emotions were real. And beads of sweat popped on his brow.

She pulled away from him and placed her hand on his chest. "Talk to me."

It was the perfect opportunity to speak. He swallowed. He opened his mouth, but silence remained. There were so many things he should say, and so many reasons not to. A lump formed in his throat. She looked at him. He'd swear she looked through him, and he got the crazy impression she understood. Which was ridiculous because she didn't know anything. Not about this.

"I thought we could go out tomorrow. Walk around town or something…"

She touched his cheek. "I think you'd enjoy it more

if you got whatever is bothering you off your chest tonight."

Damn it. He read people. She showed all her emotions. Their roles were clear. Why was she reading him? "There's nothing bothering me."

She lifted an eyebrow. "Rule three."

Crap. "Rule three?"

"Don't tell me you forgot already?" She teased him, but then her serious expression drew his attention. "Honesty. We promised each other honesty."

"I remember." He remembered everything when it came to her.

"So, why won't you tell me what's bothering you?"

"I want to."

"But?"

He squeezed his hands into fists. "I don't know how." He ground those four words out and shut his mouth before his shaking lips betrayed him.

She reached across the sofa and covered his fist with her hand.

"Will you let me help?"

How could she help? She looked so earnest, though, he couldn't keep himself from nodding. She brushed her thumb back and forth across his knuckles. Her skin was soft, the movement hypnotic.

"What's the subject?" Her voice was quiet, gentle even.

"My past."

Her hand stilled for a moment, before resuming its caress. Why'd she stop?

"Are you afraid to tell me or afraid of not telling me?"

He shook his head and looked out the window. The

sky was black and cloudy, no stars visible. He'd like to look at the stars, remind himself how small he was, how small his problems were. But right now, with Fiona so close, they were magnified. "I don't know. I want...I don't know what I want."

"I think you do."

His pulse pounded in his ears. "You know nothing about me, Fiona."

Her gaze never left his. He couldn't handle emotions.

"I think you want to talk to me but you're afraid."

She was right.

"You're afraid of my reaction and of how you're going to handle it. Because you don't know how to deal with the emotions you feel."

He swore, and she gripped his hand.

"Caleb, it's me. Tell me how you're feeling. Let me help you deal with it."

Ice ran through his veins. He was cold. "What do you want me to do?" He pulled his hand away from hers and gripped the armrest of the sofa until the carved wood imprinted on his palms. "Give in?" His spine straightened. His muscles hardened, and in the back of his mind he wondered if he'd turned to stone.

Good. The less human he became, the less he'd feel. Because if this is what it was like to feel all his emotions, he wanted no part of it.

And then she looked at him, her expression calm but filled with sympathy. "If that's what it takes to release the emotions you've kept bottled inside so long, then yes."

His vision spiraled and the distance between them widened, as if he were looking at her from a very high place. He wasn't a statue. He was a mountain. Her hands stroked his knees, swirling in circles. He met her gaze, and she wordlessly begged him for... What did she want?

"It's okay," she whispered.

He frowned. His neck warmed, and his shoulders shuddered. He wavered and leaned into the sofa cushion. His muscles seized, as if there was a seismic shift. His lungs expanded and contracted, and when he opened his mouth, the air rushed out of him, as if he'd held it for too long. As if he'd jumped from a high place and rushed to the ground, his vision shifted again, and she was right there, within touching distance. His hand twitched and desire to feel her, to hold her overwhelmed him. He reached for her, and she took his hand and kissed his palm. Unfamiliar pressure built.

The great mountain cracked, and he leaned forward, pulled her into his arms, and held on with all his might.

She climbed onto his lap and tethered him to something solid, something he could touch.

"My father was a bastard. He got off by abusing people. It made him feel powerful. He'd go after my mother and sister for every little thing." He paused, remembering silent dinners, interrupted by his father flinging an overcooked meal across the room, the plate shattering against the wall, and food oozing down the wall. The next day, his dad would scream at his mother for being a slob if she hadn't cleaned all traces of the mess. His elementary-aged sister brought a project home from school, beaming with pride, until he looked at it and laughed at its childishness, before tearing into little pieces and strewing it across the floor. Or the long nights where she would hide in his room while the sounds of his father screaming at his mother traveled through the house.

"He verbally and emotionally abused my mother for so long, she didn't have any fight left in her. Until she finally summoned the strength to leave him." As an adult, his support turned financial. The damage had been done, and while he still loved his mother, the family dynamic was off. A shard of guilt slashed through him. How long had it been since he'd visited her?

Fiona's fingers continued their hypnotic movement on his neck. Did she realize how she affected him?

"And you?"

"I learned not to show what I felt. He wanted the reaction, and when I didn't give him one, it frustrated him, drew him toward me, rather than toward them. At some point, all the pretending to not feel anything became real. I didn't have to hide my feelings any longer, and I could focus on protecting my sister and my mom. I won't let anyone I care about suffer, not if I can help it. It's why I take charge of things, protect Lexie and Steve and…and you." He made a mental reminder to check in with his mom, schedule a time to visit her. It had been too long.

Everyone understood physical bruises, but it was rare anyone understood the toll emotional or verbal attacks took. They never realized how the sound of a laugh or the clatter of a plate could bring the memories rushing back. Or in his case, how the sound of tears or a raised voice could make him flinch. He'd worked to deal with his childhood, and therapy had helped, even if now he'd enforced distance between himself and his mother. But his childhood had also helped him be successful in business, the only silver lining he could consider.

"You can't live like this, Caleb. You can't block all your emotions all the time."

"I know. In fact, it's impossible for me to be near you...hell, to even look at you, without feeling." Every time he approached her, his emotions slipped through. "It's scary and frustrating, and I can't get enough of it." At first, he'd fought it. But it was impossible. "I can't get enough of you. I thought about pushing you away, about ending our relationship, because I was so afraid of taking on more responsibility. But you're not defenseless. You're capable and resilient and it doesn't scare me." Voicing it made it true. His heart rate slowed, and his lungs filled once again with air. Confessing his past to her didn't fill him with terror.

Fiona rubbed his back. "I can also be there for you, when you need."

"I know." He let himself give her a small smile. If he had his way, he'd stay like this forever. But she needed to understand everything.

"I needed you to know what happened. Not because I'm ashamed. I'm not. I survived. And I won. Because no matter how hard he tried, he never got what he wanted from me. I learned to not break in front of him."

"But it cost you."

"It did. But it made me a better businessman, too. And I'm trying to change. For you." His chest expanded with a warmth he wasn't sure how to label. She was his beacon, and he'd do anything to keep her close.

She pulled away. "No."

"What do you mean, no." Had he scared her away? "Fiona, I'm changing, I promise. I can—"

She placed a finger over his mouth. "I know you're changing. I've seen it. But I don't want you to change for me. I want you to change for you. I want you to get to a point where you're comfortable with your emotions." She smiled. "I'm not suggesting you go to extremes."

"Like my sister."

"Like your sister. But I think there must be a way for you to express what you feel and not be uncomfortable, not think of it as 'losing.' And you have to do it for yourself, not for me."

"I don't do things for me."

"It's time you did."

Caleb leaned and touched his forehead to Fiona's. He'd admitted his greatest fear, confessed his past, and she hadn't run. "Thank you."

She kissed him, awakening all of his senses. He clutched her to him, ran his hands through her hair and tilted her head. His tongue licked the seam of her lips, and she opened her mouth, allowing him to plunge inside. Need built in him as their tongues jousted and their teeth clicked. He ran his hands along her back. She wasn't wearing a bra beneath her sweatshirt. He groaned. His fingers slipped beneath the fabric and worked their way to her back. Her skin was so smooth. He slid around to her front and pushed her away enough to be able to cup her breasts. She moaned and he flicked her nipples, which were peaked and hard against his hands. Her hips pressed against his and his jeans tightened. He'd wanted her for days, but his battered body hadn't been ready. It wasn't ready yet, but he didn't care, despite the twinge in his ribs. He needed her more than he needed time to heal. He grabbed her backside and pressed her against him, grinding his hips against her so she could feel how ready he was for her.

"Are you sure," she whispered against his mouth.

"Yes," he hissed.

She wrapped her arms around his neck, her legs around his hips, and he stood, wishing he could thrust inside her right there.

"Bedroom," she panted.

The one word freed him, and he strode with her into the bedroom. His ribs protested, but he didn't care. He fumbled for his wallet in his pocket, grabbed a condom and threw it on the bed before shucking his jeans and joining her, letting her climb on top.

Her hands were everywhere, and his body quivered with excitement. He was about to lose control, something he only did with Fiona. Did she know the power she held over him?

Someday he'd tell her, but right now, he couldn't string words together. He could only feel, and he relished the new sensation.

The tear of the packet was the last thing he heard before she pulled at his boxers and rolled the condom onto him. He jerked at her touch and then his hips started moving on their own, rolling against her. He caressed her breasts, traced kisses along her jaw, pulled her body against his. She panted, heating his neck.

"I need you inside of me," she whispered.

He flipped her onto her back, rose over her, and plunged inside. As their bodies moved together, he stared at her, watching her lids lower, watching her cheeks flush. She arched and sheathed him even farther, and all he could do was pump. His muscles tightened and need built. She shrieked a moment before he bellowed her name. Lights flashed behind his closed lids, and warmth suffused his body. He collapsed on top of her. Their bodies slick with sweat, he turned so he could cradle her against him, and the sound of her breathing sang him to sleep.

****

*Holy cow, this man...*Fiona watched him sleep; his features soft. When awake and on guard, hard lines and planes etched his face. His tight mouth and firm jaw screamed harsh and in charge. Now, his lips were soft, and he looked more vulnerable.

Sex with Caleb amazed her, but since he'd shown his emotions and talked about his feelings, the bond was deeper. He'd lost himself in her, something he'd never allowed before today. Good lord. She lay there studying his features, wanting to know everything about this enigmatic man. But so far, what she knew broke her heart. Family life wasn't supposed to be a battleground. It was supposed to be a safe harbor. And his wasn't. How he and Lexie survived amazed her.

His eyelids twitched, he blinked, and woke. She studied the milk and dark chocolate striations of his irises. They reminded her of a big tub of melted chocolate, when you combined milk and dark together.

"Hello," she whispered. Would he regret opening to her earlier? Would he be embarrassed? Nervous?

"Hello, beautiful."

His words made her face heat with pleasure. Two words were more emotional than any of her telenovelas.

Amusement made his gaze twinkle. *"This*

embarrasses you? We just had sex, and a compliment puts you on edge?"

How to explain it to him without making him uncomfortable? She moved away from him, but he pulled her close and kissed her neck. "Nope. Not getting away so easily, gorgeous."

She buried her head in his shoulder, wanting to absorb his words, and his body shook with laughter.

"This could be fun," he said.

"Remind me not to put you in charge of entertainment."

Her body pressed against his, and his cock stirred. His skin texture, so different from hers—thicker, somehow smooth and supple like fine leather—made her restless, and she wiggled against him. She wanted him and pulled his face close.

Caleb complied, kissing her until she gasped for air. Then he pulled away.

"As much as I'd love to spend the rest of the day in bed, I have an appointment at the shelter to get more information about what they need."

Disappointment and pride struggled for purchase, and pride won. He took this obligation seriously, and she couldn't fault him for it, even if her body wanted something else. He had every right to focus on himself and his business, yet instead, he gave his time to others. This was the side of Caleb she fell for, and this was the side she wanted to see. Besides, maybe she could do a quick check-in with Melanie to nudge her about the ads.

"Can I come with you?"

He held her with his gaze. "You want to?"

She nodded, and his chest expanded.

"Okay." He climbed from the bed. "I have to stop

at my apartment first for fresh clothes."

She nodded, crossing the room, and standing in front of her closet.

"I think you should go like this," he said from behind her, cupping her breasts.

"Mm, but I think it might make people uncomfortable." She reached behind her and pulled at his neck, turned, and kissed him. "Now let me get dressed."

With a sigh like a little boy being told he couldn't play with his favorite toy, he left the bedroom. Fiona grabbed a pair of jeans and a sweater. Ten minutes later, she stepped into the living room; showered, and dressed.

"—broach the subject. I'll get financials and a wish list and get back to you." He leered at Fiona and covered the phone with his hand when she laughed. "Okay, tell the others we should talk tonight." He nodded. "Seven should be fine."

Fastening a gold hoop earring, she waited for Caleb to end the call and cocked a brow at him.

"It was Alex, one of my investment partners. We're thinking of doing something with the shelter, which is why I'm meeting with Melanie today. We'll talk tonight after I gather information."

Fiona paused. "Oh, are you sure you want me going with you? I didn't realize this was a business meeting. I thought you were playing with the kids."

He stuffed his phone in his pocket and held her jacket for her to slip her arms into. "I want you to come. In fact, I'd like your perspective."

"Financial matters aren't my strong suit." She grabbed her purse and followed him.

"No, but you have a different way of looking at things than I do. Take our different approaches to the personal websites. Yours isn't a model I would have considered, yet you're more successful than I am at it."

Was. Although things had stabilized, she'd lost a significant number of clients. But Caleb's admission flattered her, and her chest expanded with pride.

"I'm happy to give you my opinion about what they need."

Caleb drove them to his apartment, where she waited in the car while he went inside to change. Once dressed in fresh jeans and a Henley, which showed off his sculpted chest muscles and made her want to peel it off him with her teeth, they went to the shelter. This time, Fiona studied it.

From the outside, it looked like any other residential building in the area. A yellow Victorian, four-floor walkup with a front porch and mailbox attached to the wall. The front door was locked, its white paint chipped, and Caleb pressed the buzzer at the door. A minute later, Melanie came to the door to let them in.

"Caleb, Fiona, how nice to see you. Come into my office where we can talk." She led them into what had once been a sitting room. It was now filled with battered but comfortable sofas, a six-person wooden table with mismatched chairs and a play area off to the side. Filing cabinets overtook every other space.

Melanie nodded to Fiona. "This is also the intake room. Most women who come in here are nervous enough without having to sit on the other side of some cold desk. So, I've made it as homey as possible."

Fiona nodded. "That makes a lot of sense."

"Oh, before you go, remind me I have our ads for your website. I didn't expect you to be here today, but if you both have an extra five minutes when we're done, I can show them to you."

"Of course," Fiona said. "I planned to remind you about them. I'm serious about my offer."

Melanie smiled. "I want to reach as many women as possible."

Fiona nodded.

Melanie turned to Caleb. "Now, what did you want to discuss?"

He cleared his throat. "I work with a group of investors, and we look for charitable organizations that make an impact, and who demonstrate real need. I wanted to learn more about your financials and your needs and then suggest to my partners we help you."

Caleb leaned on the sofa. "We are all successful in our fields and make more money than we need for our personal use. So, we take the extra and invest it. We want to make a difference, though, so a percentage of our investments is given to charity. We've financed a public therapy garden and park in a small town in Maine and a computer-coding program for at-risk youth in New York City. They provide the need; we provide the money. It's pretty simple."

Melanie frowned. "You're generous. Thank you."

Caleb's business mask fell into place. This was the Caleb Fiona had first met, and she appreciated the new version more than ever.

"As long as your financials match with our assessment. I've volunteered here for several months now, and I've seen how you help these families turn their lives around. I want to help."

"What do I have to do in return?"

"You'll provide me a copy of your current financial statements. You'll give me a list of what improvements you'd like or need to make, as well as information about the other building you'd like to purchase. I'll consult with my group and put together a proposal. Once we all agree, we'll provide you the money, and you'll make the improvements. We'll want to see how our money will be used, but you're in charge."

"This sounds wonderful." She paused for a minute. "What about publicity?" Melanie asked. "We have to avoid the public eye. You're well known, and I'd assume your partners are too. It could be problematic for us."

"We're not looking to publicize what we do," Caleb said. "We're just looking to put our money to good use. So, if you don't want attention, we won't be the ones providing it."

Melanie shifted her focus to Fiona. "Are you one of the investors?"

"I wish." Fiona smiled. "No, I'm just here because Caleb wanted the benefit of my observation as well. He and I tend to look at things differently."

"She brings a unique perspective," Caleb said.

He remained stoic, but Fiona recognized pride and appreciation in his expression. "I don't know if I'm unique," Fiona said. "I just know what I like and don't like."

"Well, this has taken me by surprise," Melanie said. "Let me show you some of the areas that need improvement and then we can come here, and I can give you copies of our financial statements. Obviously,

I still can't share any identifiable information or allow you access to certain areas of our shelter…"

"Relax, Melanie, I know your rules, and I'm not interested in going around them," Caleb said.

She led them from her office and showed the needed improvements in the public rooms downstairs—the living room, dining room, children's playroom, and kitchen.

The unmatched appliances and scuffed refrigerator drew Fiona's attention. "You could use an upgrade in here," Fiona said.

"Well, they're old, but they work," Melanie said.

"How well?"

She grimaced. "Depends on the day."

"As you know, we have a laundry area and a rec room downstairs."

"Can we see those again?" Fiona asked.

Melanie led them downstairs and showed them the rooms. "Our washers and dryers are unreliable, and I'd love to add video games or a ping-pong table to the rec room."

Upstairs, she took them to the second floor. "We've turned these rooms into a study area and library for the kids and the women. There's also an infirmary for minor injuries or illnesses. Anything serious and we take them to the hospital or a local doctor. The two remaining upstairs floors are private bedrooms."

"Do you have any vacancies?" Caleb asked. "I'd like to see what a bedroom looks like if possible."

"I do have one empty one. Let me make sure no one is around and then I can show you."

Fiona waited downstairs with Caleb. The shelter was quiet. She looked around at the peeling wallpaper, worn carpeting and used furniture. None of it mattered when you were fleeing an abusive situation, but it would be nice if the residents could have a safe and attractive place. Ideas flitted through her head, and she pulled out her phone to record them.

"Anything I should know?" Caleb asked.

"Let's wait until we're all finished, if you don't mind."

He nodded, making notes of his own.

Melanie returned. "You can come upstairs now," she said from the third step. They followed her to the fourth floor. She unlocked a room and stepped away from the doorway. Two dormer windows provided natural light. The room was arranged for an adult and a baby, with a double bed and a crib. There was an upholstered chair, a dresser, and a night table, as well as a closet along one wall.

"Most of the rooms look like this, although they can be configured for different people, depending on the age of any children who arrive."

Fiona turned in a circle. It was sufficient, but nothing matched. She peeked out the window at neighboring roofs and a few trees in the distance. More ideas percolated.

"Do you have storage facilities, either here or somewhere else, for the facility?" Caleb asked.

Fiona shook her head. Another example of how she and Caleb thought differently. She never would have considered storage space, but she recognized how helpful it would be.

"Yes, we have space in the basement and in the attic. I also have a storage unit I can rent if necessary."

She led them downstairs, flicking the hall light as

they left. "For the residents, so they know it's safe."

In her office, she opened files on the computer and pulled others from the filing cabinet. "Here are our financials for the past five years. As you can see, we get most of our money from donors."

"So, nothing steady you can depend on?" Caleb asked.

Melanie shrugged. "Well, in general, I have an idea who I can go to for what. Some years I'm more successful than others. But who we can depend upon? Not many."

"What about your wish list?" Fiona asked.

She laughed. "There's so much I want, and so much I need, I don't know where to start."

"Security system?" Caleb asked.

Melanie's face glowed. "We've got the bare bones right now, but I'd love a better one."

"What about people to help the residents move into their own places, get jobs, balance budgets, etc.?"

Melanie crossed her legs. "Some of the women who come here are well-prepared. Others aren't. I refer them to counselors who can help, but they have to take advantage of it."

"What about scheduling weekly seminars on a rotating basis to teach a variety of skill sets? Is there any interest?" Fiona asked. She could feel Caleb's attention focused on her.

"I think it's step two," Melanie said. "The women come here and need a safe home base first."

"Who helps them with legal issues?" Caleb asked.

"I have lawyers who work pro bono. It's just finding time in their schedule."

Caleb rose. "Okay, send me your materials, and I

will talk to my partners. I should have an answer for you within the next few days. Thank you for showing us around."

"Don't thank me," Melanie said. "You're the one helping me." She handed Fiona printouts of the ads she'd created.

"These are great," Fiona said. "I like the wording you've used. Email me the files, and I'll take care of it for you."

They returned to the car, and he drove in silence, while Fiona finished making notes. Caleb headed toward the beach.

"The beach? I'm not dressed for swimming."

"Not even skinny dipping?" Caleb wiggled his eyebrows.

His expression was so unexpected, she laughed. "Not even."

He parked his car and turned toward her. "Want to go over our ideas? I'm not ready to go to the office yet."

She nodded.

"As far as I can tell, they need their security system overhauled, preferably with a visual component," he said. "The kitchen appliances need an upgrade to accommodate larger groups. Same with the laundry system. What do you have?"

"The place needs to be redecorated to make people feel like it's a home. The wallpaper is peeling, and the furniture is old. Things should match. They need regular access to professionals so they can get their lives on track—attorneys, finance people, doctors, job training, therapists."

"You raised important issues," Caleb said. "I'm

glad you came with me—I told you your perspective would help me." His hands were clenched in his lap, and his shoulders were tight.

She leaned over and gave him a hug, the center console digging into her ribs and making the movement awkward. "You're doing a good thing here, Caleb."

"I just wish I didn't have to. And it was a lot easier when I blocked all my emotions. I keep thinking about how similar these women are to my family. We might not have lived in a shelter, but our backgrounds..." He swallowed.

"It's going to be okay, Caleb."

Chapter Seventeen

Caleb spent the rest of the week working. He would have liked to spend time with Fiona, but between the shelter plans, an upcoming newspaper purchase for WW Media, and Fiona's job, there wasn't time for anything other than phone calls. With a sigh, he logged onto his email.

Email to Caleb, Simon & Ted.

Re: Labor Day Get Together

Bring yourselves, bring your girlfriends and come to a Labor Day weekend BBQ at my house in Florida. Stay for the weekend. There will be beach activities, golf, a BBQ of course, and socializing. It's been too long since we've seen each other. It's time. No excuses accepted.

Alex

Caleb leaned in his chair. He loved his college friends—they were like brothers to him—but was he ready to introduce Fiona to them? Could he allow his feelings for her to show? His email pinged again.

Email to Alex, Simon & Ted.

Re: Re: Labor Day Get Together

I'll be there."

Before he had a chance to shut his computer, Alex responded.

Caleb

Email to Caleb.

Re: Re: Re: Labor Day Get Together

Bring the girlfriend. And yes, we know you have a girlfriend. We want to meet her. Especially Meg and Abby. If you leave her home, I'll send my plane. So, make your life easy and just do it.

Alex

Caleb had no doubt whatsoever Alex would make good on all the threats. He'd been the bossiest one of them in their college days, the one who always forced the issue. Every issue. When Simon had wanted to hide because of his facial scars, Alex had dragged him to a bar. Simon hadn't spoken to him for weeks afterward, and it was the one time Caleb could ever remember Alex apologizing. But his reputation remained.

If Caleb wanted control over the situation, he had to invite her. He missed her. He missed her scent, her body, and her laugh. He missed her joy and enthusiasm. He missed connecting with her on an emotional level, letting his guard down and just being himself.

But he didn't like to think about that very often, and a part of him was glad for the space. It let him push his emotions to the sidelines, making it easier for him to focus on his work and deal with the shelter in an objective manner.

If Fiona had been around, would he have been able to put his emotions back in the box? Without her, he wouldn't have released them in the first place.

He dialed Fiona. "Listen, I have a friend in Florida who's hosting a Labor Day weekend get together with our investment group. He's insisting we all join him for a BBQ, the beach, golf, and who knows what else. Would you like to join me?"

She gasped. "I'd love to go!"

He warmed at her enthusiasm. "His place is indescribable—he's a world-renowned architect, and it's beyond anything I've ever seen. I think you'll like the other guys."

"Of course, I will. If they're willing to donate all that money to charities, I'm sure they're wonderful." She paused. "I've missed you."

Relief washed through him. Confessing his feelings to her was still foreign. Maybe if they'd been in person, he'd have an easier time. But over the phone, he still needed her to say it first. "I've missed you, too. How was your day?"

As she had each day this week, she told him what she'd accomplished—how visiting the shelter had inspired her to investigate ways to empower women. She planned a series of guest posts by female experts in the field of empowerment, and she was considering featuring products made by female small-business owners. He loved listening to her talk about her job. Emotion gave her voice a lilt, and her enthusiasm spilled over to him.

"I wish I could see you," she said. "All work and no Caleb is making me sad."

All around him were spreadsheets and reports he had to tackle before he slept. "Soon."

"Let's try for this weekend," she said. "Even if we have to work through the day. At least we can work together."

He laughed; the sound was still foreign. "A working date. I like it. Hey, how are your telenovelas?"

She groaned. "I've been so busy I've had to record everything, and now I'm even further behind. It's so frustrating."

"Well, just make sure to avoid spoilers."

She laughed. "Since I don't speak Spanish, it's easy to do. Good night, Caleb."

"Good night, sweetheart."

His heart hitched as the word left his mouth. He'd been with women before, but he'd never called them anything but their names. He waited for panic to fill him, or at least his shoulders to tighten. Nothing happened. He turned off his phone, a smile on his face that for once, he didn't want to hide.

****

Friday night couldn't come fast enough. Fiona looked at her phone for the thousandth time that day, tapping it, turning it on and off, sure the clock app no longer worked. But it did. Four hours until she and Caleb would see each other. The week apart had been torture. Each time they spoke, he withdrew a little more, allowed less emotion in his voice, forced her to initiate feelings before he felt safe to do so. She wasn't surprised, but she was frustrated. She wanted to wrap her arms around him and squeeze until he yelled, "Uncle."

But then he'd called her "sweetheart." She wished she'd recorded it so she could play it over and over. She memorized the tone of his voice, the timbre of its sound, and she couldn't wait for him to call her sweetheart to her face.

Finally, the day ended, and she sat outside the guard gate. Had he given his permission for them to let her in? With a sigh, she rolled open her window and gave her name.

"You can go in," the guard said. "You're on the permanent guest list."

Her insides warmed, and she drove into the parking garage. At the second gate, it was the same, and she got into the elevator and took it to his apartment. He'd told her to come over at six o'clock, and it was five fifty-nine. He'd have to deal with her being one minute early.

The doors whooshed open, and he stood in the foyer. She gasped, his muscular arms wrapped around her like a vise, enveloping her in his unique scent. His heart thumped against her ear, and she ran her hands along his back.

"I missed you so much," he whispered.

Her heart melted. She pulled away from him and drew his head to her level. Caressing the sides of his face, moving around to his neck, and to the back of his bald head, she memorized his skin with her fingertips before pressing her lips against his. When she drew away, she was breathless. "I missed you, too. Call me sweetheart again."

His gaze darkened, and he kissed her again. "Sweetheart," he whispered against her lips. She smiled, her knees almost giving way. It was better than the last time.

He took her hand and led her into the living room. The smell of broiling steak, garlic, and other spices she couldn't quite identify greeted her, and her stomach growled.

The smile he gave her made her heart jump. "I'm glad you're hungry."

"I missed your smile," she said.

He reddened and his smile slipped.

"No, don't stop," she said. "It's me, remember?"

His lips spread and his cheeks stretched, and Fiona

laughed. "Thank you."

"Old habits."

"I know. What smells delicious?" She followed her nose to the kitchen.

"Dinner. We can't work if we're hungry."

"Oh, are we working?" She raised an eyebrow.

"There's all kinds of work," he said, staring at her until she practically melted under the heat of his gaze. Pink, purple, and orange streaked the sky and reflected on the ocean in the distance as the sun set, casting a muted haze throughout his apartment and making Fiona feel as if she were about to be swept into an enchanted spell. Maybe this was why his apartment was black and white. If her apartment offered this view, she wouldn't paint it either.

"I brought you something," she said, removing herself from the magnetic pull his stare created.

He stilled. "Why?"

"Because I saw it and thought of you."

She walked to where she'd dropped her bags by the door, expecting him to follow, but he remained frozen by the kitchen. Did no one give him gifts? She brought the shopping bag over and gave it to him.

"But it's not my birthday."

"Not all gifts are for birthdays. Besides, I don't know when yours is," she said.

"March."

"Well, you've narrowed it to thirty-one days."

He still didn't reach for it. "It's not the holidays either."

"I know. And before you say anything, you didn't do anything to earn this, either. I just saw it and wanted to give it to you."

The longer he stood still, the more nervous she grew. Her palms sweated. He turned the gift into a big deal. Finally, he reached for the bag, opened it, and removed the royal blue pillow with "Don't worry, be happy," stitched in white across it.

Maybe she shouldn't have bought it. *He's a millionaire. What does he need a pillow for?*

But then his cheek twitched.

"Thank you," he said, his voice quiet.

"You need a little color, and you mentioned you liked blue."

"Not to mention the saying," he said.

"Not to mention the saying," she repeated. She'd agonized over whether he'd think it was corny. Relief washed over her.

He walked over to the leather sofa and put the pillow on the seat. With a laugh, Fiona adjusted it, moving it to the corner, angling it, and making it look like it belonged there. It was the only spot of color in the apartment, other than the muted rays from the sunset.

"I like it," he said, coming behind her and wrapping his arms around her.

She molded herself against his body. "I'm glad." She wrinkled her nose. "Is something burning?"

With a muttered oath, Caleb let go of her and raced into the kitchen. "How important are vegetables?" he yelled.

"On the food pyramid or to me personally?" Fiona said, following him into the kitchen. She peered around his wide chest at the tray of blackened Brussels sprouts. "I'm okay with not eating these."

He scraped them into the trash. "Sorry. A

provocative woman with a surprise gift distracted me." The tray sizzled as he ran water in it, and steam billowed.

Caleb turned to her, drawing her into his arms, but she shook her head. "How about we save the distractions for after we eat. I'm starved." Her stomach growled in agreement and Caleb laughed. "Okay, sweetheart." He winked and returned to his task.

Five minutes later they sat down to broiled steak, garlic bread and a hastily made salad.

"This is delicious," Fiona said, after tasting a mouthful of the steak. "I didn't know you could cook."

He tipped his head. "I wouldn't say I can cook. I can make a steak and fry eggs. Lucky for me you're not a vegetarian."

"Ha! You can cook for me anytime." Fiona laughed, and Caleb joined in. She'd never get tired of the sound. "Are we working after this?"

"I have a surprise planned."

She leaned in the black lacquer chair. "A surprise? You don't do surprises."

"Gifts. I'm not used to surprise gifts. Experiences are a different story."

"So, this is an experience?" Fiona stabbed a piece of lettuce. "You do seem to relish those."

Nodding, he grinned.

"Can't wait." And to her surprise, it was true.

They finished eating and cleared together, Fiona washing and Caleb drying. "You cooked," she said, and he didn't argue.

"Okay," she said, when they were done, "what's my surprise?"

He looked out the window before answering. "Not

yet."

Fiona looked between Caleb and the window. "What do you mean, not yet?"

"Exactly what I said."

"You're not fair. You can't tell me you have a surprise and then not do anything about it."

"You'll get your surprise when it's ready."

"Is it cake?"

He frowned. "Why would it be cake?"

"Because cake is something that wouldn't be ready."

He rolled his eyes. "Many things aren't ready yet. Why would you jump to cake?"

"Because cake is yummy."

He looked out the window again. "Okay, let's go."

"Where are we going?"

"You are impossible."

She gave him a grin. "That's why you like me."

"Uh, sure."

She punched him in the arm. "Wrong answer."

He rubbed his arm. "You have no strength behind the punch, but man your knuckles are bony."

Leaning over, she gave his bicep a kiss. "Poor baby."

She followed him to the elevator, and this time he pushed the button. "We're going up?"

He ignored her, and she bounced on the balls of her feet. He always planned interesting surprises, and she wanted to see what this one would be. The elevator doors closed and whisked them to the roof. When they opened again, they were on a teak deck, with lounge chairs, tables, and a canopy to sit under. Next to the railing was a telescope. He led her toward it.

"We're star gazing," he said.

He bent over the telescope and began adjusting things. At least, it's what she thought he did. He twisted parts of the telescope and moved it around. Fiona observed for a moment and then used the opportunity to admire his butt. Because when a hot guy bent a certain way, what else were you supposed to do? He motioned over his shoulder for her to come over, and when she approached, he put his arm around her and guided her to the telescope.

"Look through the lens," he said. "Do you see those stars in a zig-zag pattern over there?" He pointed and she followed his finger.

"Yeah."

"That's Hydra. It looks like a snake." He pointed toward the head. "It's the longest and largest of the constellations. In Greek mythology, the water snake was the second of the twelve labors of Hercules, and it was immortal."

Fiona trembled. "Ugh, I hate snakes."

He smiled. "Well, you would have hated this one even more. It's said it had between five and one hundred heads."

She glared. "This might not be one of your better surprises."

He pointed above Hydra and to the right. "Do you see those stars clustered there?"

She nodded.

"That's Leo."

She looked through the telescope again. "It doesn't look much like a lion, does it?"

He looked and shook his head. "I guess not."

"It's still cool, though," she added. "And much

better than a snake."

"Next to it is Lynx. It's hard to see much more than the zigzag stars."

She tried. "Um, not sure."

"Okay, try this. Over there is Ursa Major." He pointed to the stars, and she looked through the telescope.

"I see it! How do you know so much about the constellations?"

He shrugged. "I've always been interested in the stars." After a long pause, when she didn't think he'd continue, he added, "Ancient people created constellation names to make things easier to understand. I was so confused; I think I took comfort in the constellations and the order they created." He shook his head. "It doesn't make much sense."

She gave him a hug. "It makes perfect sense to me." It also touched her he made such an effort to peel away his layers and show her what was inside.

They stood on the roof deck, looking at the stars twinkling in the sky, listening to the rush of the water against the shore. The night air was cool despite the high temperatures during the day, but his warm body kept the chill away. She rubbed his back, feeling the smooth texture of his muscles beneath his shirt. He rested his chin on her head, and she listened to his heartbeat.

"You okay?" she asked.

"Yeah." His voice vibrated against her head.

She pulled away and took his face in her hands. "Thank you for bringing me here tonight."

They stood looking at the ocean, the thin white line of the waves breaking against the shore and the crescent moon the only things visible in the inky blackness, other than the stars above.

"Do you come here often?"

He nodded. "I like it at night like this when there's no one around. And it's a good place to entertain in the nice weather."

"Do you? Entertain, I mean?"

"Sometimes. Lexie's more of the entertainer than I am."

Even though he'd made sure everyone at the beach had food and drink, she couldn't picture him entertaining a crowd. He was too aloof and self-contained. It was a side of him she hadn't seen, and she looked forward to it.

The elevator doors opening broke the peacefulness, and Lexie rushed over, Steve following her. "Caleb! Caleb are you here?"

She ran over to them, panting, her gaze wild, and her face streaked with tears. Caleb pulled away from Fiona and grabbed Lexie by the shoulders. "What's wrong?"

"It's Mom."

****

The second Lexie uttered the word "mom," Caleb froze. Not froze as in stopped mid-movement, like a statue. No, his insides froze. He'd swear the blood stopped moving in his veins, his organs stopped doing whatever it was organs did. There was one organ he knew about though—his heart. That organ, the one Fiona had cultivated, also seized.

"What's wrong?" His voice sounded calm. He slipped into the emotionless void in which he'd always gone to protect himself

Lexie threw herself at him, her body shaking. She spoke, but he couldn't understand what she said. God, he hated this. He looked at Steve hoping for a clue, but his gaze was trained on his wife.

"Lexie, what's going on?" Fiona's voice was like the eye of the storm, calm amidst the chaos. He looked over at her, grateful for her cool headedness.

"Lexie?" Caleb shook her. "I can't understand you unless you calm yourself."

Lexie wiped her face. "Mom had a heart attack. They rushed her to the hospital, but she wasn't breathing when the ambulance arrived. Steve drove me here to tell you."

Her face crumpled. Caleb swallowed, as a myriad of feelings threatened to overflow—horror at what happened to his mother, guilt he hadn't been able to help her, fear of what would happen next, exhaustion at the idea of dealing with Lexie. But he pushed all of them deep into the well and focused on handling the situation right now. Like he always did. "We're going to the hospital. I'll drive."

He strode away from Steve, Lexi, and Fiona, and into his apartment. Grief and worry gnawed at his belly, sending an acidic taste up his throat. He swallowed. Not now. He grabbed his keys—to his Infiniti QX80, since three people couldn't fit in his Ferrari, and his Jeep was too bouncy to deal with emotional women while driving—and led the way to the garage. In the background, he was aware of Fiona's presence, murmuring now and then to Lexie, and helping Steve calm her. He was grateful. Lexie's stifled sobs punctuated the ride to the hospital. He gripped the steering wheel so tight his hand ached, and the muscles in his shoulders tightened. He should comfort Lexie, but he didn't know how without more information.

At the hospital, they were directed to the emergency room. He turned to Fiona before going through the double doors.

"I—" His throat clogged. As much as her presence comforted him, he had to do this alone.

She touched his hand. "I'll wait for you here with Steve."

Her gaze conveyed a message, but he wasn't sure what it was—sympathy, strength, something else? He had no idea, and if he let himself think about it for too long, he wouldn't be able to deal with anything else. So, he nodded, took his sister's hand, and walked through the double doors.

Chapter Eighteen

Fiona sat in the waiting room, her gaze trained on the doors leading into the ER. Her heart hurt thinking about what Caleb, Lexie, and Steve must be experiencing. As much as she'd avoided falling for anyone who didn't sweep her off her feet, she'd fallen for Caleb. Hard. His pain had become hers. Even if he didn't show it.

The wail sounded seconds before the doors opened. Caleb, face ashen, staggered, supporting Lexie in his arms. Steve ran forward and hugged her to him. Fiona gasped and joined them. Caleb shook his head, mouth pressed together. His mother had died. Fiona turned to Lexie. "Oh, honey, I'm so sorry."

Lexie sobbed in Steve's arms, while he patted her back and whispered words of comfort. While Caleb talked to a nurse, Fiona wished she could give him comfort, too, but that would come later. Fiona stayed with his sister and Steve while Caleb made phone calls, signed paperwork, and talked to the various people who approached him. But she never took her attention off Caleb.

He'd reapplied his mask and his armor, but even with it, anyone with sight saw he suffered. His right hand shook as he signed documents. His shoulders stiffened as he forced himself erect. His left hand opened and closed, as if he were squeezing something, but it was empty. And the shell of the man she knew walked over to them, having finished everything. The rest of him disappeared, buried deep where she couldn't reach.

He wouldn't maintain eye contact with her, and she didn't force it.

"We can go now." His toneless voice rasped over each word as if dragged over rocks. All Fiona could do was follow them from the hospital.

Once again, the ride home was silent. He pulled into the apartment complex, and they walked upstairs. When Steve and Lexie left, Fiona unlocked her door.

"Come inside?" she asked, holding the door wide, desperate to help Caleb.

He shook his head. "I have to go." He turned away.

"Please?"

Stopping, he clenched and unclenched his fist. "It's late and there's a lot to do."

"Five minutes," she said.

"I have to go." He repeated the words like a robot.

"I know." She took a step toward him. His body trembled. She sensed the cost of his impassive expression. "Just five minutes."

He swallowed, and she took it as agreement. Standing toe to toe, she cupped his cheek. His jaw clenched, and she stroked it.

"I've got you," she whispered.

He closed his eyes.

"Let me help you," she said. "Please." She continued to stroke his cheek. With each stroke, he relaxed until he wrapped his arms around her and held on. They stood, silent, for five minutes. She counted. When she reached three hundred, she stepped away.

Not for her, but for him.

He walked away from her and left her apartment building. She hated every centimeter between them. He should stay with her or let her stay with him. But she knew better than to ask it of him. A man like Caleb, who had only recently learned to show his emotions, would fight tooth and nail to hide them to deal with the pain. While she planned on letting him have safe spaces to release the pressure, if she pressed him too hard, he'd push her away. So, she had to let him go, even though every fiber of her being said to run after him.

The next morning the sun had barely risen when she climbed from bed, threw on clothes, and called a rideshare to go to Caleb's. When she stepped into the hallway, she bumped into Steve just emerging from his and Lexie's apartment. He looked like he hadn't slept.

"How is she?" Fiona asked.

"Sleeping now, at last. I'm getting coffee, and I'll take her to Caleb's when she wakes."

"I'm heading over there now," Fiona said. "If you need anything, text me." She gave her number to Steve and went to Caleb's apartment. At the security gate, she paused. It was early, and he might be sleeping. The doors opened without any noise, and she was grateful. His apartment was hushed, and his bedroom door was closed. She smiled at the blue pillow on the sofa. In the kitchen, the remains of their meal from last night were strewn everywhere, and she spent the next fifteen minutes washing dishes and cleaning the mess. When completed, she made coffee and searched his refrigerator for something to make for breakfast. In the meantime, she'd wait for him.

A half hour later, his door squeaked open, and he

stepped from the bedroom, naked.

Fiona swallowed. "Good morning."

He squinted, ran a hand over his head, and retreated to his room again. "Morning. Hold on." A minute later he returned wearing pajama bottoms.

Part of her was disappointed. She handed him a cup of coffee and began making scrambled eggs.

"What are you doing here?"

"Making breakfast."

"I see. Shouldn't you be at work?"

"I'll check in later and work from here."

"I don't need you to do this for me." A muscle in his jaw ticked.

"Yes, you do." She turned her attention to the frying pan, giving him time to process her presence and her intentions. She didn't want to fight him on this, but no one should have to deal with the death of a mother on their own.

Expecting an argument, she was surprised when Caleb said nothing. Instead, he pulled bowls and things from the cabinet.

"Plates would be better," she said, her voice kind.

Shaking his head, he switched them, carrying the plates filled with food to the table. They ate in silence, and she didn't force conversation, even though she wanted to talk to him about his feelings. When they'd eaten their fill and finished their coffee, she reached across the table and touched his hand. He stilled.

"How are you this morning?"

He didn't answer. Instead, he carried dirty dishes to the kitchen. Returning to the table, he grabbed the orange juice and butter. Fiona followed him into the kitchen. He put the juice in the sink and a dirty dish in the refrigerator. With a hand on his back, she stopped him, and switched the items so they were in the right places. He swore, leaned against the sink, and let his head fall forward.

Before Fiona could do or say anything, the elevator doors opened, and Lexie and Steve entered. Once again, Caleb's emotionless exoskeleton clanked into place. Throughout the morning, Caleb assigned tasks, phoned relatives, met with clergy, and oversaw the planning of his mother's funeral. She helped where she could—placing the obituary and putting notices in online community forums; providing meals, snacks, and drinks; and making phone calls—but most of the time she remained in the background, offering silent support with her presence. At least, it's what she hoped she did. Oftentimes, Caleb would come to her, as if he needed her and then after a brief amount of time, would distance himself from her. If she were in his place, she'd be a mess. He was controlled on the outside, but what about inside, and when was he going to blow?

She listened as Caleb and Lexie reminisced while pulling photos for a display at the funeral home. Lexie was more forthright and shared more stories. Caleb's contributions tended to be a few words here or there, a nod in agreement.

"Do you remember when we started at the new high school, Caleb, you wanted to join the entrepreneur's club, but there was a fee, and you didn't want to ask Mom for it?"

He nodded, turning toward Fiona. "She didn't have any extra money to spare, and she'd already spent money on new clothes for Lexie, so I didn't want her to make any more sacrifices."

Lexie's eyes filled with tears. "Yeah, but did you know she called the club's advisor and created a payment plan so you could still join, and she could pay the fee?"

Caleb stilled. "I didn't know. I thought the advisor waived my fee because of my grades."

Lexie shook her head. "That was the excuse he and Mom created. I overheard her on the phone, and she swore me to secrecy." She fingered the edges of a photo of her mother. "Sorry, Mom," she whispered.

Fiona slipped her hand into Caleb's, and he squeezed. Stories continued late into the night, until everyone yawned.

"Visitation is at two tomorrow," Steve said. "So we'll meet at the funeral home at one thirty?"

Caleb nodded. Steve ushered Lexie onto the elevator, and Caleb turned to Fiona. "You should go home and get some sleep."

She shook her head. "No, I brought clothes with me." She turned to him and wrapped her arms around his waist. "If you don't mind, I'd rather stay here with you."

His jaw twitched. "You'll sleep better in your own bed."

"We're not talking about me."

He stared at her; his lids red-rimmed. She brushed her hand along his back. "I don't want to keep you awake," he said.

"Stop worrying about me. I'm more concerned with making sure you get some sleep. You look exhausted."

"I'm fine."

There he went again. "Caleb, please. Are we going

to argue every time I try to do something for you?"

He exhaled. "No."

"Thank you. Because my next option was going to be to forego the clothes and climb naked into your bed."

For the first time all day, Caleb's face relaxed. "Maybe I should protest harder next time."

****

Caleb eased from bed as the sun rose, every muscle in his body aching. He expected his joints to creak like a man twenty years older. He glanced at Fiona, still sleeping, and pulled the cover over her creamy, exposed shoulder. They hadn't had sex last night, but she had slept naked, and they'd held each other for most of the night. Despite his misgivings, he'd slept. But no amount of sleep could help him right now.

Fiona had awakened feelings of grief and guilt and despair he'd kept long buried and now, he didn't know how to stop them. His old methods were no longer natural to him, like stuffing a foot into a leather shoe that had gotten wet, reshaped itself, and didn't quite fit. But he couldn't let himself feel the emotions his mother's death had sparked, nor could he show them. Because if he did, he'd never get through today. So he went through the motions, not knowing how or if to let his guard down.

They were due at the funeral home this afternoon for the viewing. It was going to be a nightmare. If he were smart, he'd ask Fiona to stay home. But she'd never allow it. His luck, she'd come anyway, and her unexpected-expected presence would be worse than knowing she'd be there.

Dressed, he put the coffee on, poured himself a cup

and went onto the roof. His telescope was still there—luckily it hadn't rained—and he recalled the other evening with Fiona. Looking at the stars had been perfect. If only it had lasted.

Finished with his coffee, he grabbed his telescope and returned to his apartment. He didn't know what to do with himself.

"Good morning," Fiona said, her voice sleepy from disuse.

"Morning. Coffee is on."

She stared at him; her gaze boring into him until he thought she could see his battered soul. Without a word, she went into the kitchen.

"What's the plan for this morning?" she asked, her fingers wrapped around a mug.

"I should check into work for a little bit, just to make sure things aren't falling apart."

"Must be tough when you're the only person who can do anything," she said, a small smile on her face.

He smiled. "Humor me."

For the next hour, the two of them sat at the dining table, using their laptops. At least, he assumed she used her laptop. She might be using it as a prop, since every time he glanced over at her, she was staring at him. To be honest, he didn't get much work done, but he was grateful for the distraction. Too soon, it was time to dress for the viewing.

He stood before his closet, staring at rows of shirts, jackets, and suits. "What the hell does one wear to this," he mumbled.

Hands on his back made him jump. Fiona stood next to him and reached into his closet. "How about this?"

She'd pulled a white shirt, navy patterned tie, and a dark gray suit.

"Thanks."

He dressed. His mind scattered. "We need to get there early."

"Okay."

"You don't have to go with me."

"I'm going."

"I'm not sure who will come."

She straightened his tie, and he drank in the scent of her. "Enough people will be there."

"What do I say to them?"

"Don't worry about it. They're coming to give you support. Let them."

With a nod, he led her to his garage. He stopped, staring at the cars available. Somehow, a Ferrari didn't seem like a "viewing before his mother's funeral" type of car. Was there even one?

"How about this one?" Fiona asked, pointing to his blue Aston Martin Rapide. "I haven't ridden in it yet."

It wasn't too flashy and was appropriate for where they were going. How did she know these things? He pulled the correct key from his wallet and held the door.

"What's her name?" Fiona asked.

"Excuse me?" He pulled out of the garage.

"What's the car's name? Your Ferrari is Barbara, so who is this?"

"Astrid."

She nodded. "Any reason?"

"Goes with the brand."

"It's much more fantasy-related than Barbara," Fiona said.

She spoke a few more times, but conversation

grated on his nerves. The car fell silent again.

Too soon, he arrived at the funeral home. From the outside, it looked like every other funeral home he'd ever seen. He turned off the engine and remained where he was. His muscles tensed, and the air around him buzzed. He didn't want to leave the car.

"Ready?" she asked.

Not even close, and he never would be. He climbed from the car, and she appeared by his side before he had the chance to open her door. He didn't know whether to be annoyed or appreciative. She stuck her hand in his, gave him a small tug, and they walked into the funeral home. The funeral director greeted him at the door.

"Mr. Zeno, welcome. Once again, I'm so sorry for your loss."

"This is Fiona Hamilton."

The two shook hands, and the funeral director led them along the Victorian-style wallpapered hallway into a sitting room on the left. At the front of the room was his mother's casket. He balked and turned away. There were chairs arranged for people to sit and open spaces for…what? Mingling? Flower arrangements were placed on every available surface, making the room heavy with perfume, and an easel with the photos he and Lexie had chosen stood next to the casket. The casket he was determined not to look at.

"I'll leave you two alone with your mother." The funeral director left, and Caleb wanted to follow.

The box was not his mother. His mother was soft like the cashmere sweaters she loved to wear. The box was hard. He did not want to be here alone with it. Fiona slipped her hand in his again, and he squeezed. He couldn't do this.

"Where are Lexie and Steve?" he asked.

"They'll be here. Do you want time alone or do you want me to stay with you?"

He had no answer to the question, but he couldn't loosen his grip from her hand, so she moved closer. The scent of the flowers made him ill. Or maybe it was being here. What the hell was he supposed to do for a half hour before people came?

"Why don't we sit over there," Fiona said.

He looked at the ugly gold carpet with swirl patterns, then from the corner of his eye, he noticed she raised her arm. He tracked the direction of her arm and relief coursed through him when she pointed away from the casket. With a nod, he followed her to the back of the room. She pointed to a chair, and he lowered himself into it, feeling once again like an old man with stiff joints. His back to the casket, he could look around without worrying about what he would see. Instead, he stared at the yellow and white wallpapered walls. Who was the decorator in charge of this place? He longed for the emptiness of his clean white walls in his apartment. Did someone think it was soothing?

Fiona pressed against him. "This wallpaper is ugly," she whispered.

He huffed. Blinking, he pulled away from her, but didn't let go of her hand. He couldn't afford to let emotions in right now. Not when he had so many reasons to block them.

In the distance, the snick of a door closing, and murmured voices alerted him someone else arrived. A few seconds later, Steve and Lexie entered the room.

"Does anyone need anything," the funeral director asked.

Shaking heads prompted him to leave. With a sigh, Caleb rose and walked toward his sister. She placed her hand on the casket and dissolved into tears. He faltered. Fiona's hand squeezing his kept him in the room. His sister needed him, but she had Steve, who comforted Lexie and waited for her to calm.

"I hope a lot of people come," Lexie said, when she'd gotten herself under control again. "Mom would want that."

Caleb was pretty sure his mother wanted to be alive right now, hugging Fiona and running her fingers through Fiona's hair, taking the hand of his cousin, Ellen, and dragging her into the corner to interrogate her on about the health of her mother and the new job she'd just taken. It was also the last thing he wanted. The more people there were, the more he'd have to interact with them. Why couldn't funerals be private affairs?

Before he could state his opinion, more voices filtered in from the hallway and relatives and friends arrived. There were cousins he hadn't seen in years, friends of his mother he'd heard about, and people who'd worked with her when she'd gotten a job as a secretary in a large office. Each of them approached him and offered condolences. Many reminisced.

"Your mom always made me laugh," one of his cousins said.

He didn't recall much laughter during his childhood.

"Your mother was so proud of you," one of her friends said. "She kept her TV tuned to your stations and would yell at us if we talked about shows not produced by your network."

His chest tightened at the praise. He'd never known she admired his work. Of course, he hadn't asked.

"She was the most efficient and hardest working secretary I've ever employed," her boss said, shaking his hand. "I hated for her to retire."

Coming from a fellow business owner, it was tremendous praise. Caleb wracked his brain. Had he ever talked to his mother about her job? Doubtful.

He clenched his jaw. He'd been so busy trying to block his emotions, trying to avoid memories of the past, he'd kept his dealings with his mother to the bare minimum. And now it was too late. The knowledge of what he'd missed gutted him.

Opening his mouth, he gasped for air, and Fiona was there, as if she'd waited for this exact moment. "Let's go outside," she said.

Without waiting for his response, she pulled him toward the door, excusing them as they cut through people and avoided conversations. Outside, where no one was around, he could exhale.

"Do you want to talk?" she asked.

He shook his head. He didn't want to talk. Didn't even want her here with him. Except sending her away terrified him. So, he stood on the sidewalk, leaned on the iron railing and took deep, gasping breaths. He might look like a sea bass having been yanked from the ocean, with the life draining from him on the deck of a boat. He might look like an asthma patient. He shouldn't allow Fiona to see him like this.

But he couldn't help it.

He was thankful she didn't say anything. She stroked his arm, lending him her silent presence. And after a few minutes, he gained control.

"I should get inside," he said.

She looked like she wanted to argue with him, and he straightened his spine. Without a word, he walked into the funeral home and mingled once again with the guests.

Just as the mourners were thinning, there was a commotion at the door. An older, well-dressed man walked in, and Caleb froze.

His father had aged, but certain things hadn't changed. The set of his jaw, the proud stance, the scanning the room for attention. Caleb would know his actions anywhere. As for the rest of him, his hair was whiter and thinner. His belly was bigger. And his shoulders were starting to stoop.

Blood rushed to Caleb's face and drained. His neck chilled. He had to remove his father from here before he made a scene, before he hurt Lexie.

"Caleb." Fiona whispered the word, and his heart sank. He wished she'd stayed outside. He had to make his father leave before he discovered Fiona. Before she could ask any questions, he stalked toward his father, praying Fiona and Lexie would stay away.

"What kind of a son doesn't tell his father when his wife dies?" his father yelled. "I had to read it on the goddamn Internet."

"What are you doing here?" Caleb asked.

"Paying my respects."

"You're not welcome here."

His father's chest expanded, and his face turned red. "Oh?" He sneered.

They were attracting an audience. Lexie clutched Steve's arm. All Caleb had to do was occupy his father for Lexie to disappear into the background, or for Steve to remove her.

"She was no longer married to you. This is for people who loved my mother."

"I loved her more than anyone."

His father had an interesting memory. Then again, narcissists always created a world of their own. "You loved hurting her."

His father rushed at him, and the mourners who were around them gasped. He stood firm, allowing himself to be the target. Larger, broader, and younger than his father, he wasn't concerned about his own safety. He hoped Fiona had left the room.

His father stopped a few inches away. The vein in his father's forehead throbbed, his gaze was wild, and his chest heaved. "You have no right to tell me to do anything. You didn't even have the decency to tell me she died."

"You must have read the part that invited family and loved ones to this visitation. You're neither."

His father grimaced. "Look at you. Not even crying over your mother."

He'd never cry in front of anyone, much less this biological DNA contributor. "Leave."

His father looked around. "Where's your sister?"

God, he hoped Steve had had the sense to get her out of here. "Not here."

"You think you're better than me?" his father asked. "You're not."

He was a thousand times better than his father. "You just want credit for showing sympathy for the death of a woman you never loved. We all see you for what you are. Now leave."

No one came to his father's defense. His father's

face hardened, and he turned toward the door.

Caleb's heart pounded in his chest. He put his mask in place and turned away from his father's retreating back, ignoring the prickles running along his neck. He had a roomful of mourners he still had to deal with, and he'd never show them, or anyone, how much his father's presence disturbed him. He hoped they'd pretend it hadn't happened.

Looking around, he didn't see Fiona. His chest ached with the need to escape from here with her, but before he could act on it, one of his cousins approached and offered her sympathy. Another one nodded at him, patted his back, and left. Behind him, a voice gave him chills. His father was still here. He turned and spotted him in the hallway with Fiona. His vision tunneled, and his mouth dried. As if observing himself from a distance, he marched over to the two of them by the door. If he hurt her…

His father turned to him, a glimmer of triumph shining in his eyes. "You didn't tell me you had a girlfriend," he said. He emphasized "girlfriend" as if the word were a Pandora's box of possibilities. Possibilities too horrible for Caleb to contemplate.

The best way to shut down his father was not to engage. If his father knew how much Fiona meant to him, he would do everything in his power to hurt her. He couldn't let it happen.

"I don't."

Fiona flinched.

Caleb's stomach ached.

"She said she was," his father said.

"She's a girl, and she's my friend." A voice in his head argued, but he ignored it.

His father stared at him, and Caleb held his ground, schooling his features and praying he'd let it go.

By some miracle, he did, turning and walking away without saying another word. Caleb was too smart think this was the end.

"Caleb?" Fiona's voice came to him as if from a far distance. She'd want an explanation, but if he told her the truth, she'd try to get involved. And then she'd get hurt.

He walked along the hallway in the opposite direction from his father. Fiona followed. An empty sitting room on the left beckoned, and he entered.

"What happened?" she asked.

"It was nothing." He swallowed. His throat was raw, his chest tight.

She opened her mouth to speak, paused, and closed it. Her gaze softened, and she stepped toward him.

Dammit, he couldn't afford this either. Not now. Not when he had the rest of the day to get through. "I'm fine." He glared. He hated knowing about more emotional alternatives.

"Okay." The compassion she showed pierced his heart.

"You can leave." It would be easiest for him if she did, ensuring his father wouldn't do anything to her to get to him. His muscles tensed, waiting for her to argue with him.

"Okay." She stayed where she was. His jaw twitched. Why wasn't she leaving?

"But if you want to talk—"

"I don't." Not here, not now, not ever.

"—I'm here."

He clenched is hands at his sides, and pain radiated

through him.

She waited, never taking her gaze off him. He remained where he was, until Fiona surrendered and left the room. Still, he remained in place for a few more seconds. When he was sure she left, he fell forward, bracing himself with his hands on his knees, like a marathoner gasping for air after a race.

He shuddered. How could he continue to try it Fiona's way? Was it worth it, when, if he did continue Fiona's way, someone might get hurt?

****

Early the next morning, Fiona woke after a restless night in her own apartment. She stared out the window. Caleb had denied she was his girlfriend. Despite his pain, it hurt. His first instinct was to push everything and everyone away, but her, too? If it were any other day, she'd ask him about it, make him talk. But the funeral was today. Now wasn't the time for a relationship talk.

And his father? He'd been outgoing, intrusive, and a little smarmy. He put her on edge. He asked her way more questions than he should have in such a short amount of time. Probing questions about her relationship with Caleb. It wasn't his business, and when she'd been vague, he'd pushed her. She wasn't looking forward to seeing him today…if he came.

She planned to meet Caleb at the church. He'd told her it was better that way, since she'd need her car to drive herself home—only the family went to the cemetery, and he'd asked her not to go. Being excluded added to her hurt. No, she wasn't family, but she was important to Caleb. At least, she'd thought so. He'd shut himself off into a sealed vault, and no one, not even she, was allowed the combination.

She dressed in a dark gray dress and pearl earrings. Black pumps and a matching purse.

Inside the church, Steve flagged her.

"How's Lexie?" She stood next to him away from the receiving line.

His gaze never left his wife's face across the room, and Fiona knew he'd return to her in a minute. "A mess, like you'd expect. Caleb is stoic, as usual."

She glanced at Caleb, standing next to Lexie and shaking mourners' hands. Steve patted her shoulder. "It's not you. This is just how he is. You're helping him more than you realize."

"I wish I could do more."

Steve returned to the receiving line, and a tap on her shoulder made her turn. Her stomach dropped.

"Fiona, right?"

She nodded to Caleb's dad. "Yes."

"You're awfully dedicated for someone who isn't Caleb's girlfriend."

She swallowed and tried not to notice the gleam in the older man's eye. "I'm here to support them."

"Caleb's always been surrounded by weak women."

Fiona gripped her stomach. "Oh?"

"He likes women he can rescue. Makes him feel important."

Before she had a chance to respond, a large hand gripped the man's shoulder, and Caleb spun him around. "You need to leave," he ground out. "Right now."

His father smiled. "You're just like me, you know."

Caleb growled. As if in surrender, his father raised his hands and left the church. Caleb turned to Fiona, swallowed, and walked to where Steve stood with Lexie.

Fiona sighed, grateful for the rescue, and searched for a seat in the sanctuary. For the duration of the service, she kept her gaze pinned on Caleb. While Lexie cried, and shook, and handed her speech to the minister to read, Caleb remained, as Steve said, stoic. But Fiona had learned to read him. His left hand clenched into a fist, as if he were squeezing something. His shoulders were set a little too stiff. A small muscle twitched in his jaw. And his gaze was hollow. She longed to rush to him and hold him, but there were too many people around. Besides, he'd never allow it.

As he, Lexie, and Steve followed the casket out the door of the church, she waited for him to acknowledge her, but he stared straight ahead. She followed him from the building, but he climbed into the limo before she had a chance to reach him. It pulled away, leaving her to watch her boyfriend disappear, alone.

Chapter Nineteen

Fiona had propped her front door open, eavesdropping so she'd know when Lexie returned from the funeral and hoping Caleb would be with her. In the meantime, she puttered around her apartment, dusting knick-knacks the cleaning people had already dusted, straightening things the cleaning people had straightened, and pretty much acting useless. On the one hand, she understood why Caleb retreated, but on the other hand, his regression disappointed her. She needed to find the right balance—supporting him, but not enabling him.

She was just about to check in with Patricia at the office when Lexie's sobs interrupted her. A shadow passed her open doorway. When Fiona peeked from the doorway, Steve just shook his head and followed Lexie inside. Fiona's heart hurt for her friend's agony. But she wouldn't pry. She turned on her stove to boil water for lasagna. When baked, she'd deliver it across the hall, so they'd have a meal to eat without having to make food themselves.

Besides, it kept her busy until she talked to Caleb. She'd dialed him once, and it had gone straight to voicemail. And he didn't answer her text.

The elevator dinged, and she raced to the doorway. Caleb exited the elevator. He shuffled along the hall, shoulders hunched, head bowed, hands stuffed in his pockets. Her vision blurred from tears, and she blinked them away.

"Caleb."

He stopped. He straightened his shoulders, removed his hands from his pockets and stood ramrod straight. Nothing moved, except for his hand clenching and unclenching at his side.

"I can't," he ground out.

"I know." She wished he could talk to her. Fiona stepped toward him but stopped when he stiffened. "I'm here for you when you can. Or when you need."

His throat worked as he swallowed, and she didn't push. Retreating into her apartment, she let him pass. Only when he'd slipped into Lexie's apartment, did she shut her door, sink to the floor, and give into her sadness and frustration. She cried. His hurt was palpable, and even though she'd never met his mother, just the idea of losing a parent evoked strong feelings in her. But frustration also wrapped around her. She wanted him to talk to her, release the emotions he held in check. He'd retreated into his shell, and the change infuriated her.

As evening fell, she opened her door, planning to take over the lasagna. Caleb surprised her in the hallway, his head turning from his sister's door to her own, as if torn.

"Hi," she said, leaning against the doorframe.

"Lexie needs me."

She put the lasagna on the hall table, never taking her gaze off him. He looked ready to bolt. Her heart hurt. "Is Steve with her?"

He nodded.

"Then why don't you come inside?"

He held himself still. "I should check on her."

"You were just there, Caleb. Come inside." She stepped inside, away from the door; her gaze locked on his.

Something in his gaze softened, and he turned toward her.

Gripping the door handle, she waited for him to enter. The click of the door shutting made him flinch. He tracked the space between her and the door.

"Come here." She opened her arms, and a moment later, he stepped into her arms. He stood there as the seconds ticked by and she ran her hands along his back. She rested her head against his chest, listening to the drumbeat of his heart and wishing he'd let her help him.

"I can't do what you want."

"What do you think I want?"

"Talk about my feelings, talk about today. If I let them escape, I'll never be able to control them."

Her desire to understand their relationship would have to take a back seat. She didn't know how long she could last, but she could give him today to get over his fear. She pulled her head back and caressed his cheek. "Someday you're going to need to release your emotions, no matter how scary it might seem to you, and I hope I'll be here for you. But for now, all I want to do is help you to feel better. And if it means staying with you while you keep everything bottled up, I'll do it."

She listened to the sound of his breathing. His chest rose and fell as if he were gulping great amounts of air and his hands trembled against her waist. She drew him close again while they stood in the foyer of her apartment, waiting for him to gain control.

"What's that?" He pointed to the foil pan.

"Lasagna. I was about to take it over to Lexie and Steve."

He shook his head. "They already ate."

"Are you hungry?"

He paused, as if considering the question. His stomach growled.

"I'll heat some for you." Maybe normalcy would help him.

She fixed two plates of lasagna and brought them into the living room, where he sat on the sofa staring into space. "Want to watch a movie?"

He shrugged, so she gave him the remote and let him choose. Of all the things to pick, he chose a documentary. She raised an eyebrow but kept silent. They ate their dinner while learning about solar probes and the next research trip into space. He focused his attention on the screen. She didn't understand a lot of the technical jargon, but she got the gist and by the end of the show, the documentary had captured her attention.

He took her plate with his and went into the kitchen.

"You don't have to do this," she said, but he shook his head and rolled his sleeves, showing her branches with the words "strong" and "care."

He scrubbed not only their plates and utensils, but all the lasagna pots in her sink. By the time he finished, her spotless kitchen shone. He turned. "Thank you."

He headed toward her front door. "I need to get home."

"Do you want to come over after work tomorrow?" she asked.

"I don't think I'll be able to, but I'll let you know."

****

The next day, Caleb buried himself in spreadsheets. Whenever he couldn't concentrate, he called Lexie. When Lexie's emotions got to be too much for him, he asked her to hand the phone to Steve. He only focused on his sister. And if Fiona popped into his head at odd moments, he shifted her to the back of his mind to deal with later.

His phone rang, and he answered without thinking, assuming Lexie was on the other end.

"Hello, Caleb."

His neck tightened at the old, familiar, chilling voice. "Why are you calling me?

"I'm your father. I don't like how you treated me at the funeral. I deserve better."

"No, you deserve to be in jail."

His father laughed the same laugh he remembered from his childhood. The one that said he wasn't amused. "I don't like being the last to know when my son has a relationship with a woman. Imagine what people will think of me, being unaware of my son's life."

His father always cared what others thought of him. It's why he never tried anything with his wife or daughter in public. "I told you, Fiona and I are friends. Nothing more."

"Are you sure? Seems strange to me a 'friend' would spend so much time worrying about you."

Caleb squeezed the stress ball on his desk and shut his eyes against the pounding headache building at his temples. His father had noticed more about Fiona than he'd realized. "No stranger than you here."

"I had to pay my respects. What would people think?"

Now it made sense. His father cared about how he looked to other people. "Well, you were there. Are we done?"

"For now. I enjoyed meeting your girlfriend."

Caleb disconnected the call, hand shaking. When his father lived with them, he'd rained much of his verbal and emotional abuse on his mother. Caleb had been unable to protect her as a child, but as he got older, he deflected the man's attention to himself, especially when his father threatened his sister. Once his mother left him, and took Caleb and Lexie with her, they'd been safer. But the scars remained. His father reappeared periodically in his life. He'd always call Caleb out of the blue and then fade into the shadows. Caleb never said anything to his mother or sister because he never wanted to upset them.

With Lexie married to Steve, she had her husband to protect her. And even though Caleb would always be there for her, Steve would never let anyone harm his wife.

But now his father wanted to know more about Fiona. The man liked to figure out women's weaknesses so he could take advantage of them. It's why he'd never let his father near any of his girlfriends, and why he'd make sure to protect them by never being photographed with them. He hadn't counted on the funeral though—as if anyone could. He'd never let his father play his mind games—or take anything out—on Fiona.

He paused. Unless his father used Fiona to upset him? His head continued to pound. He didn't care about himself. But Fiona? Cutting off all contact with her was the only way to protect her. If his father thought her unimportant, he'd back off. His chest ached.

When Fiona called, he almost let it go to voicemail.

"Hey, it's me," she said. "How are you doing?"

He reached for his stress ball and paused. Releasing it, he closed his empty fist and brought it to his lap. "Fine. You?"

"I'm working and worrying about you."

"Don't. Focus on your business," he said, nodding to his secretary and signing papers she handed him. The lines swam on the paper.

"I've managed to persuade two frequent users of my site to meet with me for private appointments."

"Good," he said, opening sales data for one of his TV stations and unable to make any sense of it.

"I'm hopeful I'll be able to convince a few more. Just putting the finishing touches on my sales pitches. Do you want to grab dinner?"

"I told Lexie I'd stop by after work."

She paused before she answered. "Well, I'll be home, so knock if you get done early."

He stared at his computer after he ended the call with Fiona. He should have invented an excuse about why he couldn't see her tonight, ease her into the idea of pulling away from him. Although whether he lied or entered his sister's apartment, the message was clear. He didn't want to see her. He couldn't.

Irrational though his fear might be, he had to protect Fiona from his father. Everyone his father encountered got hurt, either with intention or as collateral damage. Once Caleb got strong enough to protect his mother and sister, his father had set his sights on him, but had never been successful. He found a way in, though, with Fiona. And Caleb would never let it happen. He had to protect her, until his father got tired of chasing his tail and moved onto something else. Right now, the best way—the only way—Caleb could protect her was with his distance.

Chapter Twenty

As he prepared to leave the office late the next afternoon, Caleb's phone rang.

"Want to go for a walk on the beach?" Fiona asked.

He stared out the window. The sun sat mid horizon, shining into his office. The special windows he'd had installed—the ones Alex had suggested prevented sun glare—enabled him to look out the window without getting blinded. It had been a gorgeous day, and he hadn't had a chance to see any of it. He wanted to go for a walk on the beach, and being with Fiona made him want to give in. But he couldn't.

"I'm going to take work home," he said. "I'm behind with all the time off I took." He rubbed the bridge of his nose, hating the lies he told.

Fiona called him again the following morning. "Caleb, are you available to help me with something for my website?"

He frowned. The last thing he should do was encourage her by agreeing to help. It would take longer for her to get the message. But she'd never asked for his help before. In fact, she usually pushed away his offers to help. Why did she ask for it now? Maybe she needed him. The urge to protect her grew so strong it almost swallowed him. Which way would be better for her? He looked at his calendar and sighed with relief. "I've got meetings all day today."

"What about tomorrow? Can you come to my office around ten?"

He checked his calendar, again. This time nothing offered him an excuse. And her persistence meant she needed him. "What am I helping you with?"

"I need a guy's perspective for a new set of articles on the website."

Did she not have any others to ask? She'd stressed to him the huge difference between his website and hers, as well as her desire to do things on her own. And now she asked for advice? "I'll see you then."

At ten the next morning, he exited his Ferrari and stared at the refurbished warehouse in front of him. Classic Fiona. Even from the front door, color, character, and charm oozed from every nook and cranny, just like her. He'd bet her clients, if they came to her office, got a sense of who they were dealing with just by standing on the sidewalk.

Shaking his head, he climbed the steps and pressed the funky looking doorbell. He'd missed her so much, his hand shook. A buzzing rang inside. The artistic doorbell had been converted to a buzzer with a camera mounted under the eaves. Clever.

A click sounded, and he tried the door. At least she was safety conscious. He opened the purple door and stepped into an entryway with a bench on the left and a set of stairs on the right. The hallway went from front to back and there were doors along either side. A decorative sign hung next to the stairs, listing the names of the various offices and their locations. Fiona's office was on the first floor.

He walked toward the back of the building. The second door on the right stood open, and he heard her voice.

"—any moment. Oh, there you are!" she said. Her bright smile lit her entire face. He stepped across the threshold. "Patricia, this is Caleb. Caleb, Patricia is my assistant and close friend."

A woman with red hair stepped from behind a carved desk. "It's nice to meet you." She stared at him, making no secret of her examination and he stood there, stoic, until she finished. "I'm sorry about your mother."

Air left his lungs. Before he could do anything but nod, Fiona spoke.

"We're going to be in the conference room." She turned to Caleb. "Come with me." She led him through the anteroom into a larger room with a fireplace, an alcove filled with two stuffed blue chairs and a side table and a large table with six chairs around it. Lace curtains covered the windows and a red rug covered oak floors. It looked more like his grandmother's parlor than a conference room.

Fiona motioned to a seat beside her laptop, and he sat. He wanted to have time to drink her in, but she opened her laptop and pointed to the screen. "We're doing a feature on men and women's relationships— whether they're men with women or men with men or women with women. I've got experts authoring articles on how to tell if your relationship is healthy; the perfect 'date' restaurants; and now I'm working on a personal essay about how to tell if someone is into you. I hoped you'd read it to give me your opinion."

"Wait a minute, personal essay as in about you and me?"

Fiona shifted in her chair. "I wanted to talk to you about it first. I'm not publishing anything without your permission, but—"

"No!" Caleb paced the office. "Our relationship is private. I don't want it blasted all over the Internet for the world to see." Not when his father was in the picture.

Fiona's gaze flashed. "I'm not 'blasting' it anywhere. How about you read it first before you jump to any conclusions?"

"There's no need. My relationship is private. You agreed after what happened with your clients."

Her face flushed. "*Your* relationship? A relationship involves two people. It's not yours. It's ours. If we even have one. I'm not saying anything in this article that violates our privacy. Your name is not mentioned, nor are any identifiable details."

He reared. "Are you serious? You can't be that naïve. You lost clients because the two of us were seen together. Anyone reading your essay will know you're talking about me."

She glared. "Maybe. But unless you read it to see my take and my slant, you have no idea what I'm even saying."

"The answer is no. It's bad enough you told your assistant about my mother, now you want to do this?"

He spun away from her and strode to the fireplace. Bracing his forearm on the mantle, he stared at his shoes, trying to rein in his temper. Since when did he let his emotions get the better of him?

Since Fiona.

Her hand on his back made him jump.

"Patricia is my friend, as well as my assistant. I had to give her a reason why I missed work. I'd never violate your privacy by telling details of your personal life. You should know me better."

Her calm, soft voice hinted at a role reversal, as if they switched places and entered a reality where emotions governed him, and she remained rational. He took a moment to review what she said.

It made sense.

When he'd taken time off because of her car accident, he'd told his secretary the reason as well. If it was okay for him, it was okay for her to do what she did as well.

Dammit.

"I'm sorry," he said, his voice quiet.

"Want to talk about it?"

"Talk about what?"

She led him to the chairs under the window and they sat together. "Your father. Your mother. Whatever has you so upset right now."

A war raged inside him. Would it be so bad to talk to her? He shook his head. She'd never understand the dangers of showing emotion, of letting people know what your motivation was. He had no idea how to make her understand his response to his father, or how essential it was he keep her safe from him. He could see it bothered her. No matter how understanding, hurt reflected in her gaze.

She reached for his hand and stroked the top of it with her thumb. The motion soothed him, and he leaned in the chair. Even hurt, she focused on him. God, he didn't deserve her.

"I can't do this, Fiona."

"Let me show you the article. If there's anything about it you don't like, I'll delete the entire thing. I'll get someone else to do a guest post using their own experience. I'll come at this from a different angle. Just read the article first."

Now calm, it was the right thing to do. His reading something wasn't going to give it to the world to see. And all he had to do was say no. He nodded.

She let go of his hand and returned with her laptop. Handing it to him, she sat next to him while he read. He disappeared into her article, awareness of Fiona fading. She was a great writer—pithy, intelligent, and relatable. She was also right. She didn't dish on her boyfriend. She gave broad examples—even if readers identified him as the boyfriend, they weren't given a window into who he was. However, the reader got a clear view of just how much she cared about him.

He swallowed. Maybe he could ask Paulo to create a recipe for eating crow, to make it taste a little more palatable. Closing the laptop, he faced her. "You're right. I'm sorry."

"Any chance you want to talk about why you reacted the way you did?"

Nope, he didn't want to at all. But she deserved an explanation. "Patricia surprised me when she greeted me the way she did. It shouldn't have, but it did. Followed by this, I assumed the article displayed my life for all to see."

"No matter how different we are when it comes to what we're willing to share of ourselves, I would never do something to make you uncomfortable. It's why I wanted you to come over and read this."

This woman meant more to him than any other woman ever. So why couldn't he answer her? Because she'd never understand. The best way to keep her safe was to keep her insulated from his father's vitriol, and now his father had re-entered their lives, he had to protect Fiona from his father at all costs.

"You know about my father; how violent he was. I don't want him to bother you. I was afraid if your article mentioned me, he'd come after you."

She played with the hem of her skirt, and he could see her brain processing his information. She stopped. "Okay."

Was that it?

She cleared her throat. "About the article…"

"It's good," he said. "You can use it. Why not just email it to me, though?"

"I wanted to be with you when you read it. I wanted your immediate reaction, not just a well-thought-out one you could formulate with time."

He nodded. "It's well-written. I can see why your clients love you."

She smiled. "Thank you. I'm going to wait until you've had time to consider it, though. I wanted your immediate reaction, but I also want you to have a chance to turn it over in your mind."

"I'm not going to change my mind."

"Maybe not," she said. "But I'll ask you about it again tomorrow. Just in case."

The next morning, he was still comfortable with the article, and he texted her permission to use it. However, his guilt continued to develop. Because he could tell she was falling for him. It should have made him happy, but he'd never had a long-term relationship with a woman, and he had no idea what to do. He didn't know how to align his feelings for her with his need to keep her safe. His father's reappearance reminded him of all the reasons he kept his feelings hidden, and like the monster under the bed, his father's presence meant he couldn't stop thinking about all the awful possibilities—his father hurting her to get to him, his father hurting her just for the hell of it, his father telling her lies to make her doubt Caleb's love. Whatever progress he'd made with his emotions before his father arrived had flown from the window after their argument. How the hell was he supposed to ignore years of strategy? And what right did he have to make Fiona suffer?

He stared out the window of his office. The safest thing for everyone was to make a clean break from her. It wasn't fair otherwise. If he continued seeing her, but pulled away emotionally, she'd never understand. She'd feel bad and think it was her fault. A clean break would be the kindest thing he could do for her, no matter how much he'd suffer.

His chest squeezed at losing the light she'd brought him. He'd never known how much he missed until she entered his life. He wouldn't just miss her physically, even though she was beautiful to look at. But she was much more. Her laughter raised his spirits. Her concern for him touched him. And somehow, she'd shown him there was room for him to feel things.

His father's laughter echoed in his head. A clean break would protect him but wouldn't allow him to protect her. Because she still didn't understand why his father was so dangerous. He wasn't sure he could explain it with any logic, but he needed the chance to at least try before he excised her from his life. She deserved an explanation, and the chance to prepare. His email pinged with a message from Alex, his friend and CAST partner, and he remembered the Florida trip.

Fiona was supposed to go with him. How could he uninvite her? Aside from the ribbing he'd take from his other friends, it would be rude. But what kind of man asked his girlfriend on a trip right before he ended their relationship? No matter how much he wanted to spend time with her...Unless he used their time together in Florida to prepare her? And maybe he'd find a way the two of them could stay together. If not, when they returned, he'd have to let her go.

****

For a man who loved expensive cars, Fiona should not have been surprised at Caleb's private jet. A Gulfstream G650, its luxurious appointments included butter leather overstuffed massage chairs, noise-cancelling headsets, polished zebrawood tables, and granite bathrooms. Like his apartment, though, everything was black and white, softened with occasional shades of gray. With the large panoramic windows, travel would be very bright. After greeting the pilot and co-pilot, Caleb led her to a seating area, and they made themselves comfortable for the six-hour flight to Florida.

Fiona couldn't stop looking around. "Wow, this is impressive. Does it have a name?"

Caleb's mouth quirked in a ghost of a smile. "Like my cars, 'it' is a 'she.' And her name is Eos."

"Pretty. What's it mean?"

"Goddess of the Dawn."

"Perfect." She rubbed her hands on the armrest, luxuriating in the feel of the leather against her palms, and looked around. "Do you use this often?"

"Mostly for business trips. Sometimes for pleasure."

She turned. "You don't seem like the kind of guy to travel much for pleasure."

"I like where I am. I prefer to have a purpose."

"But vacations are fun. And rejuvenating. And inspiring."

He patted her arm. "I manage to have fun, get rejuvenated, and inspired anyway. Sometimes I even go skiing at my house in Colorado." He handed her a set of headphones. "Here, put these on so you're not bothered by the noise."

Was he concerned for her ears, or did he just not want to talk to her? She'd respected his wishes and given him space, but it was hard. He'd pulled away from her, and she didn't know if it was because he dealt with his mother's death, his father's reappearance, or something else...like not wanting to be with her any longer. But if he didn't want her anymore, he wouldn't have brought her to Florida, right? This flight would be the perfect opportunity to ask all her questions if he'd let his guard down long enough for the conversation. Except now he gave her noise-cancelling headphones, which meant he didn't want to talk. She put on the headphones, moving aside her hair. Caleb leaned forward to help her, and his gaze softened when he touched her hair. Desire filled her and she relished his touch. It had been more than a week since he'd touched her with any type of feeling, and she missed the contact. Before she could encourage anything, he pulled away, his mask once again in place. She sighed. Did he care for anything more than the physical pleasure they got from touching each other? Was this his way of trying to end things with her? No, he wouldn't. And what about when they landed? She didn't know anything about

Alex's house, but would they share a room? A bed? The thought hadn't crossed her mind, but now, she didn't know what to think.

Outside the large window, the hangar and other planes slid by, then tipped as their own plane pushed away from the ground and took off. Below, cars, buildings, and roads became toy sized. On the horizon, clouds resembled cotton puffs. The sun glinted off the steel of the wings, making it seem as if they were touched by fire. It was glorious. If Fiona owned a plane, she'd make sure to use it as often as possible.

A steward, named Fred according to his nametag, came over with a list of beverages printed on thick stationery. Impressed, she opted for a mimosa. She wondered if the glass would tip from the inequality of expensive champagne poured into ordinary orange juice. The orange was probably gold plated, though. She almost laughed when it was served in Waterford—no crystal of that caliber would dare tip. The fizz made her nose tingle and her eyes water, so she closed them.

Without the benefit of sight or sound to distract her, she thought about Caleb. Since his mother's funeral, he'd been distant. Oh, he was solicitous and protective, like he was with his sister, but he didn't let his feelings show and every time she brought up their relationship, he found a way to divert the conversation to something else. Maybe being around his friends in Florida would relax him enough for the two of them to talk. She let herself drift, the vibration of the plane making her drowsy.

When she awoke, Caleb stared at her.

She removed her headphones. "Did I snore?"

He shook his head. "No."

Instead of continuing the conversation, he turned his attention to the work spread in front of him. With all the events of the past week, he had fallen behind. Although she wanted to talk to him, he had work to do. She stretched her legs and opened her laptop, and the two of them worked in silence for the next two hours.

When she returned from the bathroom, she tapped his shoulder. "That bathroom is nicer than my entire apartment."

"Came with the plane. Want to see the cockpit?"

She knew nothing about flying, but the instruments the pilots used to keep this fancy tin can in the air fascinated her. Maybe not tin, possibly platinum? The pilot and co-pilot performed almost balletic moves as they directed the plane east across the country.

When they landed, Caleb offered his hand to her, and they walked across the tarmac to the waiting limo. The humid air smacked her in the face, and she could feel her hair frizz right away. The limo was even more impressive, with gold plated accoutrements, Waterford champagne glasses, and a soundproof interior.

She must have shown her surprise because Caleb answered her question before she could ask. "It's Alex's. He's showy with his luxuries."

"I can see." She strapped her seatbelt. "I'm not sure I should touch anything in here."

He squeezed her hand. "You may touch whatever you want."

Her lungs contracted in surprise at the sexual innuendo after his distance the past week, and she raised an eyebrow. "Oh?" She slid her hand along his thigh.

For a moment, the old Caleb returned, and his gaze

burned with desire. But before she could encourage him, the limo driver slammed the trunk shut, and the noise jerked him to the present. Disappointment slithered through her.

As the limo pulled away from the airport, she leaned toward him once again. "Do you think Alex names his cars as well?"

"I don't think he keeps them long enough," Caleb said. "He likes to upgrade to the newest models—of everything."

"Going to be an interesting weekend."

"You'll enjoy it," he said. "I promise."

The limo whisked them through Miami Beach, onto a causeway leading to an island, through a gate, and when it pulled into the driveway of Alex's home, Fiona's mouth dropped.

"He designed it himself," Caleb said, an amused tone to his voice.

The two-story home was modern and boxy, a combination of concrete and wood with vast windows. Lawns that would make a golf course envious, with swaying palm trees and tropical flowers surrounding the home. Fiona exited the limo in a daze.

"Wow."

"You might want to release your awe here, because Alex will be impossible to deal with if he sees how impressed you are with his masterpiece," Caleb said.

"Too late, my friend!" A booming voice brought Fiona to her senses. A man who could be described as a blond surfer dude strode to them, clasping Caleb's hand and drawing him into a hug. When he turned to Fiona, her awe of him diminished her awe of his house.

He looked like a Ken doll come to life. Perfectly

coiffed, thick blond hair that ruffled in the light breeze, muscular arms and chest shown to perfection in a white linen button-down shirt open at the neck, trim waist, long legs in khaki pants, and piercing blue eyes that twinkled when he looked at her.

"Where have you been hiding her, Caleb?"

"He doesn't hide me anywhere." She straightened her spine. "I come and go as I please."

Alex laughed. "Excellent. I'll bet you keep him on his toes."

"I do my best." She winked.

Alex put his arm around her shoulders, put his other arm around Caleb, and walked with them into his house. "We are going to get along well."

"Terrific," Caleb said.

Inside, Alex turned and spread his arms wide. "Welcome to my castle."

The interior of the house was white marble walls and floors, accented with dark wood. To her right, a zigzag staircase led to the second floor. They walked through a dining room and open living area, separated by dark wood pillars. Unlike Caleb's apartment, this one oozed warmth, despite the white marble.

"I have plenty of bedrooms for you to choose from upstairs," Alex said.

Fiona glanced sideways at Caleb. Would he want them to share a room?

Alex continued. "When you're unpacked, we'll have drinks and hors d'ouevres outside."

Caleb led Fiona upstairs and chose a bedroom. It had the same marble and dark wood, with floor to ceiling windows giving a great view of the canal and bright red and white bedding. Her heart warmed at the pop of color, and that he wanted her to share his bed. Maybe her earlier concerns were unwarranted.

"This house is beautiful," she said, as she put away her things in the closet.

"He did a great job and will sell it in a year or two."

"Why? I'd think someone would want to keep a house as beautiful as this."

Caleb shook his head. "He doesn't stay anywhere for very long, and he'll design an even more beautiful, more amazing house in the next place he lands."

"It's kind of sad. Roots make us happy and keep us secure. Everyone needs them."

"Maybe someday, but I don't see it happening with Alex for a long time."

When they finished unpacking, she turned. "Before we go downstairs, can we talk?"

"I don't want to keep Alex waiting, Fiona. We'll talk later."

She followed him, but wondered to herself when "later" was, because for Caleb, it never seemed to arrive.

****

Caleb sprawled on the sofa on the patio of Alex's house, enjoying hors d'ouevres, a bottle of IPA, and the peace of the infinity pools. In the distance, the lap of water against the dock provided soothing background noise, the briny air reminding him of the beach at home. Jazz played in the background, and Alex and Fiona were talking about his house.

He knew why Alex never committed to one place or one woman for very long, but it wasn't his story to tell. For a long time, he'd been like Alex when it came to women. Fiona was the first woman who made him want to rethink his plans. But he'd have to release his emotions. And his father's presence had reminded him, again, that doing so could be dangerous, if not to him, then to others.

He gripped the cold bottle in his hands, the condensation dripping from his fingers. If only he could see a way clear to change his ways and keep Fiona safe. But he couldn't. And he had no idea how to break it to Fiona. She was aware of something; her desire to talk upstairs and on the plane proved it. He could only put her off for so long. If he were smart, he would have left her home, but Alex had persisted, and part of him hoped maybe being here this weekend would show him a way to move forward with her.

"Hey, Caleb, your long silences might work well with others, but not here," Alex called. He turned to Fiona. "How do you suffer through them?"

She snuggled against Caleb and took away the sting of Alex's words. "He's not silent with me."

"Oh?" Alex winked.

"When are Simon and Ted arriving?" Caleb wanted to change the subject and looked forward to seeing his friends in person. Video conferencing just wasn't the same.

"Ted and Abby are arriving tomorrow morning. She had a class at the community center she had to teach today. Simon and Meg are arriving tonight."

Caleb turned to Fiona. "Abby teaches computer coding for kids at a community center a few hours away from us."

"Cool. What does Ted do?"

"Ted is a cyber security expert. Just so you know,

he's hard of hearing. And Simon and Meg live in Maryland. He's a renowned landscape architect, and she's in PR. A house fire burned and scarred him several years ago." Fiona wouldn't care, but he wanted to prepare her.

He stared at the ocean. He should try to see Ted more often. Living in the same state gave him no excuse for pulling away.

A noise from inside Alex's house drew their attention.

"Speak of the devil," Alex said, "they're here."

Caleb pulled away from Fiona as Meg entered the patio.

"Alex, Caleb, it's so good to see you!" Meg said, rushing to each of them and giving them a hug. Caleb wrapped his arms around her and squeezed. Simon was a lucky man. On cue, Simon walked in, smiled at both men, and shook their hands.

"Hello, you must be the woman Caleb can't stop talking about."

Fiona's face turned bright red, and a huge smile stretched her face. "I'm Fiona. I'm not sure if he was complaining or praising."

Meg laughed. "It's true with all men. I'm Meg. It's so nice to meet you."

"Thanks, Si, I appreciate it," Caleb said.

Simon just chuckled. "You're welcome."

"Have you guys picked your room?" Alex asked. When they shook their heads, he excused himself and led them inside.

Caleb leaned toward Fiona. "Thanks for not making an issue of Simon's scars. He's still uncomfortable in public."

"I'd never judge someone for their looks." Hurt showed on her face.

He nodded. "You're right. I'm sorry." He should have had more faith in her.

Nodding, she grabbed her glass of white wine and sipped. They remained silent until Alex returned to the patio. "Dinner's on the boat tonight. We'll cast off in about an hour."

Chapter Twenty-One

Fiona stood on the deck of Alex's Dreamline yacht after dinner, watching the boat's wake and feeling the salt spray her face. The yacht was all sleek lines, bright spaces, and modern amenities, with leather, wood, and chrome. Three interior cabins, crew quarters and a garage for two jet skis, plus beautiful deck space. She could get used to this.

Could she get used to Caleb and his moods? While more at ease around his friends so far, he was still closer to the original emotionless Caleb than the new version. And why his lack of faith in her?

Maybe he was just protective of his friends. She glanced behind her to where Caleb, Simon, and Alex sat beneath the covered deck. Deep in conversation, they exuded power, wealth, and in the other men's cases, charm. Their fondness for each other was evident. So, it made sense he'd be concerned she, as an outsider, might be surprised by Simon's scars and say something by mistake. Still, a part of her still stung at his assumption. If he'd allow them to clear the air with a conversation, he wouldn't have had to assume anything about her.

She turned to the water.

"Nice life he has here, don't you think?" Meg said.

Fiona nodded at Simon's girlfriend as she joined her on deck.

"Very."

"You own the website. I love it."

"Thank you." Her funk lessened as she contemplated her website. This was something she knew and was good at. "What do you like about it?"

"You've got a lot of unique perspectives and recommendations, rather than the same old stuff in a pretty package. And speaking as a PR person, your branding is fantastic."

"Thanks," Fiona said, warmed by the praise. "Patricia, my assistant, and I have worked hard."

"It shows. Kudos on the morning show appearance, by the way. I understand it led to you and Caleb meeting as well."

Her confidence faltered. She glanced at Caleb, still deep in conversation with the other men. "I was pleased with the exposure." Fiona wrapped her arms around her waist. "He saw my interview and contacted me to arrange a meeting." Staring into her wineglass, she laughed. "I thought he wanted to be a client. Instead, he wanted to buy my company."

Meg's eyelids widened. "Whoa."

"Yeah, we didn't start in a good spot. But I thought we got there."

"Past tense?"

Fiona froze. This wasn't the time to talk about it, and Meg wasn't the right person. She shook her head and sipped her wine.

"Well, the two of you look good together," Meg said. "He's more relaxed than I've ever seen him. It's like his guard is down."

"He's more guarded than a few weeks ago."

"Probably because of his mother. And his father

appearing at the viewing."

"Oh, you heard?"

"I thought Simon planned to shoot the man, which says a lot when it comes to my super-reclusive boyfriend."

Fiona laughed. "It's not funny. The man was a jerk to him, although less so with me." She kept her voice low, not wanting the wind to carry it to where Caleb sat.

"More than a jerk, but I agree. Abby and I were talking about going to the spa tomorrow. Join us."

"I'd love to. When?"

"Three. They're taking the red eye, so they'll get here late morning."

"Sounds great." She reclined on the deck chair. "I could get used to this boat."

"Alex is good for all the luxuries. The rest of them are more low-key."

"I've noticed. Although Caleb does like his cars and airplane."

"Yes, boys and their toys."

"What about Simon? Does he have anything he likes to spend his money on?

Meg blushed.

"Oh, should I not have asked?" Fiona said. "I'm sorry!"

"No, don't be. It's just the answer is kind of embarrassing. Because he doesn't buy things for himself. He likes to spend his money on me, though."

"Aw, how sweet!"

"It is. Unnecessary, but sweet. He makes me very happy."

They relaxed in silence. The hum of the motor, the

sway of the boat lulled Fiona and her anxiety faded. Footsteps brought her to the present.

"Come watch the sunset," Caleb said.

She followed Caleb to the upper deck and to the front of the boat. His warm hand gripped hers and once again, she realized how much she'd missed his touch. He took her over to the railing, stood behind her and wrapped his arms around her, resting his chin on the top of her head. The sun descended to the shoreline, streaking the sky with blue, orange, and pink.

"Going to be a gorgeous day tomorrow," he murmured.

"Red sky at night, sailor's delight," she said.

"Red sky in the morning, sailors take warning," he answered.

She leaned into his chest, feeling his heart beat against the back of her head. A breeze blew across the prow of the ship, but wrapped in his arms, she warmed.

"Sunsets always remind me of you," he said.

"Why?"

"They're colorful and breathtaking."

She pulled away until he loosened his hold enough for her to turn in his arms. Standing on tiptoe, she kissed him, just enough to leave him wanting more, she hoped.

"Thank you."

****

As the sky darkened, Caleb realized another thing about sunsets. They were fleeting. Like his and Fiona's relationship? He didn't have an answer. Torn between wanting to put distance between them to protect her and needing her with him, he pointed to a bright light in the sky. "There's Saturn."

Fiona gasped. "Really?"

"Yup." He always took comfort in the sky. There was a pattern to everything, an expected rhythm even with something so mysterious.

"I love how you know that. Have you ever been to Cape Canaveral?"

He nodded. "In college, we came here for spring break, and I took a day and explored. It was amazing."

"I'll bet it was."

"You've never been?"

She shook her head. "No, but someday I'd love to see it."

He wished they could fit it in on this trip, but there wasn't time. Maybe they could return. He'd love to be the one to show it to her.

Or would he? If he connected too many things he loved to her, he'd be miserable when they separated, something he came closer to realizing all the time might happen. And it was selfish of him to think anything else.

Before he had a chance to probe, Alex called. "We're going to head home now."

The motor sounded and the boat made a wide turn. One hand on the railing, the other on Fiona, he steadied himself against the pull and rocking of the boat as it headed to Alex's slip. Once docked, they all returned to the house.

"Anyone interested in a movie?" Alex asked.

He led the way downstairs to the media room. It was dark, with comfortable reclining sofas and a full-sized movie screen. Caleb led Fiona to the second of the two rows of seats. She sat in one of the loveseats and patted the space next to her, so he joined her. She smelled of salt and sea and night air. It didn't matter who else was in the media room. It didn't matter what movie played on the screen or how fantastic the sound was with surround sound. The only thing he noticed during the two and a half hours the movie ran was Fiona.

Her body pressed against his as they sat together on the loveseat. The side of her soft breast touched his upper arm, the curve of her hip pushed against his upper thigh. Each time she shifted, the brush of her clothing against his echoed in his ear. Her hair tickled his neck. The change in her breathing as she reacted to the scenes in the movie—a sigh, a gasp, a series of quick inhalations—fascinated him. When the lights came on, he blinked, not because of the new brightness, but because once again, he had to replace his mask.

He was tired of it, but he didn't know what else to do.

"That was terrific," Simon said. "I'd heard great things but didn't expect it to live up to its hype."

Fiona agreed. "I loved it!"

"Me too," Caleb said, his voice soft. But he wasn't talking about the movie, and it scared him to death.

Fiona turned. "I'm exhausted. Would you mind if I turned in?"

He nodded once. His brain told him he should let her go alone. It would be easier. But his heart couldn't let her go. So, he said goodnight to Alex, Simon and Meg and followed Fiona upstairs.

She kept a steady stream of chatter as they got ready for bed.

"I like your friends. Meg is sweet and Simon and Alex are terrific."

"I thought you would."

"And Simon and Meg are adorable together. He just dotes on her. The love in his gaze when he looks at her—wow!"

He pulled his shirt over his head, glad for the coverage over his face. "They are a great match."

She climbed into bed and yawned as her head hit the pillow. "It must be nice for you to spend time with them." She yawned.

He lay next to her and reached for her hand beneath the covers. "It is." She struggled to keep her eyelids open, and he stroked her hand. "Sleep," he said. "We have a lot planned for tomorrow."

Like figuring a way to solve his problem with their relationship.

****

Fiona stretched on the massage table, Abby to her right and Meg to her left. She liked both women. Having met Abby a few hours ago, she could already tell she was whip smart and funny. The two women had accepted her into their group, including her in their activities for the day and filling her in on any information she might not know. So, an afternoon spent with them at the spa, getting massages, manicures, and pedicures, followed by shopping, was perfect.

She groaned as the masseuse kneaded the deep knots in her shoulders.

"Good, isn't it?" Abby asked.

"Amazing."

Meg groaned as well, and Abby laughed. "Jeez, what has the two of you so tense?"

"A lot of work," Meg said.

Fiona bit her lip. How much information should

she divulge?

"Spill, Fiona. It's what we're here for," Abby said.

"Definitely work, but Caleb as well."

"What's going on?" Meg asked.

Fiona told the women about her company and the issues she'd been having. "Things are much better now, and I salvaged a lot of clients quickly, but I'm still not where I was."

"And Caleb?" Abby asked.

"The two of you seem good together," Meg said.

"We are, but something's off with him. I notice it more now than I did before. And I don't know what to do about it."

"Explain," Abby said.

By now, the women had moved into the steam room and they were alone. "When I first met him, he hid all his emotions from everyone. But I could still read him. His body language gave him away. As we got to know each other better, he learned to trust me and showed more emotion to me."

Meg's eyelids widened, and Fiona smiled. "He even talked about his feelings to me. But then his mother died, and his father arrived, and of course, things changed."

The women nodded.

"I expected it. I told him it was okay, and I helped him through it. I have no expectations he'll jump back to normal. But he's getting worse. And I think it has to do with me."

"Why?" Abby asked.

"Because I know he still is attracted to me. He shows me whenever we're together."

"No kidding," Meg said, laughing. "You'd have to

be blind, deaf, and dead not to notice."

The steam room got even hotter, and Fiona ducked her head. "Yeah, well, anyway. He's trying to fight it, though. Maybe not the attraction, but the intimacy. It's like he knows his body is reacting, but he's trying to keep his heart out of it, and I have no idea why or how to fight it. I keep trying to be patient but there's only so long I can last."

"Have you talked to him?" Abby asked.

"We're rarely alone, but every time I try, he finds a reason to avoid conversation."

"So, wait until this weekend is over," Abby said. "You'll have an entire flight home. Talk to him then."

"I tried to talk to him on the flight here, but he buried himself in work."

"Don't let him," Meg said. "These guys are super successful for a reason. They could spend twenty-four hours a day working if we let them. If you need to talk to him, pull him away and make him talk."

"You're right."

"I said it before, but I think the two of you are terrific together," said Meg. "The change I've seen in Caleb is amazing, even if he's less expressive than you'd like."

"I know, and I appreciate it. I'm glad you see it, but I just wish...I don't know. I miss the old Caleb."

"Give him time," Abby said. "Ted had a hard time trusting me when we were first seeing each other. I had to remind him often I wasn't what he expected."

"Simon too," Meg said. "Believe me. The hurdle was hard to climb. But it's worth it now."

The two women nodded.

As they dressed and chose their polish colors,

Fiona stared at her two new friends. They could have backed Caleb and told her she was crazy. After all, they knew him better than her. And she could be considered disloyal for complaining. But they'd jumped to her assistance and encouraged her. Her insides warmed at this budding friendship. And she planned to follow their advice. The plane ride home would solve everything.

Chapter Twenty-two

That night, the three couples and Alex sat for dinner in Alex's dining room. Separated from the front entryway by dark wood vertical slats, Caleb could see through the rest of the house to the patio and canal. A glass-orbed chandelier provided lighting bright enough to accommodate Ted's need to read lips. The dark table was set with beautiful modern china and silver flatware, and the upholstered club chairs were comfortable. And the meal? It was fantastic. A variety of local seafood, fresh vegetables, and rice made Caleb's mouth water. The wine flowed and conversation sparkled. It should have been perfect.

When the table was cleared, Simon got a funny look on his face and stood. He cleared his throat. "May I have everyone's attention?"

The table quieted and Caleb joined everyone, turning toward Simon, and giving him his full attention.

"As most of you know, I've spent a large portion of my life alone. I've focused on developing my career, pursuing one of my passions and convinced myself my life was complete. But deep inside, I knew I was wrong."

Fiona's hand slid onto Caleb's leg and squeezed. He covered it with his own and listened to Simon.

"When Meg arrived, I fought against her attempts to bring me into the land of the living, as she likes to

295

say. After way more prodding than one man as intelligent as I am supposed to be should need—" The table erupted into laughter, and Simon waited for them to quiet. "—I listened to her."

Simon turned to Meg, and Fiona started tapping Caleb's leg. Caleb frowned.

"Meg, I love you. I love you so much, I can't imagine my life without you. Those few weeks apart almost killed me." His voice cracked, and he cleared his throat before continuing. "I know proposals are supposed to be done in private, but I've lived my life in private, and I learned from you the benefits of coming into the surrounding warmth of friends and family. So, this is the perfect place, and the perfect time, to ask you to please be my wife."

Caleb's chest constricted. He looked around the table. All the women's eyes were glassy with tears. Meg rose and faced Simon. Taking his face in her hands, she kissed him.

"Yes," she said. "Yes, Simon, I will marry you."

The room cheered. Simon slipped the ring on her finger—both of their hands shook so much, Caleb waited for the ring to slip from his grasp and skitter across the floor. But it slid onto her finger without mishap.

Caleb rose along with Alex and Ted and patted Simon on the back.

"Congratulations, Si," he said.

Others echoed his comment. The women hugged each other and exclaimed over the ring.

"It's beautiful," Fiona said.

Meg nodded. "Simon, I love it."

"The sapphire is to match your eyes," he said.

Caleb glanced at the engagement ring—a large sapphire surrounded by diamonds. He watched in awe as they showed their love for each other, seeming to not care about others. The idea of revealing that much emotion, even to his friends, made him uncomfortable.

From the corner of the living room, where he'd retreated after dinner, Caleb watched Ted and Abby. They hadn't been dating as long as Simon and Meg, but they'd been together longer than he and Fiona. Even they were swept up in the moment, holding hands and snuggling together.

He and Fiona sat on the sofa facing the electric fireplace. Their legs touched. He was in the corner, one arm on the armrest, the other behind Fiona's shoulders, extended along the sofa. But he wasn't touching her. He didn't play with her hair, or squeeze her shoulders, or stroke her upper arm. He sat. Fiona talked with everyone, seeming not to pay attention to how close they were. But she left an inch of space between her leg and his. Her hand rested on her lap, but it would be easy enough for him to touch her. It almost asked for him to do it. But she made no move toward him and neither did he. She'd drawn a line between them and dared him to cross it.

He didn't. He didn't even try.

Simon and Meg said their goodnights, followed by Ted and Abby. Fiona rose. "Coming?"

If he went with her now, there would be conversations about the engagement. It would lead to talks about their relationship. And it would lead to emotions he didn't want to feel, much less express. The only way to protect Fiona was to end his relationship with her. And he couldn't do it here. He shook his head.

"Not right now."

A fleeting look of disappointment crossed her face before she hid it with a fake smile. His stomach hurt. Had he taught her to do that? She gave him a kiss. "Okay, enjoy yourself." With a wave at Alex, she left the room.

"Join me for a cigar?" Alex asked, pointing outside.

"I won't smoke one, but I'll go with you."

He followed his friend outside and sat in one of the sofas in the enclosed patio. Silent, he stared at the series of infinity pools, each lit a different color—purple, blue, pink, and white.

"Trouble in paradise?" Alex asked.

"What do you mean?"

"You and Fiona. I thought you were happy together."

"We were."

"Were?" Alex asked. "As in past tense? What's wrong?"

"I don't see us having a future together."

****

Fiona reeled away from the balcony rail in shock. She covered her mouth to keep from making any noise. Caleb didn't see them having a future together. She supposed this was the penalty for eavesdropping. And for being a coward.

She hugged herself, halfway between the door and the balcony. Should she go inside and pretend she hadn't heard what he said? Or stay and listen more. She couldn't make herself go inside, so she returned to the railing.

Caleb was talking. "…going to work. I've tried, but

I just don't see it happening."

Fiona squeezed the square metal railing.

"Why not?" Alex asked. "Fiona is fantastic."

"She wants more than I can give."

Puffs of cigar smoke wafted her way, and Fiona had to fight the urge not to gag. Or maybe because her entire life had turned upside down. Either way, she clenched her teeth and swallowed. This wasn't happening.

"Has she told you?"

"Doesn't matter what she tells me or doesn't. She's the 'wear-your-heart-on-your-sleeve' type of woman, and I'm not. It shouldn't have lasted this long, anyway."

Adam chuckled. "I hear you. My policy is no more than six weeks." He paused and Fiona smelled another whiff of cigar smoke. "But I thought you'd settle down."

"I can't afford the responsibility. I've taken care of my mother and sister all my life. My mom is gone, and my sister is married. I can't do this again."

This time, Fiona couldn't hold back a gasp, and she raced into the bedroom. She was a burden. He never planned to have a long-term relationship with her. She tore her clothes off, her skin feeling as if it were on fire. Grabbing her suitcase, she considered packing and leaving, except it was late, and she didn't have transportation. Instead, she put her suitcase back, pulled pajamas from her drawer, and climbed into bed.

She deserved this because listening in on other people's conversations was wrong. If she hadn't been such a coward, she would have forced him to have this conversation earlier. They could have talked about their relationship before they left for this trip, or even on the airplane over here. Instead, she'd pushed it off, telling herself she let him heal from the loss of his mom, when she feared rocking the boat. Even last night, she could have propped her eyelids open and made him talk.

Their bedroom door opened, and she pretended to be asleep. Caleb paused before tiptoeing and getting ready for bed. The bed rocked as he climbed in, and she lay still, hoping he'd think she slept. He turned over and released a deep sigh.

Her heart squeezed, wishing he'd draw her into his arms and tell her a funny story about how he'd lied to Alex to save face. It wouldn't be funny, but she'd forget it when he declared his undying love for her, enabling her to make him spend the rest of his life atoning for the not-funny story. But it would never happen. Nor was Caleb the type of friend who would lie to save face.

Now she knew his true feelings, it was time to leave this mess with as much dignity as possible. It meant not making a scene for the remainder of the weekend. She'd pretend to have fun, pretend to love being here. She'd be an actress, like her idol, Barbara Morí. She'd give the performance of a lifetime. And when they left this place, she'd tell Caleb it was over.

****

Caleb sighed with relief as the sun rose on their last day in Florida. He loved visiting Alex. He always had a great time, and his friends were fantastic. But he had to get Fiona away from here. He suspected she knew. He didn't know how, but he could tell she wasn't herself.

No one else recognized the fake smile she wore to breakfast on the cabana patio. No one else knew the laps she swam were to burn off…something—anger, hurt, embarrassment? She'd jumped at the chance to go shopping with the ladies in Miami for a couple of hours to get away from him. And no one else could feel how stiff she sat next to him as they had a last BBQ before they left for the airport.

But he knew. And he hated himself for making her miserable.

"You have the most gorgeous location, Alex." She bit into a piece of swordfish kebab.

"Thanks. I'm thinking of selling it."

"Why?"

Ted laughed. "Alex always sells his houses soon after renovating them. No matter how much the rest of us beg him not to."

Alex looked uncomfortable and Caleb wondered if maybe this lifestyle of his, always temporary, was wearing on him.

"Well, someone will be very lucky to live here." She took her plate of food and walked toward the edge of the patio, staring at the water.

Caleb wanted to apologize. But this was for the best. And he suspected she left to center herself, to get a break from having to pretend nothing was wrong.

"Anyone want a last swim before we leave?" Simon asked as he and Meg dove into the water.

Caleb wasn't surprised when Ted refused—he wasn't a fan of being unable to hear around people— but what did surprise him was when Abby pulled him aside and changed his mind. The two couples enjoyed the pool, while he, Alex and Fiona remained on the patio.

Fiona returned with her empty plate. "As much as I'd like to join you all, I think I need to pack. We're leaving at three, right, Caleb?"

Caleb nodded. "Need help?"

She gave him her fake smile, the one he hated. "Nope, you stay here and enjoy your friends. I'll be fine." She waved to everyone and returned to the main house.

Alex gave him a look, but Caleb didn't want to deal right now. "You know what, I think I'll swim." He shucked his shirt and dove into the deep end of the pool, disappearing beneath the water where none of his cares could follow him. He swam the length of the pool without coming up for air. By the time he reached the wall, his lungs were about to burst, and he shot from the water, gasping.

"You look like Poseidon," Abby said, and everyone laughed.

Deciding to have a little fun, he dove under the water to where Abby stood in the shallow end. She was tiny, it was the only place she could stand and not drown. He lifted her in his arms and threw her into the deep end, laughing at her shriek. She spluttered to the surface and chased him through the water. She might not be able to stand in the pool, but she could swim. After she got in a few well-aimed, soaking splashes, she returned to Ted's side and Caleb climbed from the pool.

"I'm going to get dry and dressed. I'll see you all again before we leave."

He wasn't looking forward to facing Fiona, but there was no way for him to leave without packing. Gritting his teeth, he returned to their bedroom.

It was empty.

Chapter Twenty-Three

As Alex's gorgeous house retreated into the distance, Fiona leaned back in the taxi, eyes filled with tears. She was a coward. She'd left without saying goodbye. She hadn't thanked Alex for being an amazing host. She hadn't wished Simon and Meg well or told Ted and Abby how much she enjoyed meeting them.

She'd left a note for Caleb.

For a writer, it was a lame note. For someone big on emotion, it lacked any. For an adult, it was childish.

We both know this isn't working. I can't force what you can't give. Goodbye.

But it was the best she could do. She was hurt, angry, and embarrassed. Prolonging her time with Caleb wasn't doing anything. Better to tear off the Band-Aid than drag the pain on forever.

It didn't make it any easier, though.

"Which terminal, miss?"

She had no idea. She didn't have a reservation. "Whichever one serves domestic flights," she said, forcing the words past her aching throat.

The taxi driver frowned, his face wrinkling in the rearview mirror, and stopped at the first terminal he came to. He helped her with her bag and deposited it on the sidewalk. With a backward glance—maybe to make sure she wasn't going to crumple to the ground—he pulled away.

Two hours later, after booking a flight, changing terminals, checking in, checking her bag, and going through security, she sat at the gate. Her flight didn't leave for another three hours, and she spent the time watching other flights take off and land, studying the people around her and trying not to think about Caleb. She wasn't successful.

Every goodbye she witnessed made her think of leaving him. Except the goodbyes were bittersweet. The people were teary. They hugged each other tight. They called across the room to have a safe flight, to call when they landed and to say how much they loved each other.

It's what she wanted, and Caleb would never be able to give those words.

Smiling faces or fearful fliers filled every arrival. There were occasional reunions at the gate, and those were even more emotional than the goodbyes. Most of them involved children, and it made Fiona stop short. She didn't want children who would be afraid to show their emotions or wonder if their father loved them. She wasn't planning on having children right now, but someday, she wanted them. At least one of each, and maybe more. But if Caleb were their father, would he hide his emotions from them too? And worse, would he teach them to hide their own?

She shook her head as she boarded her flight.

She spent the flight watching a movie, a love story. The hero and heroine showed their feelings for each other, even when they were angry or didn't think they liked each other. And when the credits rolled, Fiona wiped her cheeks, wet with tears, as the hero declared his undying love. It was what she wanted. She wanted a man to sweep her off her feet. Someone who would show his emotions and accept hers as well. And it wasn't Caleb.

When the plane landed, she flagged a taxi from the taxi lane and stared out the window on the way to her apartment. The ocean looked different here. She winced when they passed where Caleb had taken her for clams. And again when they turned onto the street where they'd gone to dinner. Would every place remind her of him?

She unlocked the door to her apartment, and Lexie called to her just as she was about to enter. "Hey! How was Florida? You're early."

She couldn't do this. Not now. Not with Lexie. She plastered on what she hoped was a smile and said over her shoulder. "Good. But I'm tired. I'll talk to you later." Before Lexie had a chance to answer, Fiona closed her door.

Her colorful apartment greeted her. From the curtains to the paint to the pillows to the furniture, everything was colorful and vibrant and alive. It always made her feel cheerful. But right now, the colors gave her a headache. Dragging herself into her bedroom, she collapsed onto the bed, and went to sleep.

The next morning, she awoke where she'd collapsed. Her apartment was silent—no pounding on the door from a man begging her to take her back. She checked her phone—no text messages or voice mails begging her to give him another chance. Silence.

He didn't even care enough about her to ask why she'd left or to suggest they talk. She was done.

****

Caleb walked into his office, dropped his briefcase

on the credenza, and sank into his chair. Opening his desk drawer, he grabbed a bottle of painkillers and tossed two pills back, followed by a swig from the chilled water bottle his secretary always had waiting for him each morning. For the twenty-fifth time since Fiona left him yesterday, he resolved to remove her from his mind. Today, he planned to focus on his work.

He tried. He made a huge effort. In fact, if someone were going to illustrate how much of an effort he made, it would include a cartoon of a pulley and winch system. Or maybe show him growing huge muscles and tearing his clothes to shreds. Because every time his mind slid to Fiona—while he reviewed the performance of his Internet holdings, or looked out the window at the beach and remembered their last time there, or ate lunch in between meetings and remembered how she'd moan over the taste of her food—hell, even knowing she shared the same oxygen—he could not escape her memory.

The more he thought about her, the more positive he was right to have pushed her away, no matter how much his chest ached. It was the only way he could protect her and himself.

But he couldn't get past how she'd left him, without saying a word. The woman who always had something to say, whose emotions hung for all to see, had nothing to say to him.

When he stopped in the middle of the afternoon, his secretary popped her head in. "Your sister has called four times today. Can you please call her, so I don't have to deal with her anymore?"

"Lexie?" he asked when she answered her phone. "What's wrong?"

"I have a sneaking suspicion my brother is an idiot and I needed to confirm I was wrong."

What the hell? "What are you talking about?"

"I saw Fiona last night."

The sound of her name sent a spike through his heart. "So?"

"So, she said the trip was good."

She did? "And?"

"What happened?"

"Why would you think something happened," he asked.

"Because Fiona never says something is good. She goes into detail with me about why and how and what could have made it better. If she says something is just 'good,' it means something went wrong. So what did you do?"

"Why would you think I did anything?"

"Then tell me you didn't."

"She's the one who left early. I didn't."

"Wait a minute. She left? As in, without you? And you didn't stop her? Caleb what did you do?"

The last sentence erupted into a wail. Caleb held the phone away from his eardrum. He grabbed his stress ball and squeezed with all his might. When she finished, he spoke. "Nothing."

The sigh she gave sounded as if it came from her toes. "Caleb, why? Don't you care about Fiona?"

"Feelings don't matter, Lexie. It never would have worked between us. I can't give her what she needs and I won't run the risk of hurting her."

When Lexie sounded as if she were going to argue, he cut her off. "Leave it be, Lex."

This time she didn't give in. "We're not done,

Caleb. I'm sorry. I may not be able to prevent you from ruining your life—I think only a shrink can do that—but Fiona is my friend. She deserves better."

Blood rushed to his head. A shrink? He squeezed the stress ball so hard it popped. The outer rubber shell split and the foam inside spilled. He'd always wondered what was inside one of them. Now he knew. Frustrated, he threw it into the trashcan. "You're right. She does. And I'm not the one to give it to her."

"Are you sure? Because you two are perfect together."

"There's no such thing as perfect." And even if there were, he'd never have it.

Lexie backed down. "I'm not leaving this alone, Caleb. I'll give you a break for now. But I've never been so disappointed in you before."

He stared at the phone. She'd hung up on him. He shook his head. It didn't matter.

****

When Fiona came home from work that evening, she once again ran into Lexie. And this time, she couldn't avoid her. Without a word, she walked into Lexie's apartment, swallowing her feelings as she'd been doing all day.

"I told my brother he was an idiot."

"Ha!" The sound burst from Fiona's lips. Her gaze filled, and she blinked.

Lexie squeezed her hand. "He is."

"Why did you tell him?"

"Because he broke up with you and only an idiot would do so."

"I appreciate the loyalty, but he didn't break up with me."

"You broke up with him?"

Fiona shook her head before dropping it into her hands. "No, not exactly. But I left him." She told her what happened in Florida. "I know I shouldn't have eavesdropped, but I know what he said, and I can't go back. I'm sorry. I know he's your brother—"

Lexie stopped her with a hand on her arm. "You're one hundred percent right. I can't fault you for what you did. And you're my friend, so I'm not going to drop you just because you and my brother are no longer together. It would be stupid. There is only one Zeno family member who is stupid, and it's not me. We'll just have to be more creative in how we get together."

She hugged Fiona, and Fiona swallowed the rest of the threatened tears. She could only confess so much to the sister of her ex-boyfriend, even if the sister was one of her best friends.

"So, what are you going to do now?" Lexie asked. "You can't just hide in your apartment pining for my brother."

Fiona gave a hollow laugh. "No, I won't. In case you missed it, I have a company to run."

"You can't bury yourself in work. It's not healthy."

It might not be healthy, but it would keep her busy. "I've neglected it with the traveling. I'm not burying myself. I've always been independent."

Lexie pursed her lips, folded her arms, and tapped her foot, transforming Fiona into a cell under a microscope. Finally, Lexie relaxed. "Okay, but you and I are going shopping this weekend. There's nothing like a little retail therapy to mend a broken heart."

She doubted it would help, but she said yes anyway.

By the time the weekend arrived, Fiona had progressed from sad to angry. She'd spent the week working. And in between, she'd recalled Caleb's actions and her reactions. When she met Lexie, she was sputtering.

"I can't decide who I'm angrier at, your brother or myself."

"Well, there's a good sign."

Fiona pulled away as they stood in line waiting for coffee. "Why?"

"Because anger spurs people on to do something." She turned to the barista behind the counter. "I'll have an iced coffee with milk."

"I guess so, but it wasn't the reaction I expected."

"What did you expect?" She added sugar to her coffee, and they went outside, walking along the street to the shopping area.

"I figured you'd be upset that I'm mad at your brother."

"I told you I wouldn't be. So tell me why you're angry."

Fiona stared at a blue and white dress in a shop window. "I'm angry at him for not changing—or for starting to change and then regressing. Which is stupid. People don't change. And I'm angry at myself for pushing my own desires aside to accommodate him. It was so one-sided. And now I'm angry because I'm ignoring how you might feel because of your mom. Ugh, I'm a terrible friend."

Lexie hugged her and they went inside to look at the dresses. "You're not a terrible friend. I'm sad. I miss her so much. But Steve's been a rock, and I'll be okay."

They tried on a few different ones, and Fiona purchased the one she'd admired in the window. Leaving the store, they continued on their way.

"As for you being so accommodating," Lexie said, "it's one of the things that makes you a great friend. It's wonderful when someone looks out for you." She stopped and admired a leather purse in the window. "Let's go in."

The store had a yummy leather smell, and Fiona inhaled. Her tension slipped away. She wandered around the displays of clutches, shoulder bags, and business cases before examining the leather accessories.

"I should buy a tablet case for Patricia," she said, fingering a pink one. "Pink is her favorite color. What do you think?"

Lexie came over. "It's pretty. I'm sure she'll love it."

They made their purchases and left the store.

"As I said, being accommodating makes you a great friend," Lexie said. "So, don't hate yourself for it. You've never been one to let yourself be a doormat. Were you one with my brother? Because I never saw it, maybe what I saw was the exception."

Fiona paused. "I think I became more accommodating as our relationship progressed. And somewhere along the way, I lost myself and my need for independence."

"And my brother? How did he handle it?"

"He didn't. It was like he did things for me because he was obligated. It was one-sided, even though I was involved. Like he followed a script with his head, while his heart wasn't involved at all."

Lexie nodded. "That's what he does when he's

threatened."

"Threatened? By whom? Certainly not me?"

"I don't know. I don't have an answer. But you shouldn't berate yourself."

Chapter Twenty-four

Caleb stood on his roof studying the stars. They twinkled above but unlike usual, they provided no joy. If anything, they appeared dull. Which was weird, since it was a clear, cool night, perfect for stargazing.

Everything in his life was bland. He'd been numb, going through the motions since Fiona left. He'd hoped he'd adjust to life as it used to be, but it hadn't happened.

"Caleb?"

He turned and his heart raced. "Lexie. What's wrong?"

She walked toward him. "Can't I stop by and visit my brother without something being wrong?"

He glanced behind her. "Where's Steve?"

"Home."

"You shouldn't be alone."

She sputtered. "Are you serious? I'm a grown woman."

He clenched his hands into fists.

Her features softened and she touched his shoulder. "I think it's time you stopped treating me like I'm incapable of taking care of myself."

He swallowed. "It's my job to protect you."

"I don't need to be protected, Caleb. We're safe now."

Caleb shook his head and looked over the balcony.

"No, you're not. He came to the funeral. He can come after you anytime."

She joined him, her hands resting on the railing, the diamond in her ring winking like the stars above. "I'm an adult, now. And while I'll never be comfortable around the man, I'm not the frightened child I was. I handled him fine."

Caleb wracked his brain to remember what Lexie did at the viewing when their father arrived, but his mind drew a blank. He'd been focused on his own grief and on protecting Fiona. Had he failed Lexie? His heart thundered in his chest.

"Hey," Lexie said, grabbing his arm. "What's going on with you?"

"What did he do to you?"

"Nothing. He walked over to me after he confronted you, and I told him I had no interest in talking. Steve was with me, but Dad didn't do anything." She laughed. "I think my calmness threw him. He walked away. Of course, I fell apart afterward, but he didn't see it."

He glanced at her face. She looked at him, concern etched into her features. "I handled him, Caleb. He can no longer hurt me. You don't need to worry."

Caleb squeezed her hand. "I'm sorry I wasn't there for you, but I'm glad you were able to handle it on your own."

She hugged him, and the strength emanating from her surprised him. Had it always been there? Pulling away, she met his gaze. "You are not responsible for everyone around you, Caleb. We can take care of ourselves. You don't need the weight on your shoulders."

He shrugged. "I take care of the people I love."

"Including Fiona?"

His breath hitched. "We're not together anymore."

"I know. But you love her."

Lexie didn't question it and didn't seem surprised. Did he love her?

"It wasn't a question, Caleb. I know you do, even if you're afraid to admit it. It's in the way you look at her, how you act around her, what you do. You must let yourself believe it."

"What's the point? Like I said, we're not together. It's safer for her if we aren't."

"Safer for her or for you?"

He glared. "What are you talking about?"

"Why did you push her away?"

"Because Dad came back and showed interest in her. I needed to protect her from him because—"

"—because you love her."

He loved her. He let the idea roll around his head. He loved her. It made him want to laugh. He'd figured it out, and she was gone.

"It's not too late to get her back," Lexie said, her voice soft.

Since when had she become a mind reader? "Yeah, it is."

His sister sighed. "You know, Dad ruined a lot of things for us. I hate how he ruined this for you." She pulled him into a hug. When she let go, she met his gaze. "I know what you sacrificed to protect me. I can never repay you, but I can tell you this. I'm okay. And you deserve to be happy."

Caleb watched her leave, unable to react. What he'd done for Lexie had never been a secret, but this was the first time she'd talked about it. He didn't know how to respond to her, much less how to go about making himself happy. Fiona made him happy, but she was gone now. And without her…

Frustrated, he put his telescope away. Tomorrow he planned to go to the shelter, to see the progress being made with the CAST investment. He needed to focus on work. Because no matter what state his personal life, business always made him feel better.

It didn't. As Melanie welcomed him with a huge smile at the front door of the shelter, he opened his mouth to speak but no words emerged. Instead, he nodded. Her smile dimmed.

"Welcome, Caleb. Come on in. Wait, don't." She held out her hand. "I want to show you the new security system we have in place. When I close the door, ring the buzzer."

He waited until the front door clicked shut, then pressed the metal buzzer next to the front door. A video screen turned on, and Melanie appeared at her desk.

"Hello! Isn't it great?"

"It is."

"Hold on, I'll come and let you in now."

She opened the door. "Now I can see who is outside before I open the door. It's fantastic, and makes our residents feel so safe. Thank you."

He nodded. "You're welcome."

"Let me show you what else we're doing." She led him inside, where the walls of the foyer and hallway were stripped of the old wallpaper and the drywall was plastered. "The only thing left is paint," she said, pointing to color swatches on the wall. "Any preference?"

"Whatever you and the other women like. It's yours." He didn't care about paint. He always preferred white, but lately, the white walls he lived with looked gray. Maybe they were dirty. The color swatches she had on the wall—pale yellow, pale blue and a pale peach—were fine, but didn't do anything for him.

She showed him the cosmetic changes in the downstairs rooms. In addition to newly painted walls and brand new, matching furniture, there were new appliances in the modernized kitchen, new gym equipment in the gym area, and lots of other items Melanie gushed over. Caleb barely noticed. But she was happy, which meant the women who needed this shelter were happy.

They passed the common room, and Marcus peeked from the doorway. His face glowed. "Caleb! Did you come to play with me?"

Caleb kneeled and held out his arms. The little boy rushed into them and squeezed his tiny arms around his neck in a hug. Tears pricked Caleb's eyelids. This was the first time someone other than his sister had touched him since Fiona left. He'd missed the warmth. Setting Marcus on his feet, he tousled his blond hair. "I'd love to play with you."

Marcus grabbed his hand and pulled him into the common room. With a backward glance of apology at Melanie, he followed him, sat on the floor, and played with the trucks Marcus zoomed around his feet. The boy's laughter warmed his heart and again, for the first time since Fiona, a spark of joy ignited. After a few minutes of play, Caleb rose.

"I've got to finish with Melanie, Marcus. I'll play with you again another time, okay?"

Marcus gave him another hug. "Okay. I love you, Caleb."

Caleb froze. "I love you, too," he said, his voice no more than a whisper.

He finished his meeting with Melanie on automatic pilot and rushed home. Marcus loved him. How? His mother had been brutalized by his father, right in front of him. By all rights, the kid should be terrified of male adults. But after taking time to get to know Caleb, he loved him.

Had the little boy learned nothing? He needed to protect himself for the future. Sure, Caleb would never harm him, but others might. Marcus needed to be on his guard. Next time he went to the shelter, he'd talk to Melanie about his concerns and see if he could help Marcus protect himself.

****

When Fiona opened her email at work the next day, her heart rate increased at the sight of a message from Abby.

Hey, so, I'm going to be in town next week. Are you free for lunch?

Abby

She hadn't talked to Abby and Meg in weeks, not since she'd left without saying goodbye. What could Abby want?

To yell at me? Her message was cryptic. Why would Abby want to get together with her? She rose from her desk and paced the room before sinking once again into her desk chair and typing a response.

Hi, I'd love to get together for lunch. Name a day and time, and I'll pick a place.

Fiona

They emailed a few times, sticking to logistics for lunch and not mentioning either Caleb or Florida. She wondered if Abby had been put up to this by anyone. She wondered if Caleb knew about it. She wondered why Abby wanted to see her in the first place. By the time their lunch date rolled around, Fiona was a pile of nerves and didn't think she'd be able to eat, even though she'd picked her favorite sushi place.

She walked into the small Japanese restaurant at noon that Friday and scanned the room for Abby. Not seeing her, she chose a seat facing the front door and waited. Five minutes later, Abby rushed in, her straight hair swinging in a ponytail.

"So sorry I'm late. Traffic was brutal. How are you?"

Abby hugged her, and Fiona gave her a wide smile. "It is so good to see you." She sobered. "I'm glad you contacted me. I owe you an apology. It was rude of me to leave without saying goodbye to you and Meg, as well as everyone else. I was upset with Caleb, but it doesn't excuse my behavior to you. I hope you'll forgive me."

Abby grinned. "Men suck."

Fiona bit her lip. "I'm not sure how to respond."

"Well, would it make it easier for you if I told you after Ted and I had sex for the first time, he fired me and had me arrested?"

The water Fiona had sipped made her choke. Abby rushed around the table and patted Fiona's back until she calmed. "You have to tell me this story."

"One day I will. Right now, though, I think we should get to know each other better."

Fiona ran her finger along the edge of the

laminated menu. She'd already picked her sushi—this was a place she frequented, and she often ordered the same thing when she ate here with friends. Since she didn't need to think about what to eat, her mind wandered to other things, like why Abby pushed this friendship. The last time she'd featured something on relationships on her website, the key had been honesty. Well, friendships were relationships, and there was no time like the present.

"I don't quite know how to say this so it doesn't come out wrong, but why, if I'm not with Caleb, are you so eager to be my friend?"

The waitress took their order before Abby responded. "Wow, you're blunt, aren't you?"

"Just honest. You want to get to know me, which is great, because I'd like to get to know you as well, but I'm curious about the timing and maybe the motive. I'm sorry. I don't mean to offend you."

"Actually," Abby said, "you don't." She fiddled with the chopsticks wrapped in paper. "I liked you when I met you in Florida. We're not far from each other, and I look forward to spending more time with you."

"I'd like it, but don't you think it will be awkward?"

"Why? Do you have an issue with Ted? Because he's where my loyalty lies. I don't care who you're dating or not."

She liked Abby. She had backbone and spoke her mind. "I think we could be great friends."

Abby nodded and dug into her plate of sushi. "Good, now tell me about this website of yours."

For the rest of lunch, she and Abby talked about

her lifestyle website. Abby, being a computer programmer, was more interested in how the site worked rather than what it provided for her clients, and Fiona did her best to answer the questions.

"You're getting a little beyond my technical abilities," Fiona said.

"Sorry, occupational hazard."

"I'd love to talk to you about a feature I'm considering for a few months from now. Women's empowerment."

Abby's gaze brightened.

"I'd like to talk to women in non-traditional jobs, or in jobs where there have been fewer women in the past. How you became interested in your field, how you got where you are today, what advice you'd give women and what kind of role mentoring can play. Would you be willing to talk to me about it?"

"I'd love to. I'm assuming you're looking at areas other than just computers, though, right?"

Fiona nodded. "Yes. A woman I know who runs a shelter for abused women and their children put me in touch with a woman who provides bodyguard services, and that woman is looking into other contacts for me."

"Is this the same shelter CAST is investing in?"

"Yeah."

"It's one of the things I love about the guys. They care and they use their money to show it."

Fiona shifted in her seat. Caleb might care, but not about her. "It's a worthy thing they do."

"Back to your website, if you ever need assistance with cyber security, let me know."

"Thanks, I appreciate it."

Abby looked at her over the rim of her water glass.

"You know he's miserable, right?"

Fiona glared. "And why should I care again?"

"I just know what I hear from Ted."

"Caleb's been talking to Ted?"

"In a matter of speaking."

Her confusion must have shown on her face because Abby laughed and explained. "He's hard of hearing, which makes him good at reading body language. Way too good."

Fiona laughed.

"Anyway, when Caleb realized you were gone and then again during their video chats, well, Ted can tell Caleb is hurting. He'll never admit it, but according to Ted, anyone with sight can see it."

They paid the check and walked outside. "Look," said Fiona. "I'm sorry he's miserable, but I'm not much happier to be honest. I don't want him knowing about me. But I don't see him being happy with anyone if he keeps everyone at a distance."

"You're right. I agree with you. I thought knowing he is, though, might make you feel better."

"I hate to see anyone unhappy." Fiona gave Abby a hug. "I'm glad you suggested this. I'd love to do it again soon."

"Me too."

Abby walked away. Fiona might have lost a boyfriend, but she'd gained a friend.

****

Caleb called Melanie the next day. "Hi, I wanted to talk to you about an issue I saw when I was at your shelter the other day. Do you have time now?"

"Sure," she said. "Is something wrong?"

"Not wrong, but there's something I wanted to

bring to your attention."

"I'm listening."

He leaned in his chair and looked out his office window at the beach below. "I don't think I can continue volunteering at your shelter."

When Melanie protested, he interrupted her. "Oh, CAST is still supporting you, don't worry. But I think I should back off the volunteering for a while."

"May I ask why?"

"You know the little boy, Marcus?"

"Yes. He adores you."

"Exactly. He's grown attached to me. To protect himself, he needs to be able to erect walls, to keep himself safe from those who might harm him."

"And you would harm him?"

Caleb slammed his hand on the chair. "Never!"

"Then I'm sorry, Caleb, but I'm confused."

He rubbed his hand across the top of his head. The motion reminded him of Fiona. He clenched his fist. "I would never hurt anyone, much less a child, but he's going to get hurt if he forms attachments to people who are going to leave. He's a child, he doesn't know any better, but he needs to be protected."

"Caleb."

He had to strain to hear her whisper.

"Forming these attachments is why we have this program in the first place. Don't you remember when you first came, and I described it to you?"

He did, but somehow hearing about it and seeing it were different things. He'd never realized how painful it could be.

She cleared her throat and continued. "We want him, and others like him, to learn not everyone is going to hurt them. Sure, it will be sad when the person is no longer there, but it's a normal part of life, and it means they formed a positive attachment while they were there. It's a good thing."

"But I don't want to hurt him."

"You're not, in any meaningful way. The benefits he and the other children get far outweigh the detriments."

He squeezed his new stress ball. Was she right? "How do you know?" His voice was raw, and it took effort to speak.

"Caleb, you're going to have to trust me on this. I want you to continue to volunteer with our kids if you can. Please."

He blinked. "Okay."

"And I'm going to email you a name I think you should contact."

He ended the phone call and opened his email. Melanie had provided him with the name of a therapist.

A therapist? Why the hell did she think he needed a therapist? He shut his email and pushed away from his desk. This was the second time someone had suggested he see one.

They were crazy.

Chapter Twenty-Five

Fiona stood in the green room of the TV station waiting for her turn to sit with the morning show host. They were taping a holiday special, and Fiona would speak about the hottest restaurants to celebrate with family and friends. She paced the room, running her hands over her hair to make sure no random strand was out of place. Outside, the leaves on the trees were mostly brown by now, indicating cooler temps, even in California. She looked in the mirror they provided. Her teal wool suit with black trim made her look serious, but pretty and gave her skin a glow. Red lipstick, a hint of blush and she was ready to go on.

"Fiona, we're ready for you now."

"Thanks." With a smile, she followed the production assistant from the green room into the studio. She stepped over wires and sat on the beige sofa they directed her to, where they miked her, and a makeup artist gave her a quick pat of powder.

"You ready?" the host asked.

When she nodded, they counted down, the spotlights turned on and the host began speaking.

"My guest today is Fiona Hamilton, host of the popular lifestyle website Love, Laugh, Live. With guest reviews, great topics like relationships, gift ideas and women's empowerment, it's easy to see why she generates more than fifty thousand hits per day. She's here to talk about the best restaurants for holiday celebrations."

"Thanks for hosting me, Dana. I'm happy to be here."

"So, the holidays are approaching and that means getting together with family and friends. But it doesn't always have to be cooking for a crowd, does it?"

Fiona shook her head. "No. In fact, quite often, while the main holiday day might be celebrated at home, families and friends gather before and after at restaurants to enjoy each other's company without the stress of having to cook. And several in the area are foodie favorites."

She paused while they flashed the restaurants on the screen.

"Do you have a particular one you enjoy, Fiona?"

"Well, I've been to all of these and love them for different reasons. However, my clients have been raving about The Olive & The Dove. Its Mediterranean food is unique and divine."

"And will you be celebrating your holidays there with someone special?"

The question threw her for a loop. Should she fake an answer? She looked at the camera and winked. "Happy Holidays everyone!"

When the camera cut away, Fiona deflated in relief. She hadn't expected the line of questioning. Her "someone special" was non-existent, and she had no idea what she'd be doing for the holidays. This interview focused on promoting her business.

Thanking the host, she left the building, calling Patricia on her way from the building.

"How'd it go?" Patricia asked, before Fiona even

had a chance to say hello.

"Good morning to you, too. It went well, I think. Until she asked me about my personal life."

"She did what?"

Fiona filled her in on her last question.

"How did you respond?"

She pulled into her parking spot and rode the elevator to her apartment. "I didn't. It's fine. I should have been prepared. But regardless, I think it'll be a good spot for the holidays. I also think it will encourage other businesses to work with us, which is the second goal."

Kicking off her shoes, she disconnected her call and sank onto the sofa. Life exhausted her these days. Or, as it said on the Internet, adulting was hard. She had no appetite, slept little, and put all her energy into work. Still, things took her twice as long to do as they should. Dating a man for such a short time shouldn't affect her as much as it had. Prior to Caleb, she'd never had a problem being independent. Now? She missed him. She shook her head. She no longer wasted time pining over him. Life was meant to be lived and enjoyed.

Energized, she called Lexie and a few other women and arranged for a girls' night out the next evening. She was getting back into the game.

****

Caleb threw his remote control across the room. It hit the floor, the cover broke off, and all the pieces slid beneath the sofa. He'd turned on the TV, intending to watch his station's morning news program, but he'd been riveted by an interview with Fiona. Once again, she was on a rival network. Once again, she was beautiful and professional and made his mouth water.

Once again, he was powerless to do anything about it.

It had been months since she'd left Florida, months since they'd talked. And he realized how stupid he'd been. His talk with a therapist yesterday had sealed the deal. It wasn't his first appointment, and it wouldn't be his last, but he'd concluded he'd thrown away the best thing to ever happen to him, all because he feared letting her in. It didn't mean he was ready to let her in, or that he even knew how, but admitting it was necessary if he ever wanted a relationship with anyone.

Until he'd seen her on TV, he figured he'd have time to learn how before meeting someone who mattered. And then he'd turned on the TV and the woman of his dreams looked at him, winked, and said, "Happy Holidays."

His mouth dried. Desire coursed through him. More than anything, he wanted her. Not some other woman he could meet any number of ways. Not someone Lexie offered to set him up with. Not the owners of the flirtatious glances he navigated through every day. Not the women he used to go to for casual sex, and whom he hadn't visited in more than six months. Fiona. And only Fiona.

The one woman he couldn't have.

He stalked to the balcony.

There had to be a way.

His palms started sweating and he rubbed them on his wool slacks. He'd have to apologize. Bile rose in his throat. He'd talked to his therapist about confessing his feelings, even practiced with her. It was necessary. Hell, he'd done it with Fiona before. Before he'd seen his father. Before his mother died. When Fiona still talked to him.

Fiona was strong. She had the ability to show and feel emotions, to deal with crises and not fall apart. And she made him stronger, too. Fiona had never made him feel bad for showing his emotions. She'd shown her feelings. He could do this. He'd tell her everything, apologize, and convince her to try it again with him. Because without her, life was bleak, had been for a long time. And he was tired of bleak.

****

Fiona laughed as she stuck her key in the door. "Shh," she whispered to Ryan, opening the door to her apartment. "I don't want to wake my neighbors."

She led him inside and dropped her keys on the hall table. Turning, she wrapped her arms around his neck. It was warm. He bent and kissed her. He tasted of wine and tomato sauce. His lips were soft. She smiled against his lips and pulled away as longing for softer lips, Caleb's lips, overtook her. Her ex-boyfriend had no business haunting her during a date with someone else. Steve had introduced her to Ryan and they hit it off. After two dates, they were in her apartment for the first time.

"Do you want a drink? Or dessert?" She walked into the kitchen, turned, and almost bumped into Ryan. "Oh!"

He caressed her face. "Would it be terrible of me to say I want you?"

She stared into his green eyes, which gave away his feelings. Her tummy flipped with nerves. His hand, unlike his neck, was cool against her cheek.

She kissed him again, longer this time. It was nice. It didn't rock her socks off—she wore tights, anyway— but she liked being kissed by someone who demonstrated his emotions.

"I do have a yummy dessert here," she whispered when he pulled away.

"I can see we're not going to get anywhere unless I feed you." He smiled.

He had a great smile. It came easily and often. He laughed and made her laugh. Maybe that was it. It was too easy. His smile didn't take any work, didn't make her feel special for coaxing it from him. Was it normal?

On their first date, he'd arrived in a limousine with three dozen roses. He'd taken her to the best restaurant in town where they'd ordered from the regular menu. As she'd spoken to the waiter, she'd had an insane urge to beg Ryan to order for her. But he would have looked at her funny. Shaking her head, she pulled the cheesecake from the fridge. She had no idea if he liked cheesecake, but she'd bet he'd go along with it to make her happy even if he didn't.

They sat next to each other, him feeding her pieces of cheesecake. They talked about the movie. Ryan had suggested she pick the movie, so she'd chosen a romantic comedy. He let her be in charge. The independent side of her rejoiced. He should be everything she wanted.

He kissed her again and pulled away. "I like you, Fiona."

"I like you, too." She did.

He would sweep her off her feet if she would let him.

He looked like he wanted to say more. Instead, he nodded, kissed her one last time, and headed for the door. "I'll call you tomorrow."

She had no doubt he would. He'd followed through

on every plan he'd made. He'd made clear his feelings. She'd had fun on every date, and he had as well.

But the spark was missing. As she cleaned the dishes and the leftover cheesecake, she hoped the spark would develop. Chemistry could take time to develop, couldn't it?

There was a knock on her door. Ryan must have forgotten something.

"What did you—?"

It wasn't Ryan.

Chapter Twenty-Six

"Fiona." The one word took more effort from Caleb than any others he'd ever spoken.

She stared at him, face pale, and moved to shut the door. His arm shot out, almost as if someone else controlled it and prevented it from closing. He couldn't let her avoid him.

"Please." Did she need him to get on his knees? Because he would. For her, he'd do anything.

"What do you want, Caleb?" She stood blocking the door, her knuckles white from gripping the doorknob. He could read every emotion as it passed on her face—anger, sadness, confusion.

"May I come in?"

"I don't think so."

The back of his neck went cold, and chills raced along his spine. He had to explain. He clasped and unclasped his hands, clenched his teeth, flared his nostrils.

"I have no right to ask you to listen to me, Fiona, but I'm asking anyway. Please can we talk?"

"Why? What is there to say?"

"I need you to hear things from me." He looked behind him and at her. "And I'd rather not say them in the hall."

She sighed and retreated from the door. Walking into her apartment, he inhaled. It smelled like her—

floral and fresh—and his chest swelled. He'd missed her.

She stopped in the middle of her hallway and folded her arms around her middle. He recognized it for what it was, a protective gesture—from him—and his shoulders sagged.

"I'm sorry," he whispered. "I never meant to hurt you."

If he'd expected her to respond, he'd underestimated her resolve. Her jaw was tight, her gaze murderous. She wasn't going to help him at all.

He took a step forward, and she let him pass. He paced the apartment, almost blinded by its colors and textures. This was life, and he'd been in limbo too long.

"I never wanted to be ruled by emotions," he said. "I couldn't afford it. After my parents..." He rubbed the back of his neck. "I couldn't be like them. So, I walled off my emotions and maintained tight control over everything. It was the only way to protect Lexie and my mom. Even after we left my father, I had to protect them. Emotions affected them so damn much. I didn't want to. And then you came along and somehow found a way through my walls. You took away my control and that terrified me." He paced. "Or it should have. But somehow, when you were with me, it didn't. And then my father returned, and I realized the cost of feeling things."

"I don't understand."

"Feeling things makes you vulnerable. Building an emotional wall was second nature to me, but I hadn't counted on my father using you to get to me."

"But he didn't. He talked to me, and not even for very long."

Just like Lexie, she'd handled him. He was the only one who couldn't handle his father. "I didn't know. And I couldn't take the chance of him hurting you."

"So, you denied I was your girlfriend."

Caleb nodded. "And I resumed hiding my emotions, but it was harder this time. And then you left."

"I didn't leave."

If he were honest with himself, he'd forced her to do it by drawing away from her. Which meant he'd pushed her away. She hadn't left. "No, you didn't. I pushed you away. And once you were gone, I tried returning to my tight self-control. To my normal life, where everything made sense and fell into place, and no one was at risk because of me. Except I couldn't. And once again, I was terrified. Still am. Because now I'm feeling all these emotions and you're not there to help me make sense of them."

Fiona shook her head. "You don't need me, Caleb. That's what a shrink is for."

He stared at her across the room. "I know. I'm seeing one." Her face blanched, and he was thankful he could read her so well.

"Since when?"

"About a month now."

She nodded, almost in a daze. "Good." Her voice was whisper soft, and she started, as if she hadn't expected to say it aloud.

"But I don't need a shrink, Fiona. I mean, I do, but even more, I need you."

She was on her guard again, her body stiff. "Why?"

It was now or never. "Because I love you."

"Ha."

Her response pierced his concentration, and he jerked his head up. "A man tells you he loves you and you respond with 'Ha?' "

"When the man is a self-contained control freak who wouldn't know love if it walked by looking like a heart with legs and little cupids flying around it, yeah."

He wanted to smile at the picture she painted, even if her description of him hurt. The old Caleb wouldn't have risked it. So, he let himself smile and felt lighter than he had in a while. "Know a lot of those, do you?"

"Only one and he's enough." She turned toward the front door, and he reached for her arm.

"Fiona, please." His negotiating skills made him see they were close. Only a little further to go. Maybe. But it would never happen if he let her kick him out. "Don't give up on us now."

"Caleb, I want to be swept off my feet by someone who is madly in love with me. I don't want to be the bandage to someone's emotional issues."

Being in her presence had knocked a chink in his armor and with every look, every comment she made, waves of emotions rolled through him. Right now, he wanted to laugh at her imagery, yet at the same time, he was filled with terror at her refusal. The old Caleb would turn and walk away. Being the old Caleb was easy and comfortable. But he didn't want to be the old Caleb. Not if it meant losing Fiona.

He took her hand in his. At first, she pulled away, but he held firm, rubbing his thumb across the tops of her knuckles. After a few strokes, where he became more aware of the fragility of her bones and marveled at her underlying strength, she relaxed. Only then did he look at her.

Her eyes were sapphire, the color deep, reflecting hurt and wariness. He'd put those feelings there and now it was his responsibility to make them go away.

"You're not my Band-Aid," he whispered. "You're my fantasy come to life. You're everything I never knew I wanted in a woman. You're funny and kind and compassionate. You're brave and smart and capable. And you've shown me it's okay to share responsibility. I don't have to take it all on myself."

Her gaze lost the hurt, but she was still wary. He wanted to kiss her lips, which she bit when he spoke. But he didn't have a right to kiss her, even though he ached to take her in his arms.

"How do you know?" she asked. "More to the point, how do I know the next time something hard happens, you won't retreat behind your walls, leaving me on the outside?"

"Because I'm here."

She cocked her head to the side. "I live across the hall from your sister. Being here isn't hard."

Annoyance at her stubbornness flared, and her eyelids widened. Good, let her see it. "No, this location isn't hard, you're right. But the old me would just let you go. Being in a relationship with you requires I show you how I'm feeling, what I'm thinking. It makes me strip myself bare to you. And I'm trying. Not well, because I'm not perfect. But I'm here, after losing you, begging you to come back."

This time, she did pull her hand away and walked to the window. She stood, ramrod straight. Her shoulders rose and fell before she spun around, devastation marking her features.

"But what if I lose me?"

"How would you lose yourself?"

"By making too many allowances for your learning curve." She shrugged. "I don't know, Caleb. Relationships aren't supposed to be this hard."

He balled his hands into fists. "So, now you don't want to work hard? I need to know, Fiona, you'll meet me halfway. I get I didn't even come close to halfway before, but I'm trying. I wish I could show you how much."

Her head dropped and when she once again met his gaze, tears welled. It broke him. He strode to her and cupped her cheek in his palm. He didn't care if he had a right to touch her. If she hated him, she could make him leave. But he planned to move forward until she stopped him.

"Please don't cry. I can do anything, survive whatever I have to survive, even learn to live without you if I must, but I can't be the cause of your tears. Please, Fiona, I love you. I love you," he repeated. "I think I've loved you since the first moment I saw you on TV. Since we went clamming. I couldn't show my father I did because I didn't want him to hurt you to get to me. So, I blocked those feelings, and in the process, pushed you away. I fought against it in Florida. Opening myself to you meant letting people know how much you meant to me. But more importantly, if people knew I cared about you, they could hurt you to get to me. And I couldn't let that happen. So, I pushed you away. But I've loved you for what seems like forever, and I can promise you, no matter what you decide now, my love won't change. Oh, I'll learn to live with it alone if you force me to go, but I will still love you."

"Why are you telling me this now? I heard your

conversation with Alex."

"Because it took me until now to get my head on straight. I missed you from the moment you left. But if I had come to you then, nothing would have changed. I needed to work everything through, to learn emotions and feelings don't always mean anger. I still have a way to go, but I'm so much better than I was. Fiona, could you picture the old me ever doing this?"

She shook her head. It was a good sign, a sign he made his point. She opened her mouth, but he covered her mouth with two fingers to stop her.

"I'm not asking for praise. I'm not planning to stop working on me. But I need you to see I'm serious about the effort I'm making."

"Who are you making the effort for?"

He smiled. "Both of us." He ran his hand across his head. "Look, I'm still going to withhold emotions in the boardroom. It makes me a successful businessman, and I have no desire to change. And I'll probably withhold my feelings from other people as well."

She snorted.

"Okay, more like definitely. But from you? I don't want to hide from you. You're the one person I'm supposed to be able to trust. So, I'm trusting you. But I need to know if you want my trust. Because it does come with responsibility and—"

He couldn't say anything because she smothered his mouth with hers. Her tears dripped on his cheeks. Her lips devoured his. Her arms squeezed his neck so tight, she might strangle him. But he didn't care. Because she was his.

When he was allowed to breathe, she grabbed his face in her hands. "I love you, too."

And for the first time, he was at peace.

A word about the author...

Jennifer started telling herself stories as a little girl when she couldn't fall asleep at night. Pretty soon, her head was filled with these stories and the characters that populated them. Even as an adult, she thinks about the characters and stories at night before she falls asleep or walking the dog. Eventually, she started writing them down. Her favorite stories to write are those with smart, sassy, independent heroines; handsome, strong and slightly vulnerable heroes; and her stories always end with happily ever after.

In the real world, she's the mother of two amazing daughters and wife of one of the smartest men she knows. She believes humor is the only way to get through the day and does not believe in sharing her chocolate.

Jennifer Wilck is an award-winning contemporary romance author for readers who are passionate about love, laughter, and happily ever after. Known for writing both Jewish and non-Jewish romances, her books feature damaged heroes, sassy and independent heroines, witty banter and hot chemistry. Jennifer's ability to transport the reader into the scene, create characters the reader will fall in love with, and evoke a roller coaster of emotions, will hook you from the first page. You can find her books at all major online retailers in a variety of formats.

https://www.jenniferwilck.com

Thank you for purchasing
this publication of The Wild Rose Press, Inc.

For questions or more information
contact us at
info@thewildrosepress.com.

The Wild Rose Press, Inc.
www.thewildrosepress.com